VIOLA CANALES

PIÑATA
BOOKS

PIÑATA BOOKS
ARTE PÚBLICO PRESS
HOUSTON, TEXAS

Cecilia's Magical Mission is funded in part through a grant from the Texas Commission on the Arts. We are grateful for their support.

Piñata Books are full of surprises!

Piñata Books
An imprint of
Arte Público Press
University of Houston
4902 Gulf Fwy, Bldg 19, Rm 100
Houston, Texas 77204-2004

Cover design by Mora Des¡gn

Names: Canales, Viola, author.
Title: Cecilia's magical mission / by Viola Canales.
Description: Houston, TX : Piñata Books, an imprint of Arte Público Press, [2019] l Summary: Fourteen-year-old Cecilia worries that she will not discover her special gift before her Confirmation, especially after learning that she is expected to lift a curse tied to the village of St. Cecilia, Mexico. l
Identifiers: LCCN 2019011635 (print) l LCCN 2019015445 (ebook) l ISBN 9781518505614 (epub) l ISBN 9781518505621 (kindle) l ISBN 9781518505638 (pdf) l ISBN 9781558858770 (alk. paper)
Subjects: l CYAC: Blessing and cursing—Fiction. l Demonology—Fiction. l Angels—Fiction. l Ability—Fiction. l Mexican Americans—Fiction. l Catholics—Fiction.
Classification: LCC PZ7.C161643 (ebook) l LCC PZ7.C161643 Cec 2019 (print) l DDC [Fic]—dc23
LC record available at https://lccn.loc.gov/2019011635

The paper used in this publication meets the requirements of the American National Standard for Information Sciences—Permanence of Paper for Printed Library Materials, ANSI Z39.48-1984.

Printed in the United States of America
Versa Press, Inc., East Peoria, IL
October 2020–November 2020

4 3 2 1

Dedication

I dedicate this book to my mother Dora Casas Canales, who passed away while writing this book.

•◆••◆••◆•

Acknowledgements

I want to express my deep gratitude to those who made this book possible: my family, Dr. Nicolás Kanellos, Dr. Gabriela Baeza Ventura, Marina Tristán, Adelaida Alanis Mendoza, and the fantastic Arte Público Press team. Thank you.

CHAPTER 1

Cecilia and Julie ate chocolate bars as they sat on the front steps of their apartment building. Both eighth-graders had just walked home from the bus stop. Julie and her mother had recently moved to California from New York, after they lost everything they owned in the horrors of Hurricane Sandy. Cecilia had lived her whole life in the same San Jose apartment after her parents migrated from Mexico.

"When's your mother due?" Julie asked as she bit into her chocolate bar.

"She's in her twenty-fifth week," Cecilia said with a quick smile.

Julie wrinkled her nose. "Gosh, you look so happy. I guess you're looking forward to the new baby, huh?"

"Of course!"

"But the apartments are so small," Julie said. "I for sure wouldn't want another sibling."

Cecilia let out a short laugh. "I'll get used to it. I've been sharing my room with fifty-pound sacks of potatoes, beans and . . ."

Julie clapped Cecilia on the shoulder. "Hey, I'd gladly sleep out on the fire escape if I had a mother like yours. She cooks like magic." She added wistfully, "Boy, I've never, ever tasted anything as delicious as the *carne guisada* your mother brought over to welcome us."

1

"That's her *don*," Cecilia said.

"Her what?"

"Her talent, her celestial gift. It's a belief from Santa Cecilia, the town where my parents were born in Mexico. It's a Catholic belief, a *Mexican* Catholic belief."

"What are you getting at?" Julie asked. "That because I'm not Mexican or Catholic, I can't understand what a *don* is? Your mother cooks like . . . how can I describe it?" Her eyes darted upwards. "Your mother's cooking feels like a carnival that appears out of the blue and transforms the empty, weed-choked lot you hurry by every day and think 'How creepy!' into a joyous marvel of flashing colors, music, smells and tastes that take you to another world."

It was clear her mother's gift had cast a spell on Julie. Cecilia said, "That's a good description of what a *don*'s supposed to do." She took the last bite of her chocolate bar and, when she glanced up, she noticed the patches of bright blue sky between the soaring steel and brick apartment buildings. "A *don*," she continued, "is the gift, the special talent supposedly everyone, not just Mexicans or Catholics, is born with . . . but a person has to discover her own gift, nurture it, and then share its fruit with others. My mom's *don* is cooking."

Julie looked surprised.

This was a look Cecilia recognized. *Does she think this was weird?* Cecilia jumped to her feet, snatched her backpack and swung it over her shoulder.

"Wait." Julie grabbed Cecilia's wrist. "Tell me more."

"It's getting late," Cecilia said as she pulled away from Julie's grip. "I have to help Mom with the cooking for tomorrow's route."

"Okay." Julie scrambled to her feet. "But tell me why this *don* thing makes you look sad."

"It's because I'm coming up on my Confirmation and I have to choose a saint. . . ."

"And?"

"This saint is supposed to represent one's *don*," Cecilia finished as she unzipped her backpack and rooted around for her keys.

"And?" Julie jingled her own set of keys. "Why does this make you sad?"

"Because I have no idea what my gift is!" Cecilia dropped her shoulders with a heavy sigh.

Julie wanted to hear more but she knew that Cecilia needed to hurry to help her mother. "I'll see you at the bus stop," she said and they clambered up four flights of stairs to their apartments.

Julie thought of Cecilia's bright, fragrant kitchen. Her heart sank as she opened the door to her own apartment where her mother slept in a dark, gloomy bedroom.

CHAPTER 2

Cecilia's mother was stirring a huge pot that bubbled on the stove. When she heard a loud knock on the front door, she turned to her daughter. "It's probably your *madrina.*"

Cecilia set down the pestle of the *molcajete*, where she had ground peppercorns, cumin and garlic for the *carne guisada.* She hurried out of the kitchen into the narrow hallway.

"Hi! I'm back!" said Julie, grinning from ear-to-ear at the door.

"Is everything okay?" Cecilia asked, surprised.

"Perfect!" Julie slid past Cecilia into the living room. "Wow, it smells *so* delicious."

"How's your mom?"

"Oh, she's fine. She left a note saying she had gone to get her hair done, would be back around seven. So . . ." Julie rubbed her hands together as her nose turned towards the kitchen.

"Okay, come on in. We can use the help."

Julie's eyes widened the moment she stepped into the kitchen. "Gosh, it's just like in *The Christmas Memory!* Oh, hello, Mrs. Guerra!" Julie said and flashed Cecilia's mother Nica her biggest smile. Cecilia's mother was now kneading a big ball of dough for flour tortillas.

"Hi, Julie," Nica gave her a quick nod. "How's your mom?"

Julie repeated the story she had given Cecilia, and told Nica that her mother was grateful for the delicious food she had sent them as a welcome meal. Julie slowly examined the kitchen: there were giant silver pots on the stove; boxes of tomatoes and green peppers, and big burlap sacks of potatoes, onions and red chiles leaning against one wall; glass jars filled with cumin, peppercorns and cinnamon in a wooden rack. The sight captivated her, and so did the sounds: the bubbling of the pots, the grinding of the spices in the *molcajete*, the sizzling of steak strips on the grill. . . . And the rich aromas of spices, crackling in oil. . . .

"Julie? Say, Julie?" Cecilia said and grabbed her arm.

"What?" Julie asked.

"Mom just asked if you and your mother want to come over for dinner tonight?"

Julie's face lit up. "Really? That's fantastic!" Then she paused and dropped her head, "But . . ."

"But your mother, right?" Cecilia asked as she plopped tomatoes into the pot to blanch for the salsa.

Julie sighed and looked down at her tennis shoes, the same off-white ones she wore every day, with the same pair of jeans and the same pink pullover sweater. After Hurricane Sandy took their belongings, she selected these clothes from a pile of donated items at the shelter where she and her mom had spent several days.

"How about I put together a dinner plate for you and your mom?" Nica said. After she dried her hands, she came over and gave Julie a hug.

A wide smile broke out on Julie's face.

"I'm making *caldo de pollo* for dinner." Nica lifted the lid off the simmering pot of chicken soup.

"It smells so good!" said Julie.

"The chicken's from Doña Marta's chicken coop," Nica gave a quick smile, "so it's a magic soup because I made it with a magical chicken."

Cecilia shot her mom a sharp look before she glanced at Julie. She hoped Julie thought her mother was kidding, although she knew full well Nica was serious about the magical chicken. *Thank goodness Julie was not around when Mom said that my madrina Carmen could cure Julie's mom's depression.* That was the day Nica had concluded that Julie's mother was suffering from *susto*, shock, because of the hurricane. "All Carmen has to do is give her a few quick sweeps with her *curandera* broom, along with a dash of prayers. Then *poof!* she'll be as good as new!"

"But Mom," Cecilia had protested, "Julie and her mother are not from our culture. They would think it was witchcraft!"

Nica had raised her hand and responded sternly, "Then what? Take more and more crazy pills, sleep all the time?"

Julie cleared her throat and that brought Cecilia back to the present. Julie asked, "What's a magical chicken? Is it like an organic chicken?"

Nica winked at Cecilia with an impish grin. "Cecilia, why don't you tell Julie what a magical chicken is."

The front door swung open and footsteps approached.

"Hi, Dad!" Cecilia's father Antonio walked into the kitchen, clad in a buffalo-plaid shirt, khakis and brown boots.

"Hello, everyone." Antonio gave a broad smile. "How's your mother, Julie?"

"She's okay. Thanks," Julie said with a quick nod.

"Good." Antonio poured himself a cup of hot coffee from the thermos on the counter. "Oh, by the way, let me know if you ever need any help fixing anything in the apartment."

"Yes, thank you, Mr. Guerra."

Antonio took a sip of coffee, then left to go watch the evening news.

After Cecilia and Julie peeled the mountain of blanched tomatoes and Nica helped them transform them into a huge vat of delicious-looking salsa, Nica filled two bowls with her magic chicken soup for Julie and her mother. Julie accepted the food and made a mental note to ask Cecilia about the magical chicken.

CHAPTER 3

"**Y**es, of course. Don't worry. I'll get Cecilia to help me . . . *buenas noches*," Nica hung up the phone.

"Who was that?" Cecilia asked. She had just returned from helping Julie carry the bowls of soup to her apartment.

"It was your *madrina*," Nica said as she ladled the soup into their bowls for dinner. "She's going to the hospital. Paula's not doing well . . . she's dying."

"Paula, the lady who lives on the second floor?"

"Yes," her mother sighed heavily. "She was in a terrible accident two days ago. She and her husband were on their way to the next stop on their taco truck route when they were hit. Paula had gotten up to start prepping when *bang!* they got rear-ended by a speeding van. The truck flipped on its side and the boiling oil spewed all over Paula. Those who've gone to see her say she was burned so badly that you can see all the way to the bones in her arms." Nica slowly shook her head.

Cecilia studied her mother's pained expression, took a deep breath and stopped herself from asking more questions. *Gosh, this horrible thing could also happen to Mom.*

Cecilia picked up the ceramic tortilla holder and turned to her mother. "What did you mean when you told Madrina that you would get me to help you?"

8

"Carmen needs to spend time with Paula," Nica said in a serious tone. "She's on our community's committee for these types of emergencies. She volunteered to be on it when all the Santa Cecilia adults last met in the basement to discuss our needs. So, she can't help me with the taco truck route tomorrow. I told her that I'd bring you along to help."

"Tomorrow!?" Cecilia exclaimed. "Tomorrow's Tuesday. I have school!"

Nica wheeled around from the sink, placed her hands on Cecilia's shoulders and looked straight into her eyes. "Yes, I know you have school tomorrow, but I, we need your help."

Cecilia stepped away from her mother's grip and said in a halting voice, "But . . . what will I tell the school? It's not like I'm sick."

"Someone in our community is," Nica replied in a gentle tone. "Don't worry, I'll write you a note saying there was a family emergency."

"Family?" Cecilia asked, her eyes blazed. "I've never even met Paula!"

"Paula's family because she's from Santa Cecilia. That's all that matters. And I need to keep feeding the family with my route."

"Okay, Mom. I'll have to go tell Julie not to stop by for me in the morning."

Nica tossed her head back and let out a short laugh. "You'll be long gone by the time she wakes up."

CHAPTER 4

When her mother woke her in the morning, Cecilia scrambled out of bed and dressed quickly. She chugged down a cup of strong black coffee and helped her mother load the van with the food they had prepared the previous evening. Cecilia slept all the way to the "Taco Truck Park," where they would pick up the taco truck her mother bought years ago. When they arrived, Cecilia immediately helped transfer all the food from their van into the truck.

"Get some rest while I prepare some things," Nica suggested as she split open one, two, three, four . . . fifteen avocados with a knife. She popped the pits out with a spoon and scooped the soft flesh into a bowl. Then she grabbed an empty glass Coke bottle by the neck and used it to mash the avocado to make a chunky, creamy guacamole.

"Let me help," Cecilia offered and stepped towards the laminated counter.

Nica waved her off, then turned on the grill, "Go rest. It's still too early for you. I do this every day." She then opened the refrigerator, pulled out a metal tray and began tossing strips of fresh meat onto the hot grill, which caused it to hiss and spit, shooting swirls of smoke throughout the truck.

It smells so delicious, thought Cecilia. Her mouth watered despite how ridiculously early in the morning it was.

Suddenly, Nica spun around and startled Cecilia. She snatched a super-sized can of ground coffee from a shelf and added scoop after heaping scoop into a huge, stainless-steel coffee maker in the corner. Soon the air was filled with the rich aroma of fresh, dark brew.

Cecilia slumped in the driver's seat, caught in a delicious dream. Her mother darted to the back of the truck and plunked a square pot of pinto beans on the hot grill to reheat; they were the beans that Cecilia helped to clean and her mother cooked every evening at home. Then a second pot—this one heaping with *carnitas*, stewed pieces of spiced pork—went onto the grill, followed by others containing shredded chicken, *carne guisada*, Mexican rice, chicken soup, *menudo*. All that food had been cooked at home the night before. In a wink, the pots started to rattle and bubble. The truck was soon filled with pleasing, savory smells.

Whack! Cecilia flinched and sat up straight. *Whack!* Her mother split heads of iceberg lettuce with a machete. *Whack!—whack!—whack!* Next, one, two . . . six fat tomatoes were split, diced and tossed into a square metal tray.

Cecilia stared as her mother took a plastic bag out of the freezer, ripped it open, shook out two dozen *taquitos* into a long-handled wire basket and dunked it into the deep fryer where the hot oil whizzed furiously. Cecilia suddenly thought of Paula and the horrible pain of being burned with boiling oil. A few minutes later, Nica lifted the basket out of the oil and hooked it over the deep fryer to drip. Then, using a pair of metal tongs, she grabbed three crispy, golden-brown *taquitos* from the basket and placed them on a compostable paper plate, before she wrapped plastic all around it and set it on a rack inside a glass box. She snatched the tongs again and did the same to the rest of the *taquitos*. The glass box was quickly full.

Without the smallest break in her rhythm, Nica now dumped a jumbo bag of *jalapeño* peppers into the second fryer basket, immersed it into the boiling oil for a minute, jiggled it a bit, then hooked it next to the first basket, where it drizzled out oil. After about two minutes, she seized the basket's long handle and plopped the heap of wrinkled, oil-drained *jalapeños* into a container lined with paper towels.

After glancing at her watch, Nica posted herself in front of the grill and began scooping strips of *carne asada* into a square metal pot. She then inserted the pot into the rack on the wall that kept the food from spilling as the truck traveled from stop to stop. She next stirred and spiced the pots still heating on the grill, and, once satisfied, secured them on the rack, too.

Cecilia was amazed at how quickly her mother went from task to task. She'd never seen how hard her mother worked, how many details had to be attended to, and they hadn't even started the route. *Wow, I already feel exhausted just watching her set up.*

Cecilia scooted to the edge of the seat to watch her mother now toss disks of Mexican chocolate into a pot of simmering water on the grill. Then Nica plunged the bulb-like end of a *molinillo* into the pot, twirling its long, wooden handle back-and-forth between her hands, until it released the enchanting scent of chocolate. "How about a cup of hot chocolate?" Nica flashed Cecilia a big smile and turned off the grill.

"Oh my, yes!" Cecilia's mouth watered as she reached for the steaming, frothy cup.

CHAPTER 5

Savoring the delicious taste of the hot chocolate, Cecilia leaned back in her seat as her mother got behind the wheel.

The taco truck started with a roar, then took off. Moments later, the radio wired to Nica's sun visor played a *cumbia*. Nica smiled, bobbing her head to the music's lively beat as she steered the truck up the highway. The truck had no heater so Cecilia, still half-asleep, wrapped her arms around herself to fight the cold. Before long, the truck coasted to the curb and stopped. Cecilia checked her watch. It was six-thirty, and the moon and stars were still out.

Nica turned to her and said brightly, "This is our first stop, where we feed the workers from the shop across the street." She pointed and continued, "That's where they make Spanish clay tiles for roofs."

Nica flung the door open and jumped out. Cecilia followed and helped her raise the side panels of the truck that covered the service windows. Nica dashed back inside to turn on the grill, straighten the napkins on the counter and fetch the scuffed-up cigar box where she kept the cash.

"Juan! Hola, *m'ijo*," Nica said in a cheery tone to her first customer.

Cecilia saw a young man—a boy, really—rush over in his jeans, red sweatshirt and sneakers.

"¡*Buenos días!*" Juan flashed Nica a big smile.

"That's my daughter Cecilia," Nica flicked her chin towards Cecilia.

"Hi, good to meet you," Juan said as he turned towards Cecilia and nodded slightly.

"Um . . . hello." Cecilia wondered why her mother had called him "*m'ijo*," my son. Was he a relative?

"How about a cup of hot chocolate?" Nica asked.

"Yes!" Juan said and rubbed his hands. He looked delighted. "Cecilia," he paused. "Mexican hot chocolate is what I drank every morning back in Santa Cecilia."

He took the steaming paper cup Nica handed him through the window, brought it to his nose and inhaled deeply as the steam caressed his face. Then, he closed his eyes and took a long drink. "It tastes so good! Just like my mother's!"

Nica crossed her arms on the counter and smiled.

"This makes me feel like I'm home," Juan took another long drink. When he had drained his cup, he licked his lips, looked up at Nica and said, "Now I'm starving!"

Nica gave a short laugh, "The usual? *Chilaquiles?*"

"Please!" Juan nodded.

As Nica prepared Juan's breakfast, the two talked and joked about family, work, music, *telenovelas*, even something relating to his *don*. Cecilia watched as her mother quickly sliced two corn tortillas into square strips, tossed them onto the buttered, sizzling grill and added three large eggs, hot salsa and salt. Once it was mixed, Nica scooped the spicy, fragrant meal onto a plate and topped it off with hot corn tortillas.

"Here, *m'ijo*," Nica announced as she handed Juan his steaming breakfast through the window.

Juan reached for the heaping plate and pursed his lips. With a sheepish look, he gazed at Nica. "*Gracias*, but . . . can I pay you tomorrow . . . when I get paid? You know how it is during the week."

"Yes, of course," Nica nodded with a warm smile. She took a small spiral notebook from the shelf over the window and leafed through the pages until she found one marked with names, dollar amounts and dates. With a stubby pencil she extracted from the notebook's bent spiral, she jotted down: Juan, the dollar amount and the date.

The sound of voices made Cecilia look out the window. Another three boys like Juan were hurrying over.

"¡Hola, muchachos, buenos días!" Nica called to them.

They greeted Nica with big smiles and said, "Yes!" to cups of hot chocolate. Two asked for breakfast burritos and one for an order of *chorizo con huevos*, scrambled eggs with spiced Mexican sausage.

Nica joked and laughed with her customers as she cracked egg after egg and whipped them into mouthwatering, tasty dishes. Cecilia busied herself making change from the cigar box.

Outside the truck, engulfed in the warmth her mother cast, the men ate heartily and talked about their latest tile projects and gigs they went to when they finished work at the factory, among other things. One said he was taking his girlfriend to a dance that weekend and reminisced about the parties in Santa Cecilia. All four agreed that they longed to return to their hometown for Christmas, to see their parents, families and to catch orbs of light. *Orbs of light?* Cecilia didn't understand what they meant. They shook their heads when they discussed how their boss refused to give them any time off, that he couldn't understand why they wanted to return to Mexico. A catchy, upbeat hit by the Norteños played on the radio, and that livened up the sad moment. The men bobbed their heads to the music as they polished off their plates and finished their drinks. The sun then rose over the horizon and illuminated the clouds with shades of strawberry and honey.

For the next hour and a half the scene repeated itself in Nica's enchanted world on wheels. Young and not-so-young men, mostly Mexican, some from Central America, came over to the taco truck for their first morning greeting, a cup of coffee or hot chocolate and a hot meal they ate standing or sitting on the curb.

From what Cecilia overheard while she worked, it seemed that every single one of her mother's customers was homesick and couldn't wait to return home.

"Once I save up a thousand dollars, I'm out of here!" seventeen-year-old Luis said with chocolate bubbles clustered around his lips. "I want to buy a little piece of land for Papá . . . just big enough for a cow, a few chickens." He had come to America two years before when his mother became ill with cancer. He worked at anything and everything, seven days a week, from day laborer to dishwasher, house painter to ditch digger—even wore a black-and-white cow costume with udders once to advertise a sale on leather sofas. He wired nearly all his money home to pay for his mother's treatments, keeping only enough for a room, his food and a weekly load at the laundromat. He did this up until his mother died four months ago, around the time he got the job at the tile shop.

Nica glanced at her watch. "It's eight o'clock! Time to roll!" She leaned out the window again and said goodbye to everyone. Cecilia leapt out and shut the side panels and off they went.

The taco truck trembled as it thundered up the freeway. A fat tomato suddenly popped off the counter and rolled back and forth on the metal floor. Cecilia's teeth rattled and her entire body vibrated.

Nica glanced at Cecilia and noticed her daughter's pained expression at the roller-coaster ride of the truck, then tossed back her head and let out a short laugh.

"I told Carmen the other day," Nica shouted while touching her swollen belly, "that I'm so glad I got the truck fitted with extra-wide space; otherwise, she and I would keep getting stuck while serving our customers."

Cecilia shook her head and chuckled, thinking of her pregnant mother and her godmother—two strong, big women—wedged between the counter and the fridge.

CHAPTER 6

Cecilia remembered that cold Saturday years ago when they traveled hundreds of miles to Los Angeles to search for a food truck.

The journey began early in the week, when Nica had bolted up in bed and declared, "I've had it!"

Cecilia dashed over from her bedroom to see why her mother was yelling.

"Mom! What's wrong?"

Nica leapt out of bed and wrapped Cecilia in her arms. "It's nothing, *m'ija*, go back to sleep."

Her bleary-eyed father sighed heavily as he tossed his legs over the side of the bed and sat up. He straightened his pajamas while he patted the bed beside him for Cecilia to sit down. "*M'ija*, nothing's wrong. It's just . . . well, your mother's tired . . ."

"That's right!" Nica interrupted as she hooked a hand on her hip. "I'm tired . . . sick and tired of cooking for that chain restaurant that treats people so badly. So I'm getting a taco truck, my own little restaurant on wheels!"

Cecilia's father nodded. "Okay, if that's what you want." He then put his lips to Cecilia's ear and whispered, "There's no stopping your *mamá*."

After they had jumped in and out of dozens upon dozens of food trucks, Nica had settled on the one they now traveled in.

"Where's the next stop?" Cecilia asked as she jerked back to the present.

"Palo Alto, Oaxaca's sister city!" Nica shouted as she exited the freeway. "Ay, I wonder how Paula's doing. The accident happened here."

Cecilia imagined how the boiling oil had splattered and scalded Paula—the same fiery hot oil that now sloshed inside her mother's deep fryer. She cast her glance towards her mom's hands and arms, which now spun the steering wheel onto Palo Alto's University Avenue. For the first time, she noticed they were covered with dark, raised burns. Scars from the hot oil spitting up. Some of her fingers were crisscrossed with white lines from knife cuts. Cecilia sighed and remembered her parents' wedding picture: her mother stood next to her father and clutched a bouquet of flowers with hands so lovely, so perfect, so smooth.

Cecilia looked out the front window and caught sight of giant, glossy-green magnolia trees decked out with rich yellow flowers. The taco truck roared on, passing mansion after storybook mansion set on perfectly manicured lawns with a wealth of roses and bougainvillea in stunning colors. One house looked like a Greek temple, with white columns and a domed roof. Palm trees soared twenty-five feet high, gracing its entryway.

Nica suddenly burst out laughing and slapped her thigh.

"What's so funny?"

"I just remembered something one of my customers told me," Nica replied and shook her head slowly. "This poor man was hired to cut the grass at one of these fancy houses, and when he was doing the work, he saw a huge, fat snake slither across his shoe. He screamed and quickly grabbed the hoe and whacked the snake in half. He felt relieved and very proud of himself, but then he saw a woman, the owner of the house, run out the front door and scream at him. She was furious because he killed the family's beloved pet!"

Nica braked at a red light, fell back on the seat and groaned, "The crazy things I hear. Our people work every day in the cold or the scorching heat; they dig ditches, haul rocks, pour concrete and boil tar. Sometimes their bosses don't even show up to pay them. That's why I'm glad I have this taco truck." She shot a quick glance at Cecilia. "I know it's hard to get up at four in the morning, especially in winter, but I'm my own boss, and I get to feed many of these workers. Though it doesn't keep *me* from running into stupid, crazy stuff too."

"Like what?"

"You'll see," her mother said and pursed her lips. She kept her gaze fixed on the road as she accelerated.

Cecilia glanced at her mother's scuffed watch as she stretched out her arm: 8:20. Through the windshield, she saw a BMW and a Jaguar pull out of flagstone driveways. Then a shiny white Mercedes flashed its bright lights at them and zoomed past in the opposite direction. *Why did it flash its lights?* Cecilia wondered.

"Get down!" Nica said in a loud, sharp tone, as the truck screeched towards a stop sign.

Stunned, Cecilia gasped and doubled over.

Then the taco truck took off again. "All clear," Nica said and sighed with relief.

"What was that?"

"A police car," Nica said and arched her brow. "I was worried we might get stopped, and that we might get questioned about why you aren't in school."

Still tense, Cecilia looked out for police cars, but only saw an old, dented pick-up truck with a mess of rakes, hoes, shovels, a tree clipper and pitch fork poking up in back like cat tails chug towards them. When they got closer to it, Cecilia saw three young men squeezed inside the cab like sardines in a can. There was a sparkling, scarlet rosary dangling from the rearview mirror.

The moment Nica pulled up to the stop sign, she honked and waved at the men in the pick-up. They waved back and looked excited. When they took off again, Nica said, "Those boys do most of the yards here. The one in the middle is Jorge, the one who hacked the pet snake in half. The one driving is Diego; he hired Jorge when I told him what happened. I'm glad it worked out. They come for breakfast every day."

Further up the street, Cecilia spotted a second pick-up truck with two men in front and pool-cleaning equipment in back. Then she saw a woman pushing a double-stroller with two carrot-top babies inside. At the intersection, Nica and the woman waved at each other. Nica took off again and rolled her window down, then poked her head out and hollered greetings to a man who wore an orange vest and directed traffic around a row of traffic cones. Past the cones, Nica swerved to the curb and coasted to a halt in front of a large, noisy construction site. It swarmed like an enormous beehive with workers who hammered and drilled planks, posts and metal frames onto an ever-expanding steel-and-wood structure.

Nica killed the engine and flicked her chin towards the construction site. She snickered. "They're building town-houses for over a million dollars each."

She shook her head, took a deep breath, and punched the shiny chrome button next to the steering wheel. *Ta-ra-ra-ra-ra! Ta-ra-ra-ra-ra! Ra-ra-ra-ra-ra-ra-ra!* blared the strains of *La Cucaracha.*

"It's *SO LOUD!*" Cecilia protested and covered her ears.

"How else will they know we're here?" Nica shrugged, ". . . with all the construction noise?" Then Nica gestured towards the Spanish hacienda-style mansion across the street and said with a grimace, "That's where one of the bad witches lives."

"What?" Cecilia asked as she took in the mansion's elaborately carved, heavy front door. "A witch?"

"I call them that because they sometimes make my life miserable. They don't practice black magic, but they cast their stupid insults. They call me an illegal immigrant, an alien, a *Mexican,* as if that's the very worst thing to be, like a cockroach. That's why I play *La Cucaracha* to tell people I've arrived. They've even sicced the health department and the police on me. The one across the street did that just last week. My permits were all in order, like always," she sighed heavily, "but the whole thing gave me the biggest headache.

"And they're persistent," Nica added and opened her door. "The health department stops me out of the blue, again and again. They stick their thermometers here, there, everywhere, checking if this or that is hot or cold enough.

Anyway . . . it's time to feed my customers, so to hell with the bad witches. They want their pools cleaned, lawns clipped, their mansions built, swept and dusted; not to mention their kids coddled, fed and raised—for cheap! And to top it off, they don't even want those doing all the work to eat!"

CHAPTER 7

Stunned by her mother's words, Cecilia leapt out of the truck, raised the side panels and straightened the items that had gotten loose on the drive. Then she set a tray table outside next to the service window and placed the cash box along with the spiral notebook on top. She was still nervous about making change outside by herself, rather than next to her mother inside the truck, but there were so many customers here that she couldn't stay inside.

The drilling, pounding and hammering had suddenly stopped, including the beeping of cranes and bulldozers. Then men: young, old, middle-aged, some in hardhats, emerged from the wood-and-steel structure. Cecilia spotted three guys several blocks down who dropped their tree clippers and rakes to hurry over. They were soon joined by the woman who pushed the double-stroller that Nica had greeted at the intersection. The vested man at the traffic cones also headed towards them. Then, out of nowhere, the pool-cleaning truck Cecilia saw earlier turned the corner and screeched to a halt right across the street.

Nica stuck her head out of the ordering window, said "¡Hola!" and waved at the customers who had lined up ready to place their orders.

Bang! bang! bang! Nica belted out order after order of *tacos al carbón*, *carnitas*, breakfast burritos, *chilaquiles*, *taquitos, tortas*—even a few hamburgers. Cecilia heard her laugh and chat with her clients about everything under the sun: who got deported or divorced, who had fallen in love, who had been swindled. They shared jokes, talked about the fights, fiestas, deaths and issues with kids and families—things that happened here and there, in the United States and in Mexico. They carried on as if Nica were their mother or sweetheart. Throughout all this, Cecilia stood at the small table and furiously counted change or jotted down the names and amounts owed by those who would pay later.

During a brief lull, Nica clambered out of the truck with a pen and paper and an empty milk crate in hand. She plopped herself on top of the overturned crate next to the table and started to scribble a letter for a man named Eduardo to his wife in Santa Cecilia. As she was writing, another client came and asked for something to help with a pounding headache, so Nica sent Cecilia to the truck to bring the first-aid kit that included Band-Aids and aspirin tablets. Cecilia remembered that her mom had done the same thing at the previous stop. She had even given someone a rosary from the kit.

After Nica finished, she went back in the truck and cranked up the lively *cumbia* that pulsed from the radio as she started picking up and organizing things that needed to be washed or stored.

Cecilia thought of the witch her mother had described. When she looked up from her work, she froze. A blonde-haired woman raced over and pulled a young girl along. Cecilia bit her lip as she scanned for police cars. She dashed into the truck. Her heart pounded. Desperate, she grabbed her mother's shoulder and pointed. "Mom, look, a bad witch!"

Nica burst out laughing and slapped the counter. "No, no. That's my friend Brenda. And that's her daughter. They come for *carnitas* tacos every day."

"Nica!" Brenda said with a smile and then brushed a leaf off her sweater.

"*¡Hola!*" said Nica with a quick wave, before she gestured towards Cecilia, who was back at the table outside. "Let me introduce you to my daughter Cecilia. She thought you were a witch!"

"A witch?"

"Um . . ." Cecilia hesitated. Her stomach was in knots.

"I told her about my crazy encounters with the bad witches in the neighborhood."

"I see!" said Brenda with a short laugh as she turned to flash Cecilia a big smile. She also extended her hand.

Cecilia shook it. She felt awkward and embarrassed, but she forced a smile.

"*¿Cuántos años tienes?*" Brenda asked and gave Cecilia a gentle pat on the arm.

"Fourteen," Cecilia said, worried her next question would be about why she wasn't in school.

"This is my daughter Jessica. She's five."

Cecilia smiled.

After Nica served tacos and hot chocolate to Brenda and Jessica, she announced it was time to go. She wished everyone a good day. Cecilia picked up the cash box, notebook and table. She took everything inside the truck and shut the side panels.

It was six in the evening before they finished the route. *So many stops. So many people.* Nica had fed, fussed over, laughed, gossiped, advised and prayed with an army of workers. Not only that: she also read and wrote letters for them, and even dispensed things like nail clippers, Holy Water and recipes along the way.

It was dark when Nica swerved into a gas station. She instructed Cecilia to fill up the tank. They then drove to the taco truck park where they swept, cleaned and hosed down the inside and outside of the truck. Wet, cold and so exhausted that she could barely stay on her feet, Cecilia poked her head inside the truck to see her mother scour the grill. She knew that soon, at home, her mother would stand in front of her stove and prepare the food for tomorrow's route.

"Mom, how are you feeling?" She thought of how spent she herself felt. Even with a new baby coming, Nica had whirled round and round all day with the force of a hurricane, doing a million things.

Nica flashed Cecilia a big smile. "Thank you, *m'ija.* You worked so hard to help me today."

On the way home, Cecilia stared out the window at the night sky glowing with stars. She thought about how her mother brought a sense of lightness, laughter, even joy to her customers. That was her Mom's *don,* her gift, she thought, like the brightness of stars in the dark night sky. Then she realized that she still didn't even have a clue what her *don* might be. Cecilia was absolutely convinced that she would never find a *don* to match her mother's gift.

CHAPTER 8

"What's wrong? What happened?" Julie screeched when Cecilia opened the door to let her friend in that Saturday morning. "Why do you look so down? Did Paula die?"

Cecilia pursed her lips and tried to steady her rush of feelings, but all she could do was shake her head slightly.

Julie had never seen Cecilia this downcast before. She hurried off to look through the apartment. "Where are your parents? Did something happen to them?" Julie's heart raced.

Cecilia, with her back against the hallway wall, slid to the floor, wrapped her arms around her knees and hung her head.

"I'm calling 911!" Julie said in a panic and headed for the kitchen phone.

Cecilia reached out and grabbed her ankle.

"Okay, okay, I won't call 911, but tell me what's going on. What's wrong?!"

"My mom . . . she lost the baby," Cecilia said in a strangled voice.

Julie stared at Cecilia. She sunk down next to her on the floor.

"Gosh, I'm sorry. . . ."

"It was a girl."

Julie gave Cecilia a gentle pat on the arm. "How's your mom doing?"

"She's devastated . . . so is Papá . . . he just called from the hospital. Carmen was there, too, but should be here soon. I thought she was the one knocking on the door."

Julie nodded.

Cecilia let out a long, heavy sigh. "The call cut me like a knife. My dad was trying so hard not to cry."

Julie thumped her head slightly against the wall, feeling clueless about how to respond. The sudden sound of knocking made her jump to her feet. "Hello, Carmen," she said, opening the front door.

Carmen walked to Cecilia, who was still sitting on the floor. "I'm sorry, *m'ija*. Come to the kitchen." She took Cecilia's arm and helped her stand up.

"Can I come too?" Julie asked.

"Of course you can," Carmen said.

Cecilia and Julie sat at the table and Carmen filled the kettle with water. She turned on a burner and set the kettle on it. Then she fell into the chair next to Cecilia. Carmen placed her pudgy hand on Cecilia's head and tried to turn her face towards her but Cecilia shook her off. Carmen grabbed the back of Cecilia's head to bring them face-to-face with each other.

"Keep still," said Carmen and narrowed her eyes into a fixed, penetrating stare.

"What are you doing?" Cecilia asked in a frustrated voice.

"I'm trying to help you, to keep you from getting *susto!*"

Cecilia rolled her eyes and snickered. She tried to shake Carmen's hand from her head, but her godmother only tightened her grasp.

Wssh! The kettle whistled and Carmen got up to turn off the burner. Then she stuck her hand in her pocket and pulled out a glass vial filled with yellow and white leaves.

"What's that, Carmen?" Cecilia asked and rubbed her head where Carmen's fingers had bored into her skull.

"*Manzanilla.* I'm making you some tea. Just in case," Carmen said and scooped teaspoons of it into a green, round-bellied teapot.

"In case what?" Cecilia asked.

"In case your soul got spooked with the news," Carmen said, pouring steaming hot water into the teapot. "I'm giving you a cup too," she added, tossing her chin towards Julie.

Cecilia studied Julie's astonished, anxious expression with a sense of sadness mixed with bemusement. "It's just chamomile tea," Cecilia said and put her hand on Julie's.

"*Manzanilla* is not *just* chamomile tea," Carmen interrupted indignantly, "not when it's prepared by me."

Julie's eyes widened.

"And why's that?" Cecilia said.

"You know why," Carmen said sharply as she poured the steaming tea into three cups.

"Not really, why?"

"Because it's my *don*," Carmen said and huffed. "I'm a *curandera*, a healer," she added before she raised her cup with her right hand to slurp loudly.

Cecilia and Julie waited a bit before finally realizing that Carmen was not going to elaborate. Julie forced a slight smile. *This is yet another mystery to ask Cecilia about: Susto? And why does Carmen's don make chamomile tea more than just chamomile tea?*

Carmen plopped her empty cup down on the table. "Cecilia, come on, drink your tea. It'll soothe your soul. You need to be strong for your baby sister."

Cecilia shot Carmen an angry look, leapt to her feet, and asked, "Sister?! What are you talking about? Mom had a miscarriage!"

Julie's eyes darted from Cecilia to Carmen.

Carmen patted the chair where Cecilia had been sitting and said in a gentle, soothing voice, "Sit down. Let me explain. At twenty-five weeks it is no longer a miscarriage: it is called a stillbirth, because the baby would have survived if she had been born."

Cecilia furrowed her brow and sat back down. In a dry voice, she asked, "Did you see . . . her?"

"Yes, I did. I saw the baby," Carmen said. Cecilia wished this was just a bad, bad dream she could simply snap out of. "Please drink your tea, *m'ija*."

Julie watched Cecilia hesitate, then raise the cup to her lips and take tiny sips until she finished the tea. Julie swallowed hard, lifted her cup and chugged it down all at once.

CHAPTER 9

With the corners of her mouth curved into a slight smile, Carmen swept her gaze from Julie to Cecilia, and back again. Then she crossed her arms and said, "As Cecilia's godmother it's my duty to have a *plática*, a talk, with her about what just happened."

Cecilia leaned forward to give Julie a light tap on the arm. "Why don't you go check on your mom?"

"Oh, no," Julie replied, her eyes wide, "I'd love to stay . . . if that's all right."

"Yes, that's fine," Carmen nodded at Julie. "This *plática* will be about your sister's soul." She paused and examined Cecilia's expression to see if she was listening.

Cecilia nodded and was about to ask a question when Carmen stopped her with an open hand. "Now, before you bombard me, let me begin by saying that the day of your baptism, the day when I became your *madrina*, was about planting the seed of the Holy Spirit in your soul. Later, the talks we had when you prepared for your First Communion made that seed sprout. And now that your Confirmation is just around the corner, the seed is to bear the fruit of your soul, when you take the next step and allow your *don* to manifest. Why? To help others: your family, your community, as well as yourself. It's like what I do as a *curandera*. Like just now: didn't my tea make you feel lighter, better?"

Cecilia cleared her throat, nodded slightly and said, "Yes."

"Yes," said Julie. She flashed Carmen a big smile.

"And here you thought I was making you drink poison," Carmen laughed while she looked straight at Julie.

Julie gasped, pitched forward in her chair and said in a shrill voice, "Oh, no! No! Your tea was wonderful . . . absolutely wonderful!" She was stunned. *Does Carmen's gift allow her to read a person's mind?*

"As I was saying," Carmen continued as she grabbed the teapot to pour everyone another cup, "this particular talk— the one we're about to have—concerns Micaela's soul."

"Wait! Who's Micaela?" Cecilia asked.

"Your sister," Carmen said matter-of-factly.

"She had a name?" Cecilia asked.

"Well, today's September 29, right?"

Cecilia and Julie traded looks, then gazed fixedly at Carmen.

After a long, awkward silence, Cecilia swallowed hard and whispered, "Yes, it is." She glanced up at the wall clock and added, "And the time is . . ."

Carmen interrupted, "I see you've forgotten that too."

"Forgotten what?"

"Forgotten a flower of your culture," Carmen said.

Cecilia suppressed the urge to roll her eyes at the silliness of using the word "flower" to talk about traditions that were supposedly serious and important. She turned to Julie and said, "Carmen refers to pieces of our culture as 'flowers.'"

Julie just nodded with a rapt look.

"So," Cecilia said and faced Carmen, "today's the feast day of a saint named Micaela?"

"Close," said Carmen, smiling slightly. "Today's the feast day of Saint Michael the Archangel."

"I see," said Cecilia with a quick nod.

At that, Julie appeared to be lost. Cecilia took Julie's expression as a signal that she should interpret.

"What Carmen's saying is that, well, for example, I was born on November 22, the feast day of Saint Cecilia, which explains why I was named . . ."

"Oh, I get it!" said Julie.

"So Micaela was the name your parents chose for her," Carmen said to bring the *plática* back to Cecilia. "They also got to hold her."

Cecilia was astonished.

"I held her, too," Carmen said and tilted her head to one side with a slight sigh. "The nurse put a tiny, pink cap on her head and wrapped her in a blanket, then let your mother hold her and rock in a rocking chair. Next, your father. Then me."

Cecilia shook her head, and tried to dispel the image of the miscarriage, or stillbirth, as the bloody mess she had seen in movies.

Patting Cecilia on the back, Carmen said, "I'm Micaela's godmother, too. Father Ramón came to baptize her. Now we have to focus on taking her to Santa Cecilia to bury her."

"Santa Cecilia?" said Cecilia. "Why? She died here and . . ."

"Yes," said Carmen, "but she needs to be buried in Santa Cecilia."

"Why? Santa Cecilia is two thousand miles away, in the middle of Mexico! And we live here—here in San Jose, in the United States."

Carmen narrowed her eyes and said, "I think it's better that you ask your mother about this later, because right now we have to hurry up and start raising money to bury the baby. And . . . we need to get ready for Monday's taco truck route."

"But Carmen, listen . . . this doesn't make any sense . . . ," Cecilia continued, her face flushed. "My parents don't have the money to fly to Santa Cecilia to bury the baby. And . . . and. . . ." She exchanged a quick, anxious look with Julie. "Am I going to miss school again on Monday to help with the taco truck?"

Carmen folded her arms over her chest and nodded. She kept her eyes locked on Cecilia's. "Yes, I will need your help," she said in a softer tone. Carmen stood up and went to the stove.

Cecilia and Julie traded a puzzled look while Carmen wrenched open a can of coffee and started scooping grounds into the coffee pot.

"Why are you making coffee?" Cecilia challenged. "To fix the money problem?"

Julie's jaw dropped, not knowing if Cecilia was being serious or sarcastic.

Carmen tossed her arms in the air and groaned, "If any of the older *comadres* heard you say this, Cecilia, they would sit me right down and give me the biggest, longest scolding ever . . . for doing such a lousy job at being your godmother. What a question!"

Cecilia scrambled to her feet and started towards Carmen. "What do you mean?"

"What I mean is that, as your godmother, I'm supposed to teach you about spiritual things . . . and because I'm a *curandera*, they would expect me to have taught you the ins-and-outs of having my gift, my *don*. You should know how a person's gift works, so that you can figure out your own."

Cecilia grabbed Carmen's arm. "Carmen, I have no idea what you're talking about."

"I know you don't," Carmen said.

"So . . . are you going to explain it to me?"

"Explain what?" asked Carmen. She kept her eye on the coffee pot that now gurgled and filled the room with its rich fragrance.

"Well, how is making coffee going to help pay for the baby's burial in Santa Cecilia?"

Carmen let out a loud roar of laughter and pointed to the billowing, clattering coffee pot. "The coffee I'm making—and doesn't it smell wonderful?—is just coffee . . . coffee to drink. It has nothing, nothing to do with raining money out of the sky.

"Look, when I said your question would make the ancient ones think I had failed miserably at fulfilling my duties as your godmother, I meant that they would've expected me to have already taught you that a *curandera* not only heals illnesses of the body and the soul with teas and prayers, but also cures illnesses of the community, of families."

"But with what? Coffee?"

"By knowing everyone's business . . . and everyone's *don*." Carmen poured herself a cup of coffee.

"I still don't understand," Cecilia sighed.

"You will, soon enough." Carmen winked at her over the brim of her cup. "Ah, that was good, good coffee. I feel it coursing through my body like a lightning storm."

Suddenly, without any explanation, Carmen pulled out her cell phone and punched in a number. "Alicia . . . it's Carmen. How are you, *comadre*?"

Cecilia and Julie listened to Carmen's conversation and, when it was over, Cecilia had some questions: "What will help?" she asked.

"The bank . . . the taco truck bank. I just arranged for your mother to get jumped to the top of the list. . . ." Noticing the girls' puzzled faces, she crossed her arms on the table and added, "All the taco truck owners in the community—twelve in all—give Alicia a hundred dollars on the last Friday of every month for the Taco Truck Bank. Every month, Alicia gives the total collected to the person at the top of the list. That's how we save money. Your mother was scheduled to get the pool in December, but I just got her moved to the top of the list."

"You mean they don't have a bank account?" Julie asked. She looked incredulous.

"They do," Carmen said with a grin, "didn't you hear? It's the Taco Truck Bank!"

"But . . . but what if the person scheduled to get the money needs it too?" Julie asked.

"Well, we have a way of taking care of that. Everyone understands that shipping the dead back to Santa Cecilia is a priority, a sacred duty."

"Sacred?" Cecilia said. "Why?"

"It takes a soul nine days to get to Heaven," Carmen clarified, "and we should take that very seriously. Okay, that's enough. I really need to focus all of my attention to organize a *kermés*."

CHAPTER 10

"What's a . . ." said Cecilia.

"It's a church carnival with a soul," Carmen muttered under her breath as she hurried towards the sink with the empty cups in hand. "Just another gaping hole in your spiritual education."

Cecilia slumped back in her chair and wished she had a cheery fairy godmother. She turned to Julie and asked, "What's your godmother like?"

"My godmother?" Julie asked, looking puzzled. "I . . . I don't have one. At least I don't think so—we're Episcopalian, but we never go to church. But I sure wish we went to church," she added and gave Carmen a big smile.

"What? Are you serious?"

"You bet!" Julie said and leaned forward. "I find this so, so interesting. I never realized there was a spiritual dimension to education."

"And Cecilia still doesn't," Carmen harrumphed but then popped her index finger in the air and, in an excited tone, added, "I just thought of something: You two should put your heads together and come up with a project to investigate the 'spiritual dimension,' as Julie calls it. Does it exist, what is it, how does it work? I think most people today, especially the young ones like you, don't believe it's real anymore. They don't believe in the existence of souls, for instance."

"I don't know . . . I don't really understand what you're saying . . . ," said Julie.

Cecilia explained in a weary tone: "She wants us to test whether angels really exist."

"Really? That's a fantastic idea!" Julie said, and nearly fell off her chair with enthusiasm.

"Right? The two of you have to start working on this," Carmen said and clapped Cecilia on the shoulder. "Put your project together—"

"I can't wait!" said Julie.

Cecilia shook her head vigorously. "This is absurd. It's the biggest piece of nonsense I've ever heard." She glared at Julie and added, "Have you lost your mind? You know that Mrs. Bellows will flunk us *and* humiliate us in front of the entire class if we say we want to investigate angels for our science project."

"Don't forget the *dons*; you can do research about both," said Carmen. "You should also choose a saint to help you."

"Why stop there?" Cecilia said with a smirk. "Why not also investigate if souls really need nine days to get to Heaven?"

"Yes, why not?" asked Carmen, widening her eyes.

"Are you serious?" Cecilia could feel a headache coming on.

"Yes, I am," Carmen retorted sharply.

"And what test, or experiment, exactly, can we possibly set up to investigate this?" Cecilia rubbed her temples.

"I have some ideas, but I need to get going with the *kermés*," Carmen said as she glanced at the wall clock.

CHAPTER 11

"**B**enita, how are you?" Carmen said into the phone, explaining why they had to call a *kermés* right away.

Cecilia and Julie listened. Julie tried to catch every word, tone and gesture in an attempt to understand what this was all about.

"It's all set," Carmen said when she hung up the call. "It'll be this this Sunday . . . at Baker Park."

"Uh," Julie said and slowly raised her hand, "can I . . . can I come too?"

"Of course," Carmen said with a quick nod.

Julie smiled broadly, then caught herself and said, "Am I supposed to bring something? Or dress in a particular way?"

Carmen eyed Julie with a raised brow and said, "Well, it depends. Do you have a special ability or power?"

"Special power? Like . . . wh-what?" Julie asked.

"Let's see . . . well, have you seen Santa Cecilia's robes?" Carmen asked.

"No, what is that?" Julie asked.

"They are the most wondrous, beautiful clothes . . . veils, robes made by my *comadre* Ana. She's the most gifted seamstress we have. She was born on July 26, the feast day of the patron saint of seamstresses, Santa Ana, the Virgin Mary's mother.

"As a tiny baby," Carmen continued, "Ana's godmother started telling her stories about her patron saint, her life, her *don* for sewing. At five years, Ana cut and sewed a marvelous satin diaper for her family's ceramic baby Jesus, the one they put in the manger on Christmas Day. Suddenly word spread like wildfire about the amazing diaper she made for the baby. Every family wanted one for their baby Jesus. So just like that," Carmen snapped her fingers, "she had a small business going, with all the families in the community ordering their baby Jesus diapers from her.

"Later, as a teenager, with her sewing abilities growing even more marvelous, all the families insisted on having her sew special outfits for their ceramic Jesus toddler to wear on February 2nd for Candlemas, when they present him to the church. And now, everyone—both here and in Santa Cecilia—order their special dresses for baptisms, First Communions, *quinceañeras*, weddings, wakes—all directly from her.

"And that, Julie, is a good example of someone with a magic power. She'll be selling some of her sewing treasures at the carnival."

Julie bit her lower lip, her mind swirling with flashing images of a magic chicken . . . magic tea . . . beautiful dresses. "Um . . . ," uttered Julie, and her eyes darted at Cecilia.

"Julie, do you think you have a magic power?" asked Cecilia sarcastically.

"Why don't you first tell us yours, Cecilia. Have you found your *don*?" Carmen asked, clapping her on the back.

"I'm working on it. I still can't figure it out. I do know that Santa Cecilia, the patron saint of music, hasn't given me any musical gifts or talents."

"That's for sure," Carmen said with a snort. "Your poor father tried you first with a guitar, next a violin, then singing. You take to music as well as a pig plays the maracas."

"Thanks a lot, *madrina!*"

Julie couldn't help but laugh imagining a pig holding maracas.

Cecilia shot her a sharp look.

CHAPTER 12

"So how about last words? Has your mother tried this yet?" Carmen said.

"Last words?" Cecilia said, looking puzzled.

"Yes, last words could help you find your *don*."

"How?" asked Cecilia.

"Ask your mother about it," Carmen said and turned to Julie. "Do you like to read books?" she asked.

"I love books!" Julie said.

"Do you have any that you'd like to donate to the *kermés*?" Carmen asked. "After all, a carnival with a soul requires that the community come together to share the marvels of everyone's gifts and, in the process, raise enough money so Micaela can be buried in Santa Cecilia."

"Okay!" said Julie with excitement. She was happy to discover there was a secret, spiritual side to everything, or so it seemed.

"What about me? What should I bring?" Cecilia asked in a weary tone.

"Um, let's see," said Carmen, tilting her head up and tapping her chin with her index finger. She suddenly leapt out of the chair, crossed the room, wrenched open the refrigerator and said, "You can take this!" She handed Cecilia a *tres leches* cake. "Everyone will want a slice of your mother's magic cake."

A magic cake to add to the list, thought Julie, as she gazed at the delicious three-layered white cake. Her mouth watered.

Cecilia heard the phone ring and put the cake on the table so that she could answer it. It was her father.

"How're you doing?" he asked in a quiet, faraway voice.

Cecilia bit her lower lip, sensing her dad's sadness. "Carmen's here," she said, "and Julie. How's Mom?" Her voice began to break. "When is she coming home?"

A long silence. Then her father sighed heavily and said in a halting tone, "Your mother is . . . okay . . . better. She's sleeping. The doctor hasn't told us when she can come home."

"And Micaela? Where is she?"

"Micaela?"

"The baby," Cecilia said and shot Carmen a sharp look. *Didn't she say my parents had named her Micaela?*

"She's . . . they're keeping her here . . . somewhere," her father said in a half-whisper.

"Carmen said you held her."

"Yes," he said with a quiver in his voice.

The sadness in her father's voice affected Cecilia. She stifled a moan, then quickly changed the subject. "Carmen's planning a *kermés.* She told me to take Mom's *tres leches cake,* but I want to take something that I made myself. And, well . . . Carmen said Mom could tell me something about my *don . . .* something about last words."

"Ah," Antonio said and clicked his tongue, "Carmen's probably right. . . ."

"How did you discover your gift?" Cecilia said.

"Mine?" her father said. "I kept finding lost things, ever since I can remember: lost chickens, wedding rings, watches, a Bible, even bottles of tequila. So, from very early on, it seemed that my patron saint San Antonio was guiding me. He's the patron saint of lost things. Anyway, *m'ija*, I'll see if your mom can call you when she wakes up."

"Why can't I go see her?"

"We'll be home soon, *m'ija*. Your mother needs to rest. She's asked about you many times. Please help Carmen with what she needs."

"Okay," Cecilia said and hung up. When she turned to find Julie and Carmen gazing at her with looks of sympathy, she averted her eyes. Cecilia grasped for answers. *How can this be*, she asked herself, *that my mother never delivered, but suddenly they were mourning a baby, a baby named Micaela...?*

"The *kermés* will start at one o'clock tomorrow, right after Mass," Carmen specified. "And the committee is meeting at seven this evening in the basement. So stop by if you want to see how things are going or to help. And you, Julie," she continued and put her hand on Julie's shoulder, "can finally be introduced to Santa Cecilia."

"I'll be there," Julie's face lit up with excitement. "Should I bring the books I want to donate?"

"But what about your mother? Are you going to leave her alone?" Cecilia asked. She dreaded exposing Julie to more aspects of her culture that she herself didn't understand.

"I think so. Maybe I can even learn something that might help her."

With a quick nod Carmen then turned to Cecilia. "What do you want to eat? You must be starving."

Cecilia shook her head. "I'm fine," she said, but felt her stomach rumble. "I can fix something later. But is there something I need to cook or prepare for Monday's taco truck route?"

"Don't worry. I'll take care of all that," Carmen said. "Why don't you go take a nap? You look tired."

"I'm going to check in with my Mom," Julie said. "I'll come back at around six-thirty to go downstairs to the basement, Cecilia."

Cecilia gave her a slight nod and walked over to the living room and fell onto the sofa, feeling exhausted. Her head ached again. *When can I talk to Mom?* she wondered. She fell into a deep sleep.

❊ ❊ ❊

Cecilia suddenly wrenched her eyes open. Startled, she looked around and tried to remember where she was. The telephone was ringing. She jumped up and ran to the kitchen. Her heart pounded.

"Hi, *m'ija*."

"How are you, Mom?" Cecilia asked. Her muscles tensed when she heard the sadness in her mother's voice.

"Okay," Nica whispered.

She's trying to be strong, thought Cecilia. She stifled a sigh and then caught herself before she asked questions that might make her mother sadder than she already was.

"Have you eaten?" her mother asked.

"Yes, Mom. Don't worry, I'm fine. Carmen was just here." Then, she took a deep breath and said, "Carmen's preparing for a *kermés*, and she said I should take your *tres leches* cake to it. But I want to take something I make myself." Cecilia paused, not sure if she should bother her mother with this trifle. "Mom, Carmen said I should ask you about 'last words,'" she added, feeling a tinge of guilt, "but we can talk later. . . ."

"It's okay, *m'ija*," her mother said. "Go to my bedroom and get the Bible from my night table."

Cecilia put the receiver down and ran to her parents' bedroom. She rushed back to the phone, Bible in hand. "Okay, I got it."

"Open it to the very back. To the list of dates and names . . . and notes."

Cecilia quickly flipped to the back. "Okay, I'm there."

"Now go through all the dates and see if there's one for November twenty-second, the day you were born."

"Okay." She dragged her forefinger down the column of dates. "I found one," she said, sounding excited. "There's only one."

"Read it to me."

"It says, '*Café . . . para unir el cielo con la tierra. ¿Verdad, María? José María Guerra*'." Confused, Cecilia asked, "Who's José María Guerra?"

"One of your ancestors," Nica said in a weary voice. "Do these words mean anything to you?"

"Not really. What do they mean?" said Cecilia, staring fixedly at the smudged, black-inked words one by one.

"The last words he said before he died," Nica said.

Cecilia gasped.

"It is believed that, if a family member dies on your birthdate and says something right before dying, his or her last words might be a clue to figuring out your *don*."

A long pause ensued.

"But what could these last words possibly mean?" Cecilia said anxiously as she translated the Spanish words into English: "*Coffee . . . to connect heaven and earth. Right, María?* Who is he talking to? Who's María?"

"You need to discover this yourself . . . what these words mean," Nica said. She inhaled deeply. "The María that he's talking to concerns the other part of the belief, and that is that, when a person is about to die, someone from the spirit world comes to usher the person out of this life and into the next. That spirit might serve as a clue, too."

"This sounds crazy," Cecilia said with a groan, then caught herself, remembering what Carmen had told her. "But how did last words help you discover your gift, Mom?"

CHAPTER 13

"My birthday, as you know, is December 6th," Nica told her daughter over the phone. "That's the feast day of San Nicolás, which explains why I was named Nicolasa, Nica for short. Living in Mexico, I was brought up to believe that *Los Tres Reyes Magos*, The Three Kings, brought gifts to kids on January 6th, the Epiphany. The night before, we would put hay in our shoes for the Kings' camels—you know the three wise men traveled on camels to Bethlehem for the birth of Jesus. Then, we would wait for the magi to fill our shoes with toys and candy for us to find the next morning.

"But, after moving here to California—I was six at the time—I heard it was Santa Claus, not the magi, who brought the toys. And Santa Claus was actually St. Nicholas, my very own patron saint. All of a sudden, I felt famous, since no one seemed more loved, treasured and adored than Santa Claus—at least by kids. A few years later, my wonderful world suddenly exploded the day I found out that Santa Claus didn't exist. The toys were given by the kids' parents, not by him—the big phony.

"When I was your age, my parents and godmother were breathing down my neck, pestering me about picking a patron saint for Confirmation. Was I keeping my birth saint, or would I select a new one? 'How can I possibly stay with

San Nicolás?' I asked myself. I felt betrayed by him and associated him with the fake Santa Claus.

"When Confirmation classes began at the church and I still hadn't chosen a patron saint, my godmother was very frustrated. She told me that, if I didn't stick with my patron saint, I would also have to find a new *madrina*. During the second class, I almost fainted when we were told to write a letter to the patron saint we had selected, asking for his or her help to discover our *don*.

"I suddenly felt anxious, since the letter also had to be co-signed by our sponsor or godparent and turned in the following week, at the next class.

"'I'm just a big, stupid phony like Santa Claus,' I thought, as I dashed over to the nearby library, planning to quickly page through a book of saints and pick one—any one—just to be done with the letter. When I got to the library, I saw a sign on the door that said they were closed because of a budget crisis. My stomach dropped. I dragged myself home, cursing Santa Claus all the way there.

"Back home, my mother noticed I was upset. 'What's wrong?' she asked, taking me by the shoulders and making me sit down at the table. I tried my best not to burst into tears, but I did and I confessed everything. She grabbed paper and a pen and started to write a letter. When she finished, she put it in an envelope and addressed it to 'Doña Faustina' in big, block letters.

"'Run and give this letter to Doña Faustina,' my mother said, 'and stay until she's read it. It's a letter of introduction.'

"'Who are you introducing her to?' I asked.

"'You!' she replied with a laugh.

"'Me? Why? But what about my problem, the one I just told you about?' I asked and stomped my foot. 'The letter's due next week.'

"'This is why I'm sending you to Doña Faustina,' she said, and hurried me out the door.

"I still remember how I groaned as I slowly made my way towards Doña Faustina's little clapboard house. I knocked softly. When the door swung open and I came face-to-face with her piercing eyes, my stomach dropped. I forced a smile and handed her the envelope. She waved me inside and led me into her bright kitchen that smelled like roasting coffee. She pulled out a chair and gestured for me to sit while she read the letter. I flinched when Doña Faustina said in that low, raspy voice of hers, 'You just need to have coffee. Yes, a cup of coffee with your patron saint.'"

"'What?' I said, making a face. Without a word, Doña Faustina set about grinding the coffee in a *molcajete*. I asked her, 'You grind coffee in a *molcajete*?'

"She just laughed and said, 'I'm not grinding coffee beans. I'm putting my *don* into them.' Next, she put the grounds into a plastic funnel sitting over a ceramic pot and poured boiling water into it. After pouring cups of coffee for us, Doña Faustina sat down and said, 'Your birth saint is San Nicolás, right?' I nodded. 'And now you need to choose one for your Confirmation, one who will help you with your *don*, right?

"'Don't worry, I remember having the very same problem when I was your age. But wait,' she added. She got to her feet, opened a cupboard and waved me over. I saw stacks and stacks of envelopes tied into bundles, more than twenty of them. 'Do you know what these are? Letters of Introduction . . . just like your mother's.

"'So stop worrying and feeling miserable about not knowing what your *don* might be, what patron saint to pick.' Then she handed me the cup and insisted I drink all of it. I brought the cup to my lips and took a sip. To this day, I still remember the taste of that single sip of hot coffee. It was heavenly, something you couldn't possibly recreate by simply following a recipe.

"'How did you make this?' I asked, and took another sip, then another, and savored every drop of the incredibly delicious brew. Not only did it make me feel warm and awake, but it also made me feel whole, as though it brought all my scattered parts together and connected me to something bigger, grander.

"That's when we started talking about my birth patron saint, San Nicolás. She told me that he was indeed a real saint, the patron saint of children, and that he was not at all a phony. As for Santa Claus, his myth had been inspired by the real saint's caring and generosity towards the three daughters of a poor family, centuries back, when he tossed a bag of gold coins into the family's chimney, anonymously, three separate times, providing a dowry for each of the daughters to marry.

"Next, she asked what I loved, what I dreamed I would be as a grown-up. I thought for a minute, then blurted out, 'Chocolate . . . *pan dulce* . . . rice pudding. . . . ' Doña Faustina slapped the table and again roared out laughing. She jumped to her feet and clapped and said, 'You remind me of Sister Nicolasa, and this makes me so, so happy! 'She got up again and fetched a big, heavy book. It was a Bible with a gold cross on the cover. She opened it to the back inside cover and scanned a list of handwritten names and dates that were scribbled there. 'Here it is,' she said, 'your great-great-great aunt, Sor Nicolasa, born December 6th . . . died December 6th . . . last words: '"Jars of marmalade sparkle like the cathedral's gloriously jeweled stained-glass windows."'

"'Do you know what this means?' Doña Faustina asked as she leaned her head towards mine. I shook my head. 'Sor Nicolasa was a cook in a convent in Puebla, Mexico, in the 1600s, when it was part of New Spain,' Doña Faustina said. 'She was an amazing cook who was divinely inspired, as though angels whispered in her ears. She invented the tastiest confections and sweets, like those eaten by the highest, luckiest angels.'

"Then, Doña Faustina grabbed the coffee pot and refilled our empty cups. 'Now,' she said, 'have a cup with your patron saint, San Nicolás, and ask him to reveal who should be your patron saint for Confirmation, since a saint picks the person, not the other way around.'

"To make a long story shorter, I lifted my cup and sipped my coffee, wondering if St. Nicholas was going to pop out of it. After I had emptied my cup, I suddenly felt filled with what I would call an instinct, an understanding that the whole experience of preparing food for people to enjoy with gusto, especially the sweets, treats, confections—was a way of giving to others and delighting them. Through taste, I decided, I could transport adults to their childhood, just as San Nicolás let adults giving presents be transported back to their childhoods. Feeling excited, I looked at my cup and asked San Nicolás to please be my Confirmation saint since he represented the don I wanted.

"And that's my *don* story," Nica concluded.

"Wow," Cecilia said, pressing the phone to her ear. "What happened to Doña Faustina? Is she still around?"

"Yes. Do you want me to introduce you to her?" Nica asked as she fought against her sleepiness.

"Well . . . it might help."

"Ask Carmen, tell her I told you about my experience. See what she says . . ." Nica paused. "I have to get off the phone. The nurse just came in. We'll talk later."

After she said goodbye, Cecilia realized how deeply she missed her mother.

CHAPTER 14

Cecilia had just arrived at Carmen's apartment with her mother's *don* story on her mind.

"Hungry?" Carmen asked. "I'm making a pot of *calabaza con pollo* for Monday's route, along with some other things."

Cecilia shook her head, though chicken and squash stew was one of her favorite foods. "I just spoke to Mom," she said and forced a smile.

"Pull out a chair and sit down." Carmen ladled stew into a bowl. "You need to eat, even if it's not your mother's cooking." She placed the bowl down in front of Cecilia, a spoon beside it. "We have a lot of work to do for the *kermés*."

Returning to the stove with her back to Cecilia, she asked, "How's your mother doing?"

"She said she was doing okay, but she sounded really tired . . . and sad."

"Well, yes . . ." Carmen said.

"She told me her *don* story."

Carmen wheeled round. "Did you get an understanding about last words, how they might help serve as a clue to your *don*? To your new patron saint?"

"I got a sense of how Doña Faustina helped my mom use them . . . but is Doña Faustina still around? Is she still helping others? Mom told me to ask what you thought."

Carmen pursed her lips. "Hmm . . . she must be close to a hundred by now."

"Can I go see her?"

Carmen, who was now over the sink peeling potatoes, dropped the potato and peeler on the counter and said, "Put your coat on." Then she turned off the burners. "I'll finish cooking later. Let's hurry." And with that she led Cecilia to the front door.

"Where are we going?"

"To Doña Faustina. But we have to hurry," she said. She helped Cecilia with her coat and rushed her out the door.

Why this frantic hurry? Cecilia wondered as she started to perspire trying to follow Carmen's quick pace. *Is it because she has to be back in time for the* kermés *meeting?*

They crossed a busy intersection on a red traffic light and were honked at by an oncoming car. When Carmen didn't seem to notice the red light, Cecilia realized something was definitely going on.

"Carmen!" Cecilia shouted and grabbed her arm to try to stop her.

But Carmen just dragged Cecilia along. She turned at the next corner and said, "Let's run down the hill." She pumped her arms and increased her pace.

At the bottom of the hill, Carmen clutched her chest, panting, as rivulets of sweat streamed down her face.

"Are you okay?" Cecilia asked. She feared Carmen might have a heart attack.

"I'm fine. Fine," Carmen said and wiped her flushed face with her sleeve. She took big gulps of air until her breathing grew more regular. Next, she cast her gaze at the houses across the street.

"There . . . the lime-green one." They dashed across the street. Then Carmen started to pound on the front door loudly.

Suddenly, the door creaked open, and a bony finger appeared, followed by a tiny wrinkled face with the brightest eyes Cecilia had ever seen.

"Doña Faustina!" Carmen said and gave her a big bear hug.

"Carmen . . . is that you?" asked Doña Faustina in a low, raspy voice.

"Yes! It's been so long," Carmen answered and gave her a kiss on the cheek.

As Doña Faustina motioned for them to come inside, Carmen said, "You're still roasting coffee . . . I can smell it."

Doña Faustina nodded slightly. "Come into the kitchen," she said and shuffled down a dark hallway.

After a few steps, Cecilia also caught the scent of something roasting. Then, as they stepped into the tiny kitchen, she spotted a popcorn popper with a crank on the stove, a colander with roasted coffee beans on the counter and a burlap sack of green, unroasted beans leaning against a wall. Something that looked like butterfly wings, small and tawny-colored, fluttered through the air, everywhere. *What are those?* she wondered as she watched them float back and forth, slowly descending from above her head and landing lightly on the floor like the tiniest of feathers.

"Cecilia, come sit down." Doña Faustina pulled out a chair at the kitchen table. *How does she know my name?*

"Doña Faustina . . . ," Carmen said with a wary look on her face, "Cecilia wants to ask you a question."

Doña Faustina didn't react. Instead she shuffled towards the sink with a kettle in her hand. After she filled and set the kettle on a burner, she turned around and fixed her penetrating eyes on Cecilia. "Angel wings," she said.

Angel wings? Did she say, "angel wings?" Cecilia felt that she could not possibly ask Carmen without Doña Faustina overhearing.

Doña Faustina suddenly stopped and bent down to pick something off the floor. She shuffled over, opened her hand over the table, and said, "Angel wing."

Cecilia was bewildered by the tiny, translucent, golden-brown object in Doña Faustina's hand. She looked up and saw that Carmen was watching her with a knowing grin.

Cecilia swallowed hard and tried to summon the courage to ask her real question, the one concerning her *don*. The sooner she did, the quicker she would be able to extract herself from this stressful situation.

Just then, the kettle started to whistle, and Doña Faustina prepared and served the coffee as she had once done for Cecilia's mother. Cecilia stared at the steaming cup in front of her and wondered if Doña Faustina was now going to tell her to have a *plática* with her patron saint, Santa Cecilia.

Carmen pitched forward and raised an eyebrow at Cecilia, as if to say, *We are waiting for you to say something.*

"Um . . ." Cecilia began in a low, tentative tone, "how did you know my name, Doña Faustina . . . when Carmen didn't introduce me to you?"

"I know because I dreamt you were coming to see me."

Startled, Cecilia blurted out, "You dreamt of me? What . . . what was I doing in your dream?"

"You'll see. Just drink your coffee."

Cecilia leaned forward and said, "Are you saying I should have a *plática* with my patron saint, like you had my mother do when she was my age?"

Doña Faustina gave a quick nod and, with Carmen's help, walked to the far end of the kitchen, where they halted in front of the back door.

"Carmen and I are going outside to see the coffee tree," Doña Faustina said. "We'll be back soon."

"But," Cecilia said as she scrambled to her feet, "before you go . . . tell me about the angel wings. I mean . . . where are the angels?"

Doña Faustina reached into the sack of green coffee beans and, lifting a single bean into the air, said, "Each one has an angel. You'll see when you start your apprenticeship." She placed the bean back in the sack and added, "Ask your patron saint to explain this."

After Faustina and Carmen shut the door and stepped into the garden, Cecilia dropped back down into her chair and forced herself to gaze at the cup in front of her, and then at the cup across from her, the cup set for Santa Cecilia. *What do I do now?* She sighed heavily.

The coffee does smell good. She realized that Doña Faustina and Carmen would not let her leave if she didn't finish this *plática*. So, she took a sip, and another, until she emptied the cup. Every sip filled her with an increasing sense of well-being and hope. Yes, hope! It was hope that this *plática* might actually help her. But how strange this all felt to her, to talk to a steaming cup of coffee!

Could she really be here? Santa Cecilia? Cecilia stared at the cup, then all around the room. She looked out the window and saw Doña Faustina and Carmen standing next to a tree, touching its green leaves, talking.

"Santa Cecilia," Cecilia said in a halting tone, turning her gaze back to the cup, "can you help me . . . choose a Confirmation saint?" She paused and thought how this might have come off sounding rude. "Don't think I'm wanting to replace you," she added. "It's just that, well . . . you're the patron saint of music . . . and I'm terrible at music . . . sorry . . . but. . . ."

Cecilia gave her head a brisk shake, unsure of what to do or say next. She studied the empty chair, the steaming cup, and suddenly she got an idea. Bending forward, she reached across the table, took Santa Cecilia's cup and drained it in several long chugs.

Cecilia set the cup down and inhaled before she broke into a big smile. She felt she had just drunk the answers to her questions, that now it was only a matter of sitting quietly and waiting to interpret any signs Santa Cecilia might reveal to her. After several intense minutes, as if suspended in a spell, she jumped up and dashed out the back door to join Carmen and Doña Faustina.

"I-I got it!" Cecilia said as she rushed towards them. "I picked my patron saint!"

Doña Faustina's face brightened, but Carmen asked in a suspicious tone: "Really? Or are you saying this just to get back to your schoolwork?"

Cecilia was startled that Carmen had read her mind, again. "No . . . I'm serious," she said as she gave Carmen a hard look. *Oh, no*, Cecilia told herself, making every effort to remain calm, *Did Carmen blab her godmother "troubles" to Doña Faustina? Did she complain about how Cecilia wanted* the Confirmation process to be over as soon as possible so she could focus on her school, her friends and her priority—getting into a good college? How Carmen thought Cecilia was "Americanized?"

"So then you start the day after the *kermés*," Doña Faustina said.

"What?" Cecilia said, taking a step back. "What do I start the day after the *kermés*?"

"We'll start with this little tree," Doña Faustina said and gestured at a tree with a sweep of her hand. "I'll tell you its story and I'll show you the bundles of letters. But for now," she added, and started towards the back door with Carmen at her side, "let me help you with the *kermés*."

Cecilia went to Carmen's other side, tapped her on the shoulder and whispered, "What's this all about? What's going on?"

"Cecilia just asked me what this is all about. What you're up to," Carmen whispered loudly with a snort into Doña Faustina's ear.

Cecilia felt stricken when Doña Faustina suddenly stopped and faced her. She said, deadly serious, "I'm up to hurrying, hurrying because I have no time left." Then, she shuffled off again, Carmen at her elbow.

Cecilia was more confused than ever when she caught up with them in the kitchen. Doña Faustina asked her to weigh a half pound of green coffee beans on a brass scale and then put them in the popcorn popper.

"Start cranking the crank," Doña Faustina ordered, "the moment I switch on the flame." Cecilia nodded and quickly glanced at Carmen, who sat at the table writing something.

"Now!" Doña Faustina shouted as she pointed to the flame under the pot and caused Cecilia to jump. "Start cranking! You don't want to burn them!"

"Right!" Cecilia said and swallowed hard as she grabbed the crank of the popcorn popper with one hand, the popper's handle with the other, and started to work the machine.

"Faster!" Doña Faustina ordered as she hovered over the pot. "Don't burn them!"

"Okay!" Cecilia said and cranked harder, much harder, while her heart pumped faster, faster. All of a sudden, she heard Carmen's cackle behind her. *Is she laughing at me?* Cecilia wondered and that made her muscles tense with frustration. She glanced at Doña Faustina and detected a hint of a smile on her lips. *At least I'm cranking fast enough for Doña Faustina*, she sighed with relief, and cranked and cranked.

Her thoughts drifted to school, the heap of homework that waited for her, especially the science project she hadn't even started that was due soon.

"Faster!" *Doña* Faustina said.

Keep cranking! Keep cranking! Cecilia repeated over and over to herself, like a drumbeat. *I just have to get through this as quickly as possible . . . as quickly as possible. . . .*

"Faster!" Doña Faustina repeated and rapped Cecilia on the head. "Stop daydreaming! Focus on the coffee beans! Remember that every bean has its own angel."

Cecilia squared her feet and cranked as fast as she could. The hand she cranked with ached. *Pop!* Cecilia jumped back, startled, and glanced at Doña Faustina for a clue.

"Keep cranking!" Doña Faustina said in a stern voice.

"What was that sound?" Cecilia asked.

Doña Faustina lifted the lid by its wooden knob. A plume of smoke shot out and swirled in the air like an escaping genii, and emitted a sharp, roasted scent. Doña Faustina raised herself on the tips of her toes, leaned over the pot and peered inside. The beans, whirling round and round, were now the color of dark chocolate.

Pop! Pop!

"Take the pot off the stove!" Doña Faustina commanded as she switched off the burner.

Excited, though a bit nervous, Cecilia quickly lifted the pot.

"Dump the beans into this." Doña Faustina placed a metal colander on the counter. "Then start shaking it over the sink."

Cecilia squinted, not fully understanding, as she took the lid off the pot and poured the roasted beans into the colander, where they clattered and smoked up the room.

As she carried the colander over to the sink, Doña Faustina shuffled behind her, and she noticed Carmen still scribbling away at the table.

"Faster!" Doña Faustina said and gestured for Cecilia to shake the colander back and forth over the sink.

Flakes, translucent and tawny-colored, fluttered off into the air as Cecilia shook the colander. "Are those the angel wings?" Cecilia asked.

Doña Faustina nodded as her lips formed a bright smile.

Carmen looked up for a second, then returned to her mad scribbling.

"How long do I keep shaking the colander?" Cecilia asked.

"Until all the wings fly off," Doña Faustina said as she reached up and caught one.

After a few minutes, Cecilia said, "I think they're all off." Her arms were aching.

Doña Faustina examined the colander, nodded, then opened a cupboard and took out an empty Mason jar. "Put them in here," she ordered.

Cecilia tipped the colander and guided the beans into the jar with her hand. "Do I put the lid back on?"

Doña Faustina shook her head. "Not until tomorrow. The beans need to breathe, to exhale their air." She then slid the jar to the back of the counter.

"Now come here," said Doña Faustina. She waved Cecilia over while she opened another cupboard.

Cecilia's eyes widened with astonishment. It was filled with jars of roasted coffee beans the color of dark chocolate.

"These are for you, to take to the kermés," Doña Faustina said. One by one, she started taking jars out of the cabinet . . . until there were ten jars in front of her.

"You say they are from me . . . and you," she added, and tapped Cecilia's shoulder with her finger for emphasis.

Cecilia watched in confusion, as Doña Faustina pulled a burlap sack from a drawer and placed the coffee jars into it, slowly, carefully, as if they were precious jewels.

"From me?" Cecilia asked and pointed at herself.

With a slight nod, Doña Faustina took a piece of cord and tied the top of the sack.

Cecilia glanced at Carmen, but was startled to find her godmother staring at her with tears in her eyes. What's going on? Then she felt her arm being pulled. Doña Faustina handed her the sack.

"I'll tell you more later," she said. She shuffled over to the table and fell heavily into a chair.

Carmen jumped to her feet, placed a hand on Doña Faustina's back and said, "Are you okay?"

Doña Faustina shut her eyes and fell back on her chair, breathing heavily. Cecilia had stopped breathing, when suddenly Doña Faustina opened her eyes and fixed them on Cecilia. She said in a raspy whisper, "I have to hurry . . . so come." Then she shut her eyes again.

Cecilia was stunned. She wanted to know what Doña Faustina meant, why she seemed so grave.

"Don't worry. I'll make sure Cecilia's here," Carmen promised.

Doña Faustina opened her eyes again, briefly, and raised her arm towards Cecilia. Cecilia felt confused but took her hand and tried to smile.

As Cecilia headed home with the sack of coffee jars slung over her shoulder, her head was full of questions. *Why was Carmen almost crying? Why is Doña Faustina so serious and in such a hurry? What am I going to start after the kermés? What craziness have they gotten me into?*

"You can leave the coffee here," Carmen said as she unlocked the door to her apartment, "we'll take it to the basement later, when we meet with the *kermés* committee. We'll eat dinner before then, around six."

Cecilia placed the sack on Carmen's kitchen table and asked if she could help with dinner. Carmen shook her head and said she was fine, but that Cecilia might go see whether Julie wanted to join them for dinner. Cecilia thanked Carmen and left for Julie's apartment.

Julie opened her door and said, "Oh my god, where have you been?"

"You're not going to believe it," Cecilia said, before she lowered her voice and added, "Your mom? How is she?"

Julie's face fell. "She's having a migraine."

Cecilia was bursting to tell Julie everything, but she did not know where Julie's mom was and she didn't want to disturb her. "Let's talk out here in the hallway for a minute."

"Okay, now tell me everything!" Julie said as she stepped out. "What am I not going to believe?"

She told her about the "last words" that had helped her mother discover her *don* and about her mother's *plática* with her patron saint. Then, she told her about her experience at Doña Faustina's house and how she had made Cecilia have a talk with her patron saint.

"But now she wants me to come see her again the day after the *kermés*," Cecilia said. "Can you believe it? This whole thing has only gotten worse and worse. I thought I would just go along with the *plática*, then pick a saint—any saint—so I could finally put all this nonsense behind me and do my schoolwork. That friggin' science project, you know . . . it's due soon. But . . ."

"Oh my god!" Julie slapped her hand over her open mouth. "Are you saying you faked it? That you lied to Doña Faustina and Carmen when you told them that your *plática* with Santa Cecilia helped you pick your new patron saint?"

"The Confirmation letter is due next week!" Cecilia said. Her face flushed. "And I'm behind in all my classes. . . ."

"But . . . ," Julie said and raised her arms in the air.

"But what?"

Bang! The two tensed at the loud sound that echoed from inside Julie's apartment. "Julie! Where are you?" A shrill voice pierced the air.

The blood drained from Julie's face as she wheeled around and flung open the door. Inside, Cecilia heard Julie yell out, "Mom, what's wrong!" before Julie's and her mom's voices grew fainter and fainter.

Cecilia looked down at her hands, took a deep breath and shut the door. She wondered if she should wait for Julie to return or head back to her apartment and wait there for Julie to call. Had something happened?

Then, Julie popped back out. "Mom fell, but she's okay," Julie said in a muffled tone. "She took some pills . . . and is back in bed."

Cecilia nodded.

"Mom okayed me going to the meeting, but, till then, I better stick around here . . . in case she wakes up. I can't wait to hear more about Doña Faustina because I just got a great idea!"

"Wow, I can hardly wait to hear it," Cecilia said, trying not to sound too sarcastic. "Anyway, can you stop by Carmen's at six-thirty? I don't want to disturb your mother by knocking on your door."

Julie nodded. Then, thinking of her strange visit with Doña Faustina, Cecilia hurried back to her apartment to wash her face and rest a while.

CHAPTER 15

"Gosh, these are so good," Julie said before she bit into the second *carnitas* taco Carmen had saved for her. While Julie ate, Cecilia and Carmen labeled the jars of coffee at the kitchen table. "I'm so jealous of you," Julie said to Cecilia the minute Carmen stepped out of the room.

"Why?" Cecilia asked and looked up from writing "Doña Faustina's Roasted Coffee" on a label.

"Because you have a *don* that your mother, godmother and now Doña Faustina are helping you discover. You also have the perfect science project!"

Cecilia glared at Julie. "Why are you mocking me?"

"*Mocking* you? What are you talking about?"

"Look, I've been telling you—how many times now?— that I'm really behind in all my classes, and especially my science project. And here you're saying that you're jealous of me because I'm spending all my time getting trained to do something that has nothing to do with school . . . or even the real world. And now you claim I have the perfect science project?!"

"What's your perfect science project?" Carmen asked as she entered the room.

"Ask Julie," Cecilia said with sarcasm.

"Julie, what's Cecilia's perfect science project?" Carmen asked.

"Oh," said Julie, "I . . . I was just telling Cecilia how much I envy her . . . for having so many people interested in her *don* . . . and . . . because Cecilia told me you once cured her of a terrible eye infection with an egg, after the eye specialists couldn't do anything to help."

"And?" asked Carmen.

"And that she saw you make a tea that helped a woman have twins, after doctors told her she couldn't have children. So I think a perfect science project would be for her to test the reality of such marvels since . . ."

" . . . Everyone thinks this is just Mexican superstition?" Carmen added with a cackle.

"Oh, no!" Julie said with a gasp. "I believe it! Really I do! That's why I think it's the perfect science project . . . 'cause it'll show others that it's for real . . . that it works."

"She wants me to go around investigating, like *Harriet the Spy*," said Cecilia rolling her eyes.

Julie dropped her head and sighed. She thought it was useless to argue with Cecilia in front of Carmen.

Carmen stood up and put her arm around Julie. She looked at Cecilia and said, "It does sound like the perfect science project . . . for the both of you."

The girls exchanged stunned looks. *Is Carmen serious?*

"And you can start your project right now," Carmen added as she put the newly labeled jars in the sack, "by heading down to the basement and meeting the *kermés* committee."

The trio exited the apartment and headed downstairs. With each step, Julie felt her heart beat faster and faster. *What's down there?* In the past, she had heard muffled sounds from the basement, like the beat of festive music or cheers at the soccer matches being broadcast from a TV set. On a more somber note, she had also seen men and women dressed in black and looking sad head down there.

When they reached the dark basement, Julie took a deep breath as she watched Carmen open a heavy metal door. The loud sound of the hinges creaking made her jump back and stumble into Cecilia.

"Come on," Cecilia said as she regained her balance and pulled Julie inside.

Julie blinked rapidly, trying to adjust her eyes to the brightness of the room. She bumped into someone and almost knocked them down. "I'm so sorry," Julie said as she reached out. It was a girl about her age, height and even weight.

"Have you all met?" Carmen asked Cecilia and Julie. She placed her hand on the girl's shoulder. "This is Lebna. She and her mother just moved into our building. They're from Ethiopia. Her name means heart, spirit."

Cecilia and Julie smiled and shook Lebna's hand.

"Julie," added Carmen, "you're wondering why Lebna gets to visit the basement so soon after arriving here, when you've been here much longer. Right?" Carmen gave Julie's arm a gentle squeeze and continued. "It's because I ran into her mother in the laundry room. We started talking, and she asked if I knew any girls her daughter's age. I told her I would introduce the three of you. That's why. Lebna's also starting at your school; she's in eighth grade too, so you can take the bus together."

At the far end of the room, Cecilia saw four women—Imelda, Tata, Cristina and María, the kermés committee—huddled around a table. They were talking and picking through a huge pile of things.

Lebna gestured at the sack Cecilia was carrying over her shoulder and asked, "Want some help?"

Cecilia shook her head and replied, "It's not too heavy . . . just some jars of coffee."

"Coffee?" Lebna said, her voice suddenly sounding brighter.

"Yes." Cecilia cocked her head to the side. "Do you like to drink coffee?"

"Absolutely! It's considered the bread of my community," Lebna smiled and then suddenly seemed sad. "Well, it was . . . back in Ethiopia."

"Hurry! Bring Doña Faustina's coffee over here!" boomed one of the women around the table and frantically waved Cecilia over.

"Do you know how long it's been since I've had a cup of her coffee?" another said, after she and the other kermés committee members gave Cecilia their condolences. "Not since I was fifteen years-old! Almost a century ago!"

"Same for me!" a third woman said and smacked her lips.

"These jars will go like gold!" a fourth woman added. "Especially now that she's starting to train Cecilia. We know what that means!"

Confused at the over-the-top reaction to a batch of roasted coffee beans, and especially at the mention of her training, Cecilia set the sack down on an empty chair by the table. She ached to ask Carmen what the women were talking about.

"Mmm . . . it smells so good," one woman said after she unscrewed the lid on a jar and took a deep whiff. She passed it around for the others to smell. All of them shut their eyes as if they'd fallen into a swoon.

"Wait! I have a great idea!" another announced, her eyes ablaze with excitement. "Since these may be Doña Faustina's last jars—now that she has an apprentice, we may sell them for more. Right?"

The three women leaned forward and nodded, hanging on her every word.

"So let's hold a raffle . . . a big one!"

"Yes!" The other women cheered and clapped each other on the back. They lifted the jars up to the light and gazed at them as if they were filled with jewels.

Oh, no, thought Cecilia. *Me, an apprentice? What does this mean?*

"Cecilia should pick and announce the raffle winners," Carmen said.

"Yes!" the four agreed after they looked at each other.

"So everything's set for Sunday," Tata said to Carmen. "We've let everyone know . . . donations are coming in . . . like that chicken you're carrying, among those other things over there," pointing to a long row of laundry baskets heaping with an assortment of baby shoes, toys, hammers, small appliances and jars of canned fruits.

"Doña Carla even sent her grandson over to tell us that she was going to pawn her gold earrings first thing tomorrow morning to help," Imelda said. "I told the boy, no, not to let her, to tell her that we would raise enough money so that she didn't have to pawn her only earrings. But he said his grandmother had insisted, saying she was over a hundred years old, so she didn't need flashy earrings . . . and the baby hadn't even lived a minute. She was counting on the baby welcoming her up in heaven soon."

"And Velma called," María said, "to say she was breaking her piggy bank that she was saving for a new dress she had put on layaway . . . that this was more important."

Cecilia felt overwhelmed. *All this over a miscarriage—or, what had Carmen called it, a stillbirth?*

Julie felt confused.

"Now let's summon divine help," Tata said. She crossed to the far end of the room and the others followed.

"Where are we going?" Julie whispered to Cecilia as they proceeded through a door into total darkness, Lebna close at their side.

"You'll see," Cecilia said as the light switched on.

Julie suddenly gasped.

Carmen placed her hand on Julie's back and gently pushed her forward. "Julie, let me introduce you to our patron saint, Santa Cecilia." She pointed to a three-foot-tall statue on a highly polished wooden table.

"She's lovely," Julie said, her eyes tracing the saint's serene face, her hands clasped in prayer, her scarlet velvet robe and the bright flowers all around her. *But what are those shiny objects pinned all over her robe?* As Julie bent closer she made out the shapes of hearts, heads, arms, legs, a pair of eyes, even a truck.

"So let's pray," someone behind her said.

When she turned around, Julie saw the committee members close their eyes and bow their heads slightly. She caught Cecilia's eye and she saw her give a shrug as Lebna shut her eyes too.

"Lord, bless, protect and guide Micaela's soul," Tata said, "and help us send her soul to you in heaven. And once there, we pray that she intercedes for us, to help bless, protect and guide our community. Amen."

"Amen," everyone added and opened their eyes.

"Okay, so we'll see you all at the *kermés*," Tata said as she led the group back into the main room.

"But what about the chicken?" one of the women said, when it leapt onto the table.

"I'll take it," Carmen said and scooped it up.

The girls followed Carmen up the stairs. She suddenly turned around and asked, "Julie, did you see a demon or a ghost? What spooked you?"

Julie grabbed the handrail to steady herself and asked, " . . . a demon . . . a ghost?"

"Yes, there are demons," Carmen said casually as she stroked the chicken in her arms. "So what did you see?"

"You might be wondering why I'm stopping you here in the cold and dark stairwell," Carmen eyed the three girls and said, "but I have a reason . . . a good reason. So tell us, Julie, what made you gasp all of a sudden?"

"It was something I saw on TV . . . right before coming to your apartment," Julie said, nervously shifting her weight from one foot to the other. "A report about Breezy Point . . . this place in New York . . . It showed the houses that burned down because of Hurricane Sandy. But . . ."

"But what?" Carmen encouraged her to go on.

"Well, all you saw . . . everywhere . . . was devastation, total devastation: houses reduced to rubble, trees uprooted, debris scattered all around. But . . . in the middle of all this horror was a statute of the Virgin Mary with her arms outstretched as if offering help and comfort . . . and hope. It was amazing!"

"Yes," said Carmen and started walking up the stairs again.

— — —

Back in Cecilia's kitchen, Julie asked Carmen, "Why do you think the statue of the Virgin survived the storm . . . and the fire?"

"You tell me, Julie. What do you think it means?" answered Carmen.

"I don't know," Julie said and gave her head a firm shake.

"What about you?" Carmen asked Cecilia. "Do you know what this means?"

Cecilia shrugged. "Maybe that angels were around? I don't know."

Carmen nodded. "And?"

"Maybe it's a sign," Cecilia said.

"A sign of what? Angels?" Julie asked.

Carmen tossed her head back and huffed. Then she tapped Julie on the shoulder and said in a half-mocking tone, "Hope this talk isn't getting too crazy for you. See, for us, the Santa Cecilia community, the spiritual is real, as real as real can be. But my goddaughter Cecilia seems to be stuck between two worlds."

"What do you mean?" Julie asked.

"Ask her," Carmen said and cocked her head towards Cecilia.

Brrrring! Cecilia leapt up and grabbed the phone.

It was her father. Her mother was asleep, he said, and would come home tomorrow. "Have you eaten?" he asked.

"Yes, Dad. I ate at Carmen's," she said. "We're getting ready for the *kermés.*"

"Okay, I'll let you get back to it, but first let me speak to Carmen."

Carmen took the phone and said they should not worry about Cecilia, that she would come over to spend the night with her at their apartment.

"He's sleeping at the hospital?" Cecilia asked when Carmen hung up the phone.

"Yes, he's keeping your mother company. But I'll be staying here with you, so don't worry."

"And the chicken?" Cecilia asked as the chicken strutted across the linoleum floor.

"She'll be spending the night here too. And I hope she lays a magic egg."

CHAPTER 16

The following morning Cecilia and Carmen were at the kitchen table having breakfast, when they heard a loud knock at the door. Cecilia opened it to find Julie there.

As she stepped inside, Julie wiped tears from her red, puffy face. "Have you heard?" she asked.

"Heard what?" Cecilia replied. "Is your mom okay?"

Carmen heard the commotion and came to the door. "Is your mother all right?" she asked.

Julie gave a slight nod. "She's okay. It's . . . it's . . ."

Carmen took Julie by the elbow and led her down the hallway into the kitchen, where she pulled out a chair at the table and made her sit down. She poured her a cup of coffee and sat down next to her. "Here, drink this."

Julie's hands trembled as she reached for the cup, then took a sip.

Carmen stuck her hand under the cup and said sharply, "Drink it all down."

Julie looked at Carmen with bloodshot eyes and swallowed hard, then slowly lifted the cup to her lips and took another sip, and another, until the cup was completely empty.

"Okay now, what's wrong?" Carmen asked. "Did something happen to your mother?"

Julie only hung her head and sighed heavily as if she was too exhausted to say anything.

Carmen caught Cecilia's eye and said, "Stay here with Julie. I'll be right back." She hurried out of the apartment.

"Want some more coffee?" Cecilia asked and tugged at Julie's sleeve.

"No . . . thank you."

"How about some scrambled eggs . . . or toast?"

Julie managed a weak smile. "You haven't heard . . . right?"

"Heard what?" Cecilia said and furrowed her brow. Then she suddenly jumped to her feet. "Oh, no! My mother! It's about my mother!"

Bang! The front door slammed shut. Carmen rushed over with a stricken look on her face.

Cecilia grabbed Carmen's arm and pleaded, "What happened to Mom? Tell me! What happened to her?"

"Your mother's fine. This is about something else," Carmen said and then turned to Julie. "There was a shooting at an elementary school . . ."

"What?!" Cecilia asked.

Carmen sat down and pulled Cecilia's arm to make her sit too. "It happened this morning at a school in Connecticut: twenty kids were killed, also teachers and the principal. I just saw it on the news."

"That's why you were crying?"

Julie bobbed her head slightly, then said in a strained, barely audible tone, "It hit me because the school has the same name as the hurricane that destroyed my home—Sandy Hook."

"Hmm . . ." Cecilia said, "two Sandys in a row . . . now . . ."

Carmen raised an eyebrow and asked, "You're thinking about that old saying that things come in threes? Wondering what the third Sandy will be?"

Cecilia shrugged and asked, "So what can we do?"

"The sooner you discover and realize your *don*, the faster you can help people," Carmen said. She cast a sharp look at Cecilia.

Julie swallowed hard and leaned towards Carmen. She asked in a low, tentative voice, "Can I help too? Please?"

"What?" Cecilia asked with a groan. "You're not even Catholic!"

"That has nothing to do with it," Carmen said sharply and thumped her hand on the table.

"Confirmation and *dons* have everything to do with being Catholic, at least in this community. Even *I* know that!" Cecilia scowled.

"Of course Julie can help," Carmen said. She clicked her tongue. "She doesn't have to be Catholic. All that's required is that she discover her *don*. Everyone is born with a gift or talent, not just Catholics."

Julie's face brightened.

"But if you're going to help people," Carmen said, getting to her feet, "you must know everything you can about what you're up against, like the evil behind what just happened at that school. So let's see if we can find some clues." She placed her hand on Julie's shoulder and added, "You think you can stomach watching the scenes on TV?"

Julie's shoulders tensed before she nodded, as if she had to steel herself for what she was about to experience.

Carmen gave Julie a warm smile, crossed the room and switched on the small TV sitting next to the stove. The school shooting was on the news.

"*Se le metió el diablo*," Carmen said. She gave her head a firm shake while she turned off the TV.

"What?" Julie asked.

"The devil got into him," Cecilia translated.

Carmen then pulled out a piece of paper and a pen from her pocket and started writing. Cecilia wondered if that was the same paper she had been writing on at Doña Faustina's house.

"The devil got into whom?" Julie said in a hushed tone so as not to disturb Carmen.

Cecilia rose from her chair and peered over Carmen's shoulder. "Carmen, what are you doing?" she asked.

Carmen slapped her hand over the sheet of paper and said in a reproachful tone, "'The devil got into whom?' 'What are you doing?' Your questions only go to show how much the two of you don't know."

"Not again," Cecilia said and sighed.

Carmen explained in exasperation, "This is my letter to you, for your Confirmation."

"I thought *I* had to write the Confirmation letter," Cecilia said, "about the saint I was picking."

"That's right," Carmen said, "but as your first godmother, since you still haven't chosen your Confirmation sponsor, I still have the duty of guiding and supervising your spiritual education. Confirmation is about taking the next step, after Baptism and after making your First Communion."

"Step to what?" Cecilia said spreading her hands in a gesture of frustration.

"I've told you many, many times how important it was to spend Saturday mornings with me, learning these things. But, no, you couldn't, because you had homework to do, or a school project or a test."

Cecilia took a deep breath and said as calmly as she could, "Yes, I wouldn't be asking so many questions if I had spent Saturday mornings having *pláticas* with you. But I didn't. So can you, please, just tell me what's going on?"

Carmen pursed her lips, then turned towards Julie and said, "Let's not keep you with all this 'crazy talk,' as I'm sure Cecilia has described it to you. If you want to go check on your mother . . ."

"Oh, no!" Julie shot back. "I would love to stay . . . really I would!"

"I bet Cecilia would love to trade places with you," Carmen said with a short laugh, "so she wouldn't have to hear another word from her godmother."

Cecilia rolled her eyes and wondered how Carmen had read her mind again.

"Okay," Carmen said. She sat up straight. "Let me begin with explaining the steps. The Holy Spirit enters a person's soul at baptism, like a seed—the first step. It sprouted when you made your First Communion. At Confirmation—the next step—it starts to grow so that your *don* can bear fruit."

Carmen took in Julie's baffled expression and added, "What's the Holy Spirit? The divine in a person, her highest self, the seed that contains her sacred talent or *don*. And why is Confirmation important? Because it kick-starts a person's quest, her journey to discover, grow and ultimately fruit her *don*. Not just for herself, but to share with her family, her community, the entire world."

Julie was transfixed, while Cecilia slumped in her chair and wondered if this was just Mexican superstition or a big, fat story that had been told so many times over so many years that it had morphed into a myth.

"Don't forget," Carmen said, cupping Cecilia on the shoulder, "how all those medical doctors, even specialists, couldn't cure your eye infection, remember? You couldn't stand the pain, you thought you were going blind. But then I came along and, with an egg and a couple of prayers, you were cured."

Cecilia grudgingly answered, "Yes, I remember, but I also remember you saying that I suffered from a curse." Then she paused and, as if suddenly realizing something, sat up and said: "Are you saying that you think the devil got into the killer . . . the killer at the school?"

Julie inhaled sharply.

Cecilia turned to Julie and explained, "Carmen thinks that people are sometimes attacked by the devil and his demons."

Carmen thumped the table with her hand and declared, "That's right. Me and Jesus believe this because that's what He said."

"So . . . ," Julie said, "the devil made the killer shoot the children? Is that what you're saying?"

"Well," Carmen said and lifted her chin, "evil exists, and what the killer did was certainly evil. I don't know if he was on drugs, too, or mentally ill. But this is not a one-time freak thing that people can say is shocking, then dismiss it, believing it won't happen again. This is an evil that we must face and we must fight."

"But how?" Julie asked anxiously. "How do you fight evil?"

"By using your *don*. I'll let Cecilia explain this to you."

"What?" Cecilia said, disoriented for a minute. "It . . . it started with Saint Benedict, right?" Then, glancing at Carmen, who gave her a slight nod, she added, "Who told the monks to pray for powers, for things they needed . . ."

"Like what?" Julie asked.

"Well . . . like healing. If someone, for instance, was suffering from an illness, an illness the monks couldn't cure, they would pray. They would ask that the power to heal the illness be granted to one of them. In other words, they believed that God would care for them in every way, that all they had to do was ask for what they needed—just like Jesus said in the New Testament: 'Ask and it'll be given.' Something like that."

Carmen nodded her on, so Cecilia continued. "Because of our belief that God will provide if we ask, our community doesn't feel it needs to look elsewhere to find the help it needs. We have faith that the ability to help will be given to someone in the community. But . . ." Cecilia paused suddenly.

"But what?" Julie said, leaning closer.

"But, assuming the gift is granted, the task is then to find the person to whom it's been given . . . and to get the person to use it to solve the problem. There, I'm done."

"No, you're not done," Carmen said, banging the table. "You left something out, something very important."

"What did I leave out?"

"The complications, obstacles . . ." Carmen instructed.

"Oh, that," Cecilia said. "But complications and obstacles often prevent the gift from ever being used to solve the problem."

"Like what?" Julie said.

"Well," Cecilia said, feeling increasingly frustrated about all the time she was wasting having to translate and explain everything to Julie. "The person who gets the gift might not believe in this relationship with the spiritual . . . or might refuse to share it with others . . . or a person who didn't get the gift might go around fooling everyone, saying that they did."

"How about depression?" Julie whispered.

Carmen gave Julie a gentle pat on her hand and said, "Yes, that can also be an obstacle, when life's stresses eventually crack or even break a person's spirit, their will to live. But," she added as she glanced at the wall clock, "it's getting late, and I bet your mother is wondering where you are. So let's say a prayer for the souls of those killed at the school, as well as for Micaela, since it takes nine days to get to heaven."

"Nine days to get to heaven?" Julie asked, as if trying to understand something said in a strange language.

Carmen nodded and said, "Yes, it takes a soul nine days to get all the way up to heaven. If it wasn't so late, I would have my godchild explain this to you too. But for now, let's join hands and pray."

A few minutes later, the two girls stood in front of Julie's front door. Julie whispered to Cecilia, "I wonder where the souls of Micaela and the kids from the elementary school are now."

Cecilia looked up at the ceiling, thought for a moment and said, "I don't really know." She looked back at Julie and added, "I'll ask Carmen and let you know."

Julie nodded and said, "Gosh, I'm so jealous."

"Of what?"

"Of you! Your culture! Of having someone like Carmen for your godmother!"

Cecilia leaned on the wall and said, "I guess I am lucky . . . in a weird way, but you don't know the half of it. This culture takes so much time . . . I still have no clue about the science project."

"It's staring you right in the face."

"What are you talking about?" Cecilia asked. "Don't tell me you're still serious about testing the spiritual world."

"I'm dead serious!" Julie insisted. "We can test whether a prayed-for gift actually comes true."

Cecilia shook her head slowly.

"And I've got the perfect problem to ask for help with!" Julie added.

"What?" Cecilia said, rolling her eyes. "Finding your perfect boyfriend?"

"No! My mother!"

"What are you talking about?"

Brrring! It was Julie's cellphone. "Oh, hi, Mom! I'll be there in a minute. I'm just saying goodbye to Cecilia. Okay, I'll let her know. See you in a bit."

Julie snapped the phone shut and said, "Mom wants you to please give her deepest condolences to your parents. I have to run, but I'll tell you my science project idea tomorrow!"

CHAPTER 17

The rich scent of brewed coffee woke Cecilia up the next morning. Carmen poured her a cup when she came into the kitchen.

"Sit down," Carmen said as she placed the steaming cup on the table and pulled a chair out for Cecilia. "A cup of Doña Faustina's coffee will wake you right up."

"I thought the coffee was for the raffle," Cecilia remarked, then dropped into the chair and lifted the cup to her lips.

Carmen waved her hand. "Drink it. You'll need it now that you're Doña Faustina's apprentice. That's why I'm keeping a jar for you here."

Cecilia took a sip. It was electrifying.

"Go on, keep drinking,"

After she emptied her cup, Cecilia leaned back in her chair and gazed at Carmen, who was now cooking something on the stove. "Thanks for staying with me, *madrina*," she said. "I can't wait to see Mom and Dad."

Carmen wheeled around, wooden spoon in hand, and said, "The sofa wasn't too bad. And this morning I found the chicken had laid an egg."

"Is that what you're cooking? The egg?"

"No. I'm taking the egg to the *kermés*. As well as the chicken."

"To sell them?"

"No," Carmen said, as she filled two plates with eggs scrambled into *chilaquiles*. "You'll see what they're for when we get there. But right now we need to hurry and eat breakfast." She set the plates on the table along with a stack of hot flour tortillas.

Cecilia stared at her steaming plate and sighed. She missed her parents and the little sister she didn't get to have.

"Start eating before it gets cold," Carmen ordered.

Cecilia lifted her fork and took a bite. The *chilaquiles* tasted good, although not as good as her mother's. "Um . . . Carmen," Cecilia said, wiping her lips with a napkin, "when does a baby get a soul and its guardian angel? At birth, right?"

"At conception," Carmen answered. "So, Micaela has a soul and her own guardian angel, if that's what you're asking."

Cecilia wondered how Carmen had read her mind again.

There was a knock at the door. Cecilia leapt from her chair and raced down the hallway, hoping her parents were home earlier than expected.

"Oh, hi!" said Lebna. She cradled a long-necked pot in her arms, along with two cloth sacks. "I want to show these to Carmen, to see if I can bring them to the *kermés*."

Cecilia nodded, then led Lebna into the kitchen, where Carmen had poured herself another cup of coffee.

"Good morning!" Carmen flashed Lebna a warm smile. "Have you had breakfast? Would you like some coffee?" she offered, reaching into the cupboard. "And what have you got there?"

"Thank you. I'm not hungry, but a cup of coffee would be great," Lebna said. She placed the items on the table and sat down.

"Carmen made a pot of Doña Faustina's coffee," Cecilia said as Carmen handed Lebna the cup.

Lebna took a sip and smiled. "Wow, it's so good. I can tell it's freshly roasted."

"How do you know?" Carmen asked.

Knock—knock—knock! Cecilia dashed to the front door again. When she opened the door, she saw Julie with a stack of books in her arms. "Oh, hi! I just stopped by to show these books to Carmen, to see which can be sold at the kermés."

Carmen immediately poured Julie a cup of coffee and served her a heaping plate of chilaquiles.

"Yum!" Julie said and dropped the books on the table. She attacked the food like a starving cat. "The coffee's fantastic!"

"It's Doña Faustina's coffee," Cecilia said.

"Really?" asked Julie, as she set her cup down. "I thought her coffee was for the raffle."

"Carmen's keeping a jar for me," Cecilia said with a shrug. "She says I'll need it as Doña Faustina's apprentice. Whatever that means."

"What?" Lebna asked. "You're an apprentice?"

Cecilia nodded, then filled in Lebna about her experience at Doña Faustina's house. As the girls talked, Carmen leaned back in her chair. She scrutinized Lebna's every gesture in response to hearing about Doña Faustina's ritual of roasting coffee beans, how mothers and godmothers had sent their children and godchildren to her for generations. Lebna seemed mesmerized.

"Carmen described Doña Faustina's coffee as 'celestial,'" Cecilia said.

"It can be if it helps you find your *don*," Carmen said with a huff as she got to her feet and refilled everyone's cup.

As soon as the girls finished their coffee, Carmen addressed them: "I hope drinking Doña Faustina's coffee will help all three of you—not just Cecilia—discover your special talent." Then she picked up one of the books Julie brought and said, "So tell me what you have here."

Julie scooted to the edge of her chair and said with a stammer: "These are my books . . . some of them. And I came to ask you if I can bring them to the *kermés*."

Carmen quickly flipped through the book in her hand, then another . . . and another. They were laid side by side on the table, until all the book covers were facing up. "Which one is most like you?"

Julie pointed a finger at herself. "Um . . . which one is most like *me*?"

"Yes, which book best mirrors your life?"

"Um . . . " Julie said, and shot a glance at Cecilia to beg for help.

Cecilia leaned towards Julie and said, "Carmen thinks that *Harry Potter and the Sorcerer's Stone* mirrors my life because it reflects that our community lives in two worlds, where others, like the muggles, live in only one."

Julie tried to absorb what Cecilia had just said before she scanned the books on the table. "I guess this one," she said and handed it to Carmen.

"*Harriet the Spy*?" Carmen asked. "Why?"

"Because the girl lives in New York . . . where I grew up," Julie said in a tentative voice. "And like me, she had a nanny who raised her while her parents . . . like my parents . . . spent their time working or socializing at parties. And she wanted to be a writer, so she went around spying on people to figure things out . . . to see how the world worked."

"Okay," Carmen said. After she snapped the book shut, she gave Julie a gentle tap on the back. She then turned to Lebna and asked, "What about you? Tell me about the items you brought for the *kermés*."

"These," Lebna gestured towards the long-necked clay pot and the two sacks, "represent my mother culture of Ethiopia, where I was born."

"Yes!" Carmen said and tossed her arms in the air. "They are wonderful! What are they?"

"This is an Ethiopian coffee pot," Lebna continued as she tapped the pot's belly. "And these are green coffee beans, from Ethiopia." She opened one sack and pulled out a fistful. "The other sack is filled with corn kernels."

After Carmen prodded her, Lebna began to describe the Ethiopian coffee ceremony.

"But what's the corn for?" Cecilia asked.

"For popcorn," Lebna said.

"Popcorn?" Julie snorted.

Lebna fixed Julie with a steady gaze and said, "Yes, it's part of the ceremony. We serve popcorn—"

Brrring! Cecilia dashed to the hallway and grabbed the phone, thinking it would be her parents. But it was for Carmen. After she left Carmen chatting on the phone, Cecilia returned to the kitchen and confronted Julie and Lebna.

"I know, I know," Cecilia said and shook her head, "you have a zillion questions."

"And I'll be happy to answer all of them," Carmen said. "But not now. Irma called to say that we have to hurry up and jump-start the *kermés*."

Julie looked at her books and said, "Um . . ."

Lebna touched her coffee pot and said, "Uh . . ."

"Oh, yes," Carmen said, as her eyes darted between Lebna and Julie, "about what to take to the *kermés*." She tapped her chin in thought and said, "Julie, select three or four books but leave me *Harriet the Spy*. I'm going to read it first. Okay?"

"Of course," Julie said.

"And Lebna, I want to hear more about your coffee ceremony. But do you think you could pop some corn and bring it in small bags to sell at the fair?"

"Sure," Lebna agreed.

"Okay, so we're all set," Carmen said. She pulled a fat roll of tickets from her apron pocket and handed it to Cecilia. "These are the raffle tickets for Doña Faustina's coffee. You'll have to sell them. And, as for me," she added, then plucked what looked like a cord from her other pocket. "Where did she go?" she asked as she bent over to look under the table.

"Where did who go?" Cecilia asked.

"The chicken!" Carmen said as she rushed into the hallway and returned moments later with the tawny chicken tucked under her arm. "Hold still," she added while she fastened the cord around its neck. "It's a leash, and now I only have to put a fresh diaper on her. So you two," she gestured at Julie and Lebna, "come to Baker Park at one o'clock this afternoon. Cecilia and I will be waiting for you across the street, in front of the church. She and I first need to attend Mass, then get the chicken blessed before the *kermés* starts.

"So let's all hurry." She now scooped the chicken into her arms and headed towards the front door. "Cecilia, I'll pick you up for Mass later."

"What can I say?" Cecilia asked and flashed her friends a wry smile as the front door shut. "Never a dull moment. But," she added, "the two of you don't have to put up with any of this, whether it's Carmen's crazy *don* talk or nonsense about the magic of this or that or coming to the *kermés*. I, unfortunately, have to. I am her godchild. But the moment this is all over—the burial, my Confirmation—we can just hang out . . . and catch up with school work."

"Are you crazy?" Julie said as she clutched Cecilia's arm. "This is the most exciting stuff I've ever experienced. It's like stumbling into Harry Potter's world and discovering it's for real."

Cecilia studied Julie's face for a trace of irony or sarcasm, but found she was entirely serious. When Cecilia glanced sideways, she saw Lebna was just as serious, or even more so.

"Okay! Okay!" Cecilia said, trying to keep her balance. "But don't say I didn't give you a chance to walk away," she added and shook free of Julie's grip. "So if at any time either of you feels you've seen or heard enough, just tell me so I can tell Carmen that you're no longer part of this harebrained 'Stop the Third Sandy' nonsense. Okay?"

Julie nodded vigorously as her face broke into a joyous smile.

"Um . . . ," Lebna said, "what exactly is this 'Stop the Third Sandy?'"

"Oh," Julie said, "it's . . . it's—"

Cecilia broke in and said, "I'll fill her in, while I walk her back to her apartment."

With that, the girls headed off.

CHAPTER 18

At the park the girls saw treats, treasures and surprises everywhere. Their mouths watered as they passed a glass box filled with translucent, candied fruits—orange, apricot, fig, pumpkin and even cactus—that glinted like gems. There were stands that sold *cajeta*, creamy caramel whipped from goat's milk; sesame and pumpkin seed brittle; *cicadas*, coconut cakes; bars of dark chocolate; coiled fruit leather; squares of *ate*, fruit pastes of quince, guava, pineapple and lime.

Nearby, a man in a straw hat and overalls soared an amazing scarlet bird in the air with one hand, while dangling blue, green and orange ones in the other. Suddenly, a voice boomed over a loudspeaker and startled the girls: "*Just one or two drops of this magic tonic cures baldness, bloating, belching, bad breath, even bad husbands. Yes! Bad everything! And those are just the B's! Come get yourself a bottle— and quick! They're selling like hot tamales! Only two dollars!*"

A bright yellow bicycle cart swooshed by, driven by a young man who sold strawberry, pineapple and coconut *paletas*—frozen fruit bars on a stick. Then the girls almost crashed into an old man holding a pinkish piglet in his arms. Kids hawked tiny packages of bright, Mexican chewing gum, four pieces per pack. They whirled and weaved throughout the crowd.

Everywhere there were makeshift stalls, fold-up tables, ironing boards, spread-out blankets, baskets, tarps, crates, cardboard boxes and sacks. People sold pork rinds, salted shark, radishes carved to look like jaguars or fantastic birds, banana leaves for wrapping *tamales*, corn bread, crispy *buñuelos*; strange and exotic fruits such as *mameys* that resembled miniature footballs and *chayote*, shaped like spiky green apples. Of course, chili peppers, fresh and dried, were for sale, as were tortillas as big as pizzas and slathered with beans. The variety of foods seemed endless.

Charcoal smoked. People grilled *fajitas* and other meats, heated *mole* and beans, blistered chiles and toasted corn on the cob, sending intoxicating fragrances into the air that piqued the girls' appetite.

They walked on and saw so many other unusual sights— at least they were unusual for Julie and Lebna: fortune-tellers, a *tamal*-eating contest, a *piñata* whacking tournament, a pet and owner look-alike contest, a woman braiding hair for a dollar, another writing letters at a fold-up table.

A group of *mariachis* in dazzling *charro* outfits suddenly stood before them. "Carmen!" the one carrying a guitar called out and came up to shake her hand.

"Rodrigo! Thanks for coming!" Carmen said and introduced him to the girls.

"Do you have a special request?" Rodrigo asked, bowing his head slightly to Cecilia.

When she saw Cecilia's stunned expression, Carmen said, "Why don't you play '*Cielito Lindo*'?"

Rodrigo nodded and turned to the *mariachis* behind him—four with violins, the others with a *guitarrón*, a *vihuela*, a brass trumpet and a wooden harp—and said, "Okay, muchachos, 'Cielito Lindo' for my friends! ¡Uno, dos, tres!"

Ay, ay, ay, ay, canta y no llores . . . porque cantando se alegran, Cielito lindo, los corazones . . .

The music electrified the air, blending with the delicious, rich aromas of food and brewed coffee. Carmen shut her eyes and swayed to the music as if inside a beautiful dream. People rushed over from all directions, the music pulling them with the force of a powerful magnet. *Was this Rodrigo's don?* Cecilia wondered with amazement.

The song ended to a burst of applause.

"Ah, that was magical," Carmen said and gave Rodrigo a big hug.

"What was magical?" Cecilia asked Carmen as the *mariachis* waved goodbye.

"The music you just heard," Carmen said.

"But how was it magical?"

"It took me back to Santa Cecilia, to the *zócalo*, the town plaza where we used to stroll beneath the flowering trees."

"Are you Cecilia?" a completely bald woman asked as she approached.

Cecilia stepped back in surprise.

Carmen stepped up and draped her arm around the bald woman's shoulder. "Inés! It's great to see you. And thank you so much for donating your beautiful copper hair."

"Also my eyebrows," Inés said and arched her brow.

"And your eyebrows!" Carmen said with a chuckle. "Yes, this is Cecilia, with her two friends."

Inés shook hands with all three girls, then she faced Cecilia and asked, "Is it true that you are selling raffle tickets for jars of Doña Faustina's coffee?"

"Yes, it's true," Cecilia said and pulled the roll of tickets from her coat pocket.

"I'll take ten," Inés said. She handed Cecilia a crisp ten-dollar bill.

Cecilia thanked her and counted out ten tickets.

"I hope I win!" Inés said as she waved the string of tickets in the air like a banner. "And I'm looking forward to sending my daughter over to you in a couple of years, since I hear that Doña Faustina has chosen you to be her apprentice. How about the two of you?" Inés asked, glancing at Julie and Lebna. "What are your gifts?"

Julie's eyes widened. Lebna started coughing.

"Well," Cecilia said, "they're working on it."

"That's right," Carmen said. "And I have a hunch," she smiled as she placed one hand on Lebna's shoulder and the other on Julie's, "that their *dons* are going to come together in the most amazing way!"

Inés wished them luck with their *dons*, then waved goodbye as she headed off into the crowd.

Cecilia followed Carmen's lead and tried to answer the heap of questions Julie and Lebna bombarded her with as they made their way through the fair.

"What in the world are Inés' hair and eyebrows for?"

"For Santa Cecilia, the statue in the basement. So she can wear a new wig on her feast day," Cecilia answered.

"What did Inés mean when she said she would send her daughter over to see you?"

"I have no idea."

"What about Carmen's remark that our *dons* will come together in the most amazing way?"

"I don't know. I told you," Cecilia said to her friends. "Isn't this all bonkers? My life's impossible. That's why it would be outrageous to propose a science project where we test the spiritual world."

"No, a place like this is perfect, what with all the fortune tellers and people who read minds and do other magical things!" Julie said.

Cecilia hung her head when she noticed that Lebna had nodded eagerly.

"I told Lebna about the science project and how this is a great place to start testing it," Julie said.

"Great? Tell me what you're talking about," Cecilia said in disbelief.

"Well," Julie reached inside her purse, "I have two dollars here. And since a fortune costs fifty cents, and you're in search of your *don* . . . and Lebna and I want to discover ours . . . let's each get our fortunes read . . . and . . ."

"And we'll spy on how he does it?" Cecilia said with a hiss.

"We'll get to see what happens, right?" Julie asked and looked to Lebna for support.

"Yes, Lebna, what do you think about this crazy project?" Cecilia asked.

"I . . . I love it!" Lebna said with a slight smile.

"What?" Cecilia groaned. "Are you serious? It's like we're three kids on a mission to see if Santa Claus really exists."

"But Santa Claus does exist!" Julie said in a burst of emotion. "Didn't Saint Nicholas toss gold coins into a poor family's chimney so their daughters could marry?"

Cecilia pressed her head between her hands and took a deep breath. "That's the supposed story, the legend of that saint, but. . . ."

"Oh, Cecilia," Julie said with excitement, "you'll never know how happy you made me with that story. I grew up really believing in Santa Claus. I owned every kid's book about him, which I read over and over again, not only at Christmas, but all year round. Then Santa became especially important to me when my parents fought a lot and later divorced. Whatever happens, I told myself, I'll always have Santa.

"And then I started getting bullied at school with kids jeering at me, yelling that Santa Claus was a fairy tale like the Tooth Fairy. I got back in their faces, swearing Santa Claus was real, that they were just rotten kids and that's why Santa Claus never stopped at their homes. My mother would always reassure me, saying I was dead right, that the bullies were just jealous.

"Then, in second grade, I remember the teacher calling my mother at home one evening. I overheard my mother say she wouldn't tell me that there was no Santa Claus. After she hung up, I rushed to her and insisted she tell me the truth, if Santa Claus was real or not. She swept me up in her arms, crossed her heart and promised me that Santa Claus was real.

"A year later I found out the truth and felt betrayed . . . really betrayed. I screamed at my mother and asked her why she had lied to me and made me a total fool at school.

Do you know what she said? That she hadn't meant to hurt me. That she felt guilty about the time she spent away from me after the divorce and that I needed to believe in a bit of magic. . . . Until I heard the story of Saint Nicholas . . . I hadn't really forgiven her."

"So you want to believe in Santa Claus again?" Cecilia said in an incredulous tone. "Is that what you're saying?"

"I want to believe this other world exists: the spiritual world."

"Like Harry Potter?" Cecilia said with a brisk shake of her head. "So we can pretend we're fighting a war against Satan? That we must find our *dons* because, otherwise, the planet is going to become a sandbox like Mars? Is that what you're thinking?"

"But what if it's true?" Julie asked.

Cecilia turned to Lebna. "What do you make of this nonsense?"

"I . . . I want to believe it too," Lebna said with a quick nod.

"What?" Cecilia asked, startled. Then she swept her hand across the entire expanse of the crowd and added, "Look, let me tell you both something: I know, or at least have seen, all the people here, and they are the same people who leave our apartment building every morning to go work as cooks, maids and janitors. Many work two or three jobs every day, coming home super late at night. What kind of *dons* are those? Huh? They're not wizards, that's for sure! Those are not gifts I want."

A long, tense pause ensued. The three girls stared at each other.

"But what's there to lose?" Julie finally sputtered. "Aren't you curious about your fortune?"

Carmen walked up and asked, "What did you decide?"

"Um . . ." Julie said raising two dollar bills in the air.

"Wait," Cecilia said as she pulled Julie's hand down before she faced Pancho the fortuneteller. "Don't you . . . work as a janitor?"

Cecilia next shot a quick glance at Carmen and saw not even a trace of anger or shock on her face, or on Pancho's.

"Yes, I do work as a janitor," Pancho said.

"But, he's also the healer of our animals," Carmen said and placed her hand on Pancho's shoulder. "Pancho is short for Francisco like his patron saint San Francisco, the saint with the *don* for animals."

"Are you the man who cured my cat years ago?" Cecilia asked. She felt stunned and slightly embarrassed.

Pancho nodded.

Julie spread her arms before her and asked, "Does everyone here have *don* jobs too?"

"That's something to investigate," Carmen interrupted, "but we have to hurry. So, what are you going to do about the fortunes?"

"I'd like my fortune told," Julie said and handed Pancho a dollar. She avoided Cecilia's gaze.

With a slight bow, Pancho gave Julie fifty cents in change before he took something out of his breast pocket. He then took his pet canary out of its cage and placed it inside a second cage where there was a box with small slips of paper.

The bird immediately jumped to the bottom of the cage, hopped over to the box and took one of the slips. Pancho opened the cage and pulled the paper from the bird's beak, then handed it to Julie.

"Is it in Spanish?" Cecilia asked Julie.

"Um, yes." She handed the fortune to Cecilia. "What does it say?"

"'You'll reconnect with your childhood innocence and help change the world.'"

"Really?" Julie asked. She snatched the fortune and beamed.

Cecilia shrugged, then cupped her hand over the side of her mouth and whispered into Julie's ear, "So I guess you're going back to believing in Santa Claus."

Unshaken, Julie handed Pancho fifty cents and said, "This is for Cecilia's fortune."

Cecilia sighed and thought there was no use protesting since Julie was almost as stubborn as Carmen. Pancho repeated the process with the canary.

"So let's see about your fortune," Pancho said, handing the paper to Cecilia with both hands as if it was a priceless treasure.

Cecilia stared at it.

"Well, what does it say?" Julie asked.

"Yes, tell us," Lebna said as she peered over Cecilia's shoulder.

"The two of you really must learn Spanish," Carmen snorted. "Cecilia could make anything up to fool you."

Cecilia stared at Carmen. *Does she really have to read my mind all the time?* "'Your two friends are wasting their precious time over a big piece of nonsense.'"

"Here, let me see the fortune to make sure Cecilia isn't pulling your leg," Carmen said and reached for the fortune but Cecilia held onto it.

"So what does it really say, Cecilia?" Julie asked, all excited.

Cecilia took a deep breath before she let out a prolonged, audible sigh. "It says that I'm 'off on a magical mission.'"

"Wow!" Julie said as she snatched the fortune and handed it to Carmen, who glanced at it and nodded.

"That's great!" Lebna said and flashed Cecilia a big smile.

"Yes!" Julie added and tossed her arms in the air in victory.

"One more." Julie gave Pancho the second dollar bill. "For Lebna's fortune."

After he handed Julie her change, Pancho performed the same steps as before.

While Pancho took the paper slip from the bird's beak, Cecilia leaned towards Julie and Lebna and whispered, "This is the third time, and we're still clueless about how he does it."

"But they've all been good fortunes. I sure hope mine is too," Lebna said.

Cecilia read the fortune: "'The secret of your culture is the world's culture.' But don't ask me what that means." She then passed the slip to Carmen.

The girls' heads spun towards Carmen, anxious to hear what she would say.

Carmen pursed her lips as she read the paper. "You'll have to figure it out," she said with a quick wink at Pancho.

"Yet another mystery," Cecilia said. She rolled her eyes at her friends. "And we still have no idea how the bird picks only good fortunes."

"They're all good," Carmen said and winked again at Pancho, "if you make them so."

Cecilia faced her two friends. "I'm fine, for now, translating Spanish into English for you. But as far as making sense of everything Carmen says, I've been trying to do that for years."

"You would have figured this out long ago," Carmen said, "if only you had done what I've been asking you to do for years: spend Saturday mornings with your godmother, learning about the spiritual side of things."

"I would've been there every Saturday," Julie beamed at Carmen.

"So, Carmen, what do you mean when you say we have to figure out Lebna's fortune?" Cecilia asked.

CHAPTER 19

Father Ramón appeared before Carmen could say anything. "Just in time," he said. He threw his arms high in the air and flashed Cecilia a lopsided smile. "Many people have stopped by, asking where to buy the raffle tickets for Doña Faustina's coffee. They're so excited. Do you have the coffee?"

"Yes," Cecilia said and handed him the burlap sack she had been carrying.

"Wonderful!" Father Ramón said. He opened the bag to look inside. "Now, come over by me and arrange the jars on this ironing board while I go fetch the microphone and announce the raffle."

Cecilia nodded awkwardly, startled at the priest's excitement over the coffee. She began to place the jars on the creaky ironing board. She tried to keep them off the bent spots so they wouldn't roll off and break.

"And Father Ramón," Carmen said, "these are Cecilia's friends, Julie and Lebna. One is selling popcorn and the other is selling storybooks."

Almost immediately, Father Ramón's voice boomed throughout the park: "*Raffle tickets are now on sale for a chance to win a jar of Doña Faustina's coffee. A dollar a ticket!*"

People right across the park suddenly stopped in their tracks and hurried towards Cecilia.

"I'll take five!" . . . "Ten!" . . . "Twenty tickets for me!" People ordered faster than Cecilia could count and tear off ribbons of tickets and collect five-, ten-, twenty-, even fifty-dollar bills and shove them inside the scuffed cigar box Carmen had given her.

In what seemed like the wink of an eye, Lebna sold all her bags of popcorn, and Julie the books she had brought. Cecilia counted off the last five tickets on the roll and waved for Carmen to come over. She pointed to the line of people in front of her waiting and said, "I'm out of tickets!"

Carmen reached into her pocket and pulled out a new roll of tickets, to the sound of applause. Cecilia got back to selling with Julie and Lebna making change from the cigar box.

"This is so amazing," Julie said as she took a twenty-dollar bill from a woman who gave her tickets a loud, smacking kiss.

"I'll say," Lebna added, shaking her head in disbelief. "You would think they were buying tickets for a jar of gold or a genie's lamp."

Cecilia turned to Julie. "This seems to be the perfect time for you to be Harriet the Spy. So go on, go out there and nose around. Find out what all the excitement is over the coffee."

Julie waited till Cecilia handed the tickets to the next person before she bent close to her ear and whispered, "But how? I don't know Spanish."

"I knew it," Cecilia said, "this science project you're so excited about will wind up falling entirely on me. I'll have to do all the work, because neither you nor Lebna know any Spanish."

"Gosh, no," Julie blanched.

"So prove it by going out there," Cecilia said in a biting tone. "You don't need Spanish. Many people speak English too. And if you don't get to it," she added, "I refuse to go along with your insane science project."

"Okay, okay." Julie held her hands up to Cecilia and stepped back. "I'll give it a try."

Julie looked around the park and spotted Carmen, who had rolled a sheet of newspaper into a cone. *What's that about?* Julie walked over, relieved to spy on someone she knew. But she gasped when she saw Carmen insert the small end of the paper funnel into a man's ear, light the other end with a match and set it on fire.

"Oh my god!" Julie ran towards Carmen and waved her arms wildly in the air. "Carmen!"

"Okay, it popped," Julie heard the man say as she got closer. Then Carmen snatched the burning newspaper away from his ear, flung it to the ground and stomped the flames out.

"Julie," Carmen said glancing at the girl's stricken face, "what's wrong?"

"Um . . . ." Julie's heart pounded as her eyes darted between Carmen and the man. "I thought something was wrong . . . seeing the fire."

"Oh, that," Carmen said matter-of-factly. "I was just doing some *curandera* work. Right, Sam?"

"Yes, Carmen just cured my earache." The man touched his ear and smiled.

"Oh, I see," Julie said. Then she remembered Cecilia's threat, so she swallowed hard and added, "Did she . . . cure you with the paper cone, the one she set on fire?"

"Yes."

"I . . . I see," Julie stammered.

After the man thanked Carmen, he handed her some money to help with the *kermés*.

Julie turned to her and asked, "How did you do that?"

"With a match," Carmen chuckled.

"I guess this is a mystery too? Huh?"

Carmen replied in a serious tone. "Don't think I talk in what Cecilia calls riddles to drive you all crazy. I do it for a reason, an important reason—"

"Carmen!" a woman suddenly called out as she jogged towards them. "Can you do something about this?" She rolled up her sleeve and showed Carmen a mess of red spots all over her arm.

Carmen studied the spots, pursed her lips and nodded. Then she turned to Julie and said, "Run along and continue your spying while I attend to her."

Julie wished that she could have spied on Carmen some more. While she looked around for her next target, she noticed that, as Cecilia tore off long strips of tickets, the line seemed only to get longer and longer. She glanced back at Carmen and now saw her with a sad-looking woman. Julie suddenly got an idea. *Yes,* she thought and hurried towards Carmen, *it's worth a try.* Five feet away, she halted and waited until the woman walked away with a glimmer of a smile on her lips.

"Carmen," Julie said and stepped closer.

"Julie!" Carmen said, a little surprised. "How's the spying going?"

"Well . . . I was wondering," she said as she took out a five-dollar bill from her coat pocket, "if I could pay you . . . for some *curandera* work."

"Hmm," Carmen said as she studied Julie's face and tapped her chin. "A true *curandera* doesn't charge, though donations are okay, like for a *kermés*. But what's wrong? How can I help you?"

"Oh, it's not for me," Julie said with a quick shake of her head. "It's . . . it's for my mother. You know, her depression."

Carmen nodded and placed her hand on Julie's shoulder. "Okay, come with me."

Julie tried to hand Carmen the five-dollar bill.

Carmen shook her head. "After our little *plática*, you can, if you want, buy a raffle ticket as a donation. Okay?"

"Yes, of course," Julie said. She wondered if this explained the long line for raffle tickets. Was it because the people who offered their *don* work all over the park had asked those they helped to buy raffle tickets to donate to the *kermés*?

"What strikes you most?" Carmen asked as she waved at a woman who held the hand of a laughing seven-year-old girl.

"Strikes me most?" Julie asked with a confused look.

"Yes, what do you see that's interesting or unusual?"

"Well," Julie replied, glancing around, "the children. They seem so happy, so loved and appreciated."

"I see," Carmen said with a quick nod. "And your mother? Tell me about her . . . about when she was a young girl around seven."

"Gosh," said Julie, "I think she spent all her time with her nanny, since her dad was always working. Her mother was away, too, at teas and charities."

"Was this how it was for you too?"

"Um, I guess so . . . at least until my parents divorced."

"I see," Carmen said in a softer tone. "And when was your mother happiest?"

"Happiest?" Julie asked, her brow furrowed.

"Do you recall a time when she was happy? Or did she ever mention such a time?"

Julie looked up and tried to remember. "Yes, the morning I went off to summer camp. It was as if . . ."

"She couldn't wait to get rid of you?" Carmen said with a slight chuckle.

"Yes!" Julie said and grimaced. "That's right!"

"Come on," Carmen said. She grasped Julie's hand before they headed off again. "And what did your mother do while you were away at camp?"

"I have no idea. I only know she was happy I was not there."

"Ask her next time."

"What?" Julie said, stopping. "You want me to ask my mother why she was happy to get rid of me?"

"You asked me to help your mother, right?" Carmen replied as she stepped in front of Julie. "That's what I'm doing: trying to get a sense of what her *don* might be. And it isn't to get rid of you. So next time you have a chance, ask her what she did while you were away at summer camp. Okay?"

"Okay, I'll try."

"You'll try?" Carmen snickered. "You told Cecilia you want to be a spy, figuring out our culture's mysteries, but you'll only *try* to figure out yours?"

"I . . . we don't have a culture," Julie said and swallowed hard. "At least not anything like Santa Cecilia's . . . unless . . ."

"Unless, what?"

"Unless making money, getting college degrees and joining clubs and charities is a culture." Julie crossed her arms over her chest.

Carmen said in a gentler tone, "Well, ask her, and let me know." Then she glanced at her watch, "Let's go see how Cecilia and Lebna are doing. The raffle winners will be announced in about fifteen minutes."

"I want to buy five tickets," Julie said as she hurried after Carmen.

"It's up to you if you want to buy tickets," Carmen replied, "but I'm still working on your *curandera* problem. And who knows? You might win a jar that could help your mother."

"What do you mean?"

"Well, this is Doña Faustina's coffee."

Julie asked, "So, if I win a jar and my mother drinks a cup, she might discover her *don*?"

"I wish it were that easy." Carmen stopped suddenly. "Look, there's a long line for the raffle tickets. Maybe you should get in line if you want a chance to win the coffee."

"You're right." After a long wait, she was finally next. "I'm going to get five," Julie announced, smiling at Cecilia.

"Five what?" Cecilia asked.

"Five tickets!" Julie responded. She handed Lebna a five-dollar bill.

"Okay." Cecilia counted out the tickets. "And what earth-shattering clues did you spy out, Ms. Harriet? Huh?"

"Well, here's one weird thing I've noticed . . ." Julie took the tickets.

"What?"

"I am the youngest buyer of your raffle tickets."

Cecilia tilted her head in thought. "You're right. But why are you buying tickets?"

"Because Carmen's working on a *curandera* case for me . . . for my mother."

"We'll talk later," Cecilia said when she noticed the line was still long behind Julie. "The winners will be announced in just a few minutes."

"Want me to help sell tickets?" Julie moved aside as a woman asked for ten.

"Please stand next to me. I want to tell you something."

"What?"

"I asked Carmen earlier if you or Lebna could help me sell tickets, but she said no, because part of the reason the tickets are selling like crazy is that Doña Faustina has asked me to be her apprentice."

"And they're selling like hot cakes! It's amazing!" Julie said. She moved over to stand next to Lebna.

Lebna nodded. "It's more amazing than you think."

"What do you mean?"

"Well, that elderly woman who bought twenty tickets pawned her gold earrings, her only pair, just to buy tickets. And—"

"*Ten minutes left! Ten more minutes before the raffle winners are announced!*" Father Ramón's voice boomed through the loudspeaker. "*So be sure to get your tickets for a chance to win a jar of Doña Faustina's marvelous coffee! And the winning tickets will be drawn by her handpicked apprentice: Cecilia Guerra! That's right, folks. Doña Faustina has finally chosen her apprentice, and we all know what that means!*"

Cecilia, Julie and Lebna exchanged astonished looks as people suddenly raced throughout the park to get in line. Julie shook her head as she watched Cecilia tear off strips of tickets faster and faster, while Lebna received bill after bill.

"Since I can't help Cecilia with the tickets, I'll help you make change," Julie told Lebna.

"How about I take the bills, while you make change?"

"Okay."

"You heard that Doña Faustina chose Cecilia to be her apprentice, right?"

"What does that mean?"

"I don't know, but I bet it's something astonishing," Lebna said.

"You got that right!" Julie declared. "But I'll tell you one thing . . ."

"Let me guess," Lebna suggested. "You're going to make sure you're there, right in the middle of Doña Faustina's kitchen for Cecilia's first lesson."

"How did you know?"

"Because I'm thinking the same thing."

"Really?" Julie said. Her eyes brightened. "That means that we now have to work extra hard to convince Cecilia to make this our science project . . . for all three of us."

"And how exactly do you suggest we do that?"

"Oh, I have an idea!" Julie clapped her hands with excitement. "How about we—you and I—write up the proposal. And once it's approved, we'll show it to Cecilia and she'll be. . . ."

"Ecstatic?" Lebna asked as she glared at Julie. "Are you crazy? She'll kill us!" Lebna tried to keep her voice down. "And what do you suggest we say in the proposal? That we want to conduct an experiment to determine if Mexicans or Mexican Americans have a spiritual world that's weird but true? Or that it's just wishful thinking, a big piece of nonsense? And. . . ."

"And what?"

"Well, you know how strict Ms. Bellows is. She'll laugh her butt off at us. And, as I said, Cecilia will kill us when she finds out."

"Lebna! I've never heard you talk so much! Anyway, you don't have to do this, you know."

"But that's the whole point," Lebna said as she took a quick glance at Cecilia and found her completely focused on thanking people, counting and tearing off strips of tickets. "I want to learn more about Cecilia's culture, but we'll blow our chance if we cook up a plan that upsets her. You know how badly she wants to rush through her Confirmation just to get back to her schoolwork. The science project is all about digging deeper into her culture; that's what she wants to run from, while we're positively intrigued by it. At least with what we've seen so far."

"I see what you're saying. But then how do we do it?"

"*That's it!*" Father Ramón's voice thundered. "*It's time to pick the raffle winners!*" He then invited Cecilia to bring the tickets over.

With Cecilia at his side, Father Ramón picked up the glass pitcher that contained duplicates of all the tickets sold. *"Cecilia, Doña Faustina's apprentice, will now select the winning tickets. So come on up,"* he added and waved everyone over.

People in the crowd searched their pockets, purses and bags for their tickets.

"Now, the winner of Doña Faustina's first jar of coffee!" Father Ramón announced.

Cecilia took a deep breath, reached into the glass container and quickly snatched a ticket. As she handed the ticket to Father Ramón, the crowd fell silent. He brought it up close to his eyes and said, *"The very lucky winner is number 1021—1-0-2-1! Look at your tickets!"*

"Bingo! I got it! I got it!" shrieked a woman's voice from somewhere in the middle of the crowd that suddenly parted like the Red Sea as the woman raced towards Father Ramón and waved her ticket in the air.

Father Ramón raised his arms and said, *"Elvia, you won! Congratulations! Now, please accept this jar of Doña Faustina's coffee from her apprentice."*

Cecilia smiled as she presented the jar to Elvia. She recognized her as a member of one of the families who lived on the second floor of their building.

The woman lovingly cradled the jar in her arms as if it were a newborn baby, looked straight at Cecilia and said, "I'll be praying for you . . . for your apprenticeship . . . that it'll all work out." Then she lifted the jar high in the air like a trophy and the crowd roared with applause as she made her way back.

That's how it went as they raffled off the other jars: the crowd was riveted, Cecilia picked a ticket and Father Ramón called out its number, triggering a joyous shout from the lucky winner and riotous applause from the crowd.

"Now for the very last jar!" Father Ramón said and raised it up in the air. *"Who will be the final lucky winner?"*

He swept his gaze across the hushed crowd and then gave Cecilia a quick nod. Cecilia felt a thousand eyes bore straight into her as she reached into the pile of tickets and dug her hand deeper and deeper to the bottom of the container.

Julie's heart sank as she realized that she had no chance of winning, since her duplicate tickets had fallen on top of the pile, not the very bottom, where Cecilia's hand swirled the pieces of paper around. She sighed when she saw Cecilia hand the last winning ticket to Father Ramón. How desperately she had wanted to win one of the jars. She had imagined she would serve her mother a cup of Doña Faustina's magic coffee, watch her drink it, then ask her when she had been the happiest.

"1600! Number 1-6-0-0!" Father Ramón's voice roared as Julie watched the sea of bowed heads study their tickets.

"Who's got the winning ticket—number 1600?" he repeated as his gaze swept from left to right across the crowd. Heads turned as they looked for the winner—a raised hand, a shriek.

"Oh my god!" Julie screamed and slapped her hand over her wide open mouth. "I won! I can't believe it!" She rushed up and thrust her ticket at Father Ramón. *It's a miracle,* she thought.

Father Ramón looked at the ticket and shook Julie's hand. *"Congratulations to the last winner!"*

The crowd erupted in thunderous applause. "It's a miracle!" Julie said to Cecilia as she took the jar and gave it a quick kiss. She said this over and over as she returned to stand by Lebna.

"Thank you all for coming! For making this kermés *possible, especially with such short notice,"* Father Ramón said as he smiled and waved at everyone. *"Plus many thanks to the* kermés *committee for organizing it!"* he added before he handed the microphone to Cecilia.

Cecilia gave Father Ramón a startled look.

"Just say a few words," Father Ramón encouraged her, "on behalf of your family and your little sister."

Cecilia gave a slight nod, then raised the microphone to her lips and said in a halting voice: *"I'm grateful . . . very grateful to you all . . . thank you . . . on behalf of my family . . . and Micaela."*

Cheers and clapping ripped across the crowd as several people hurried towards Cecilia. Father Ramón then handed the microphone to the head of the *kermés* committee who thanked everyone and officially ended the fair.

People approached Cecilia to shake her hand and give her warm hugs. They offered comforting words, such as Micaela would be in heaven soon and that she could then intercede to help their community.

After ten minutes of this, Carmen popped up out of nowhere and took the microphone. "Mil gracias *to all of you,"* she said in a strong voice. *"Now I have to take Cecilia home to receive her mother back from the hospital. We'll see you all at the funeral. Again, thank you all so much!"*

On the way back to the apartment, Carmen congratulated Julie. "It's wonderful you won one of the jars!"

"I know!" Julie said. "And it's like a miracle, since I bought some of the last tickets and Cecilia took the winning ticket from the bottom of the pile."

"That's because it was meant for you," Carmen said. "And don't forget about our *plática*," she added as she clambered up their apartment building's front steps.

"Of course! I won't forget!" Julie said, then dashed up the steps and opened the door for the others.

"I can't wait to see Mom," Cecilia said and hurried through the door. "Maybe she's back already."

"You go on up, Cecilia," Carmen said. "I'll stop by in a minute." Then she turned to Julie and said, "You might want to brew some coffee for your mother."

"I was thinking the same thing!" Julie held the jar up. "Also, I'm really looking forward to continuing our *plática!*"

"What about you?" Carmen tapped Lebna's arm, sensing the girl wanted to ask a question.

Lebna hesitated for a moment and exchanged a quick look with Julie. "We . . . that is Julie and I, were wondering . . . wondering if we could. . . ." Lebna suddenly dropped her arms heavily at her sides and sighed with a look of total defeat.

"Could what? What are you and Julie wondering about?" She took both girls by the arm. "Hurry up and tell me because it's getting late and your families will worry."

"We want to," Lebna cleared her throat, " . . . if it's possible . . . to witness Cecilia's apprenticeship with Doña Faustina."

Carmen huffed, then shook her head slowly from side to side. "So, while Cecilia can't wait to get this whole thing over with, so she can get back to the real world, the two of you can't wait to get a taste of her apprenticeship. Am I right?"

"Well," Lebna coughed into her hand, "we thought that we might be able to connect the two. Right, Julie?"

"Oh!" Julie said, blushing before facing Carmen. "Yes, we were thinking of how to team up with Cecilia . . . the three of us . . . to work on the science project, you know . . . the project we need to do for school? And Lebna and I think that the apprenticeship could be the perfect project."

"Yes," Lebna interjected. "But we still don't know how to convince Cecilia about this . . . and . . ."

"And you think Cecilia will not only laugh at your great idea, but will also want to kill you for suggesting it. Right?"

"You think it's a stupid idea, right?" Julie asked.

"Not at all. I like your idea," Carmen said. She hurried the girls up the stairs.

"You mean it?" Lebna asked.

"Yes," Carmen said sharply. "It'll be good for all three of you, as well as for our community."

"Our community?" Julie asked as she tried to catch her breath. "How?"

"That's something you have to figure out," Carmen said, "while you work on your science project." She suddenly stopped and caused the girls to bump into her. "I'll talk to Doña Faustina . . . about Cecilia's first day of training."

"But even if she lets us come, Cecilia will still say no," Lebna said.

"Who said anything about telling Cecilia?" Carmen snorted.

"What?" Julie and Lebna asked in unison.

"She'll kill us," Julie said.

"That's true," Lebna agreed.

"Come on," Carmen said as she continued to rush the girls up the steps. "Don't worry. I have a duty to Cecilia's spiritual education. And the way I see it, the two of you will help me with it. So let me talk to Doña Faustina and I'll let you know."

"If . . . if you think so," Lebna said and inhaled deeply as she tried to keep up with Carmen.

"Yes, if you think it's a good idea," Julie agreed.

At Julie's floor landing, Carmen opened the metal door. "This is where you get off, Julie." She waved the girls through, then followed them to Julie's front door.

"Thank you, Carmen, for everything." Julie waved good-bye when she heard her mother's voice call out to her.

Carmen next escorted Lebna to her apartment, and, as soon as she got to her own place, she telephoned the head of the *kermés* committee and then dialed Doña Faustina's number.

"Well?" Julie asked as her mother set down the cup of Doña Faustina's coffee.

"Well, what?" Marie responded, squinting at Julie while she pulled the covers up to her neck. As usual, her mother was in bed and her room was in total darkness.

"The coffee? How was it" Julie inquired. She sat perched at the edge of her mother's bed and scrutinized every inch of her face for some sign.

"Hot. It's too hot to drink." Marie stretched her arms out, then let them fall heavily by her side.

Julie got to her feet and went to the night table. The cup was as full as when she had handed it to her mother.

"How about I make you a sandwich while the coffee cools?" Julie asked as she considered the mess of pill bottles on the same table.

"I'm not hungry, honey."

"Mom, you hardly eat anymore. I'm worried about you."

"Okay." Marie rubbed her eyes. "Make me a cheese sandwich if it'll make you feel better."

Julie went to the kitchen and tossed two slices of bread on the griddle. She was getting the cheese from the fridge, when suddenly she heard her mother yell: "Julie! Come here!"

Julie raced down the hallway, her heart pounding. "What's wrong?" Her mouth dropped open, shocked to find her mother sitting up in bed, smiling. Even her eyes looked as if they were sparkling. Julie could not remember when she had last seen her mother smile.

"Any more coffee?" Marie lifted her cup.

"Yes . . . but . . ."

"Will you pour me another one, please?" Marie said with an even bigger smile.

Julie stared at her mother. She was eager to ask her a million questions. Then she remembered the toast she had left on the hot griddle and rushed to the kitchen. She was relieved to see that the bread only had a few traces of char. She quickly scraped the dark spots off before she melted slices of cheese between the pieces of toast. Then she sliced the sandwich diagonally and placed it on a plate and took it to her mother. After that, she returned to the kitchen to make her another cup of coffee.

While Julie waited for the kettle to boil, she decided to make two cups of coffee, one for her mother, the other for herself. *It might help me think about what to ask Mom if I have a cup too*, she thought. So she ground and brewed two cups' worth, then placed the steaming cups on a tray and hurried back to her mother's room.

Surprised to see her mom's empty plate, Julie's mood brightened because the cheese sandwich was the first substantial thing she had seen her mother eat in quite a long time.

"How was the sandwich?" Julie handed her a cup.

"Really good," Marie answered. She brought her nose close to the steam that rose from it. "Oh, it smells so good!" She took a sip. "What brand is it?"

"Does it taste different?" Julie asked, stunned to see her mother look so lively, her face flushed with color, her eyes so alert and bright.

"This is really good coffee, but . . ." Marie searched for the right words.

"But what?"

"Well, like I said, it tastes like good coffee, but it also makes me feel lighter . . . and . . ."

"Happier?" Julie suggested.

Marie let out a slight chuckle that sounded, to Julie's ears, like the faint heartbeat of a person who had been presumed dead. "Oh, Mom!" Julie exclaimed as she jumped to her feet and embraced her mother.

Marie took Julie's hand in hers and squeezed it. "It's not exactly happiness I feel. It's more like . . . hope."

"Would you like a third cup?" Julie asked because her mother's cup was almost empty.

Marie shook her head and said. "No, sweetie, I shouldn't have even had the first, it being, what . . . ten already?"

"You don't need to sleep!" Julie said. "That's all you've been doing!"

Marie grabbed Julie's arm and pulled her towards her. "Sit. Please," she said. Julie dropped on the bed and faced her. She felt excited that her mother was so animated.

"Yes, it must seem that way to you . . . that I've slept my life away, lately."

"Oh, gosh, I didn't mean to be critical," Julie groaned.

"I wish I were happy . . . not sleeping so much . . . so I could be there for you."

"All I want is for you to be happy," Julie said. "Don't worry about me."

"I'm supposed to be the mother, the adult here, making things safe and happy for you."

"Know what you could do to make me happy?" Julie asked.

"Oh, sweetheart," Marie's face darkened, "I wish I were stronger, since there's nothing I want more than to be a good mother to you."

"Mom, when were you the happiest . . . the strongest?"

"When?" Marie knit her brow.

"Yes, was it . . . when you got married?"

"Um . . . I guess it was when I was nine years old," Marie said, closing her eyes, "and riding Chocolate."

"Chocolate?"

"Yes, my pony!" Marie's eyes lit up.

"Wow! I've never heard you sound so happy!"

Marie dropped her head and added wearily, "But that was years ago, when I was a little girl. . . ."

"And?" Julie squeezed her mother's wrist.

"I don't know. That was just kid stuff, fairy tales and make-believe."

"You mean that growing up caused everything to fall apart?"

"It's part of growing up." Marie looked sad all of a sudden.

"Please don't get sad again!" Julie handed her cup of coffee to her mother. "Here, drink this!"

Marie took a sip, then gazed directly into her daughter's eyes. "Julie, life is hard. There's no Santa Claus or Easter Bunny or magic like in the Harry Potter books and movies. We just lost everything, *everything,* in that horrible, horrible hurricane."

"I know, I know," Julie said softly. "But what if magic is real? And Santa Claus? And . . ."

"What are you saying? Did you drink something strange at your friend's church fair? Tell me!"

"No," Julie shook her head vigorously. "I just think that magic might actually exist. It's part of a science project we're doing."

Marie was relieved her daughter had not been doing anything bad.

"The pony that made you happy," Julie said, "tell me more about her and you when you were nine years old."

Marie looked at the clock on the night table: eleven-fifteen. She was about to say that it was too late to talk, that Julie needed her sleep. Instead, she raised herself against the headboard, took a long drink of coffee and proceeded to tell her daughter about the pony.

CHAPTER 21

Cecilia flung open the apartment door and found Carmen on the landing. "Oh, I thought it was Mom and Dad. They're supposed to arrive soon, right?"

"Yes," Carmen said as she hurried to the kitchen.

"Carmen! Is something wrong?"

"Wrong?" Carmen asked as she filled the kettle with water and pulled out a small bag from her pocket.

"Is that for Mom?" Cecilia's voice was strained. "She's still coming home today, right?"

"Yes, of course."

"What are you making?"

"Tea."

"Just tea? Or is it *curandera* tea?"

"Yes, I'm making tea, and I am a *curandera*."

"Oh, come on, Carmen, can't you just be straight with me? I'm so tired . . . so confused . . ."

"Exactly," Carmen said. She crossed the room and dropped into the chair opposite Cecilia. "To answer your question, I am making what you call *curandera* tea. It's chamomile, for you and your mother, who'll walk through the front door any moment now."

The lock suddenly clicked. Cecilia leapt to her feet and ran to the door just as her father shouted out: "Surprise, we're home!"

"Oh!" Nica said, kissing her daughter. "I couldn't wait to hug you, *m'ija!*"

Cecilia stepped back and looked her mother over from head to toe. She felt a burst of relief wash through her. *Wow, Mom can even smile, stand and walk, and she's not the crumpled up, fragile person I imagined.*

"How do you feel, Mom?"

"Your mom just needs some rest," her father said as he took a suitcase to the bedroom.

Carmen chimed in. "Welcome home!" She kissed her sister on the cheek. "I'm making tea, so come sit down."

Carmen and Cecilia both tried to help Nica to a chair, but she shook them off and said, "What are you doing? I'm no invalid. I'm fine, fine."

"Why are you shaking your head?" Cecilia whispered to Carmen.

"Because you have a very stubborn mother."

Nica lowered herself into a chair at the table as Carmen poured a stream of yellow tea into a cup and set it in front of her.

Carmen looked at Cecilia and ordered, "Sit here," and filled a second cup for her.

"*Manzanilla* tea," Nica said, after a sip. "Tastes good, soothing. It's good for *susto*, too, right?"

"Yes," Carmen said and dropped into the chair next to Nica.

"Do I have to drink this?" Cecilia asked with a frown.

Nica took a long drink and leaned back in her chair. "We just lost a family member. The tea will help comfort our souls."

Cecilia turned to Carmen, who nodded. *The soul? That must be the biggest difference between what I learn in school and this home-brewed education: there's no such thing as a soul at school because it's invisible, imaginary.*

"By the way, Doña Faustina chose Cecilia to be her apprentice." Carmen flashed Nica a broad smile.

"What? That's incredible!" Nica said, overjoyed. "That's such an amazing honor, *m'ija*."

"She starts her apprenticeship tomorrow."

"Yes, that makes sense," Nica nodded. "I guess she thinks it's time to go rest since she's now . . . what . . . in her nineties?"

"Ninety-five," Carmen said and pursed her lips. "You should've seen the raffle at the *kermés*. It was amazing. And all because Doña Faustina donated jars of her coffee and announced that she had selected Cecilia to be her apprentice."

"Mom," Cecilia said, "I don't have time for this . . ."

"Time for what?" Nica said. She caught sight of Carmen's eyes, whose expression warned her to tread lightly.

Cecilia bit her lower lip, ready to voice her concerns, when her father walked in and announced: "Time to go rest. I've turned down the bed and put your things away."

Nica nodded, but then said, "Antonio, join us for a moment. Have some of Carmen's *manzanilla* tea, and hear the great news: Doña Faustina just chose your daughter to be her apprentice. Her training starts tomorrow."

"That's wonderful!" Antonio beamed as he patted Cecilia on the back.

"But," Carmen said sharply, "Cecilia thinks it's a big waste of time to train with Doña Faustina."

"A waste of time?" Antonio echoed. "What do you mean, Cecilia?"

Cecilia pushed her chair back and felt everyone's eyes drill into her. "Well, you . . . Dad and Mom . . . have always told me to take school seriously. Right?" She raised her eyes to meet her parents' stares. "So what I want to say is that I've gotten so behind on my school work . . . that spending my afternoons at Doña Faustina's . . . making coffee . . ."

"Making coffee?!" Carmen spat out.

Cecilia flinched not knowing what to say.

"I'm really sorry," Carmen said and shook her head slowly as she addressed Cecilia's parents. "I have tried so hard to be a good godmother to your daughter, but she's been so clever at finding all sorts of excuses to avoid her *pláticas* with me: her school work, this test, that project . . . that's why her questions are those a seven-year-old asks her godmother, not those a young woman who is about to make her Confirmation asks."

Cecilia felt her blood freeze in her veins. Never, ever had she seen Carmen so upset.

Suddenly there was a loud knock at the front door. Cecilia leapt to her feet and ran to open it. It was Julie.

"Is Carmen here?" Julie asked as she caught her breath. "She didn't answer when I knocked on her door."

"Yes, I'm here!" Carmen's voice boomed from the kitchen.

Julie hurried towards her.

"Oh!" Julie stopped at the threshold of the kitchen. "I'm so sorry. I didn't mean to intrude. I thought you were still . . ."

"Don't worry, you're not intruding." Nica smiled as she waved Julie over. "It's good to see you."

Antonio nodded and gave Julie a warm smile.

"Gosh, I'm really sorry about the . . . the baby," Julie stammered.

"Thank you." Nica pursed her lips. "What did you come to see Carmen about? You sounded so excited."

"Um . . . ," Julie said, "it's about . . . my mother."

"Did you make her some coffee?" Carmen said as she lugged an extra chair to the table and gestured for Julie to sit down.

"Oh, thank you," Julie looked at the chair and said, "but I can't stay. I . . . I just wanted to tell you," and she looked at Carmen, "that the coffee made my mother suddenly brighten up. It's the happiest I've seen her in the longest time."

"You made her a cup of Doña Faustina's coffee, right?" Carmen said and raised an eyebrow at Cecilia, who was slumped back in her chair.

"Yes, from the jar I won at the raffle," Julie said.

"And isn't it true that you would do anything to witness Cecilia's apprenticeship?" Carmen asked with a sly grin.

Julie's mouth dropped open.

"Yes, I'm guilty of revealing a secret," Carmen said, "but sometimes that's what it takes to keep something alive, to keep it from dying. See," she continued as she fixed her eyes on Cecilia, "I told Julie I wouldn't tell you that she and Lebna would be showing up at Doña Faustina's for your first day of training. It would be a total surprise. Julie is dying to be there. Right, Julie?"

"Yes," she squeaked in a barely audible voice, her eyes cast down at her sneakers.

Nica turned to Julie and asked, "What about your school work?"

"School work?"

"Yes, Cecilia claims that the apprenticeship will put her behind in school. That she'll never be able to catch up with her homework."

"Ah, well," Julie replied, aware of Cecilia's angry glare, "my mother has a college degree from an Ivy League university and . . . she's terribly unhappy . . . deeply depressed. Yes . . . school is important . . . but . . ."

"But what?" Carmen prompted her.

"Well, it doesn't necessarily make you happy. And I haven't seen my mother so happy as when she drank Doña Faustina's coffee."

Nica nodded and said, "Both are equally important: your school work and your *don* education."

"That's right, you have to balance both," Antonio chimed in.

"Cecilia, we'll be able to combine both with the science project," Julie blurted out.

"Don't start," Cecilia grimaced as she jumped to her feet and flashed her open hands at Julie. "Just don't, okay?"

"What's this science project about?" Antonio asked.

"Um . . ." Julie hesitated as she saw the fury in Cecilia's eyes.

Antonio stroked his chin, trying to understand what was going on between his daughter and her best friend. He had never seen Cecilia looking so enraged. "So tell us, *m'ija*," he said to his daughter, "tell us about the project."

"Oh, Dad," she sighed, "it's a pointless, stupid idea, which will only make us all look ridiculous . . . and superstitious."

"That's not true!" Julie stomped her foot.

"Wait!" Nica raised her hand like a traffic cop before she turned her head to face Cecilia. "What do you mean by saying that it'll make us all look ridiculous and superstitious? Who's us?"

"You! Me! Dad! Carmen! And the rest of the Santa Cecilia community!" Cecilia said, exasperated.

Nica, Antonio and Carmen were startled. Julie covered her face with her hands.

"Come here," Carmen said. She took Julie by the elbow and guided her into a chair at the table. "Now drink this. It's chamomile tea."

Julie raised her head and wiped the tears from her eyes with the tissue Carmen had just handed her. She drank down her tea, paused for a moment. "I . . . I don't want to make fun of you . . . of your community. I want the exact opposite. I would do anything to be part of it." She dropped her head.

"Thank you," Nica said and gave Julie's hand a gentle squeeze. She turned to Cecilia. "Now, m'ija, tell us what you meant."

"Well," Cecilia finally responded, then coughed into her hand and hesitated even longer, "it has something to do with testing . . . investigating if the spiritual really exists. Like Doña Faustina's coffee: seeing if it really helps people find their *dons*. Plus investigating if *dons* are for real or just magical thinking. Right, Julie?"

Julie stammered. "Um y-yes. I guess . . . that's the heart of it."

Brrring! Cecilia got up to answer the phone, then returned shortly. "That was your mother, Julie," she said. "She wanted to know if you were here. And . . ."

"And what?" Julie asked and her eyes clouded with concern. "Is she all right?"

"Yes, she's fine," Cecilia said. "It's just that she went on and on about the coffee, thanking me and sounding so happy! She sounded really different from her usual self."

"See? I told you!" Julie beamed. "It's like a miracle! Like magic!"

"Like magic! Sounds like great data, don't you think, Cecilia?" Antonio interjected.

Cecilia stopped herself from rolling her eyes. "What about you, Dad? What proof of magic can we investigate as to your *don*? Huh?"

"I would be absolutely honored to be studied for your project," Antonio replied.

"I bet others would be too!" Carmen seconded. "And don't forget Lebna, the third member of your team."

"Lebna? She wants to do this?" Cecilia asked.

"You bet your tacos!" Carmen said. "Right, Julie?"

"Yes, she's excited about it."

"And this will all weave itself together in some perfect, magical, cosmic way, right, Carmen?" Cecilia shook her head slowly, afraid that she would be laughed at and bullied at school for her backward and stupid Mexican ways.

"I hope so," Carmen said and crossed her arms. "But I still need to have my *plática* with Lebna."

"You've already had yours?" Cecilia shot Julie a stern look.

"We started it. Right, Carmen?" Julie asked.

"That's exactly right!" Carmen smiled at Julie. "The *plática* is a process, not just one tiny talk like Cecilia wants to think."

"Why can't this all wait?" Cecilia asked, spreading her hands in front of her. "Why does Doña Faustina have to go rest all of a sudden? What, is she moving to Florida to retire?"

Everyone in the room immediately froze at Cecilia's words.

"Wh-what's going on?" Cecilia stammered.

Antonio rubbed his eyes as if rousing himself from a deep sleep. "By rest, we don't mean retire."

"Oh," Cecilia said, pursing her lips. "I see."

"What do you see?" Julie asked.

"We'll talk about it in our next *plática*," Carmen said.

"Okay." Julie got the hint not to pry further and jumped to her feet. "It's late, so I better get going. But thanks so much for letting me come visit."

After they said goodbye, Cecilia walked Julie to the door, where Julie waved Cecilia out into the hallway.

"What?" Cecilia asked.

"What do they mean, huh? Saying that Doña Faustina needs to go rest?

"Carmen's explaining this to you at your next *plática*," Cecilia insisted.

"I want to know now!"

Cecilia sighed. "She . . . she's ready to pop off."

"Pop off to where?"

"To the spirit world."

"What? Like, as in, dying?" Julie's eyes widened.

Cecilia gave a quick nod.

Julie's mouth dropped open.

"Oh, come on," Cecilia said in a sarcastic tone. "Just a minute ago you were all gung-ho about investigating the spirit world."

CHAPTER 22

"**W**ell," Carmen said after she glanced at the wall clock, "I better go too. I have a ton to cook for tomorrow's route."

"I'll help you with the cooking here. And I plan to go with you tomorrow." Nica grabbed the edge of the table to pull herself to her feet.

"No way, Nica! You're crazy! You have to rest." Carmen took her sister by the elbow and tried to lead her back to the chair.

"Carmen's right," Antonio said.

Nica thrust her arms out and freed herself from their grips. "Don't tell me what to do!" Then she clenched her jaw in pain and doubled over.

"Nica!" Antonio exclaimed, grabbing her by the shoulders.

"Sit down!" Carmen demanded, setting the chair directly behind Nica.

Nica clutched her forehead with one hand and her stomach with the other while she slowly eased herself into the chair.

"See?" Antonio said, stricken. "It's too soon. You're still recovering."

"Here," Carmen added, handing Nica a glass of water.

CECILIA'S MAGICAL MISSION

Cecilia returned to the kitchen and dashed over to her mother. "What's wrong?!"

At the sound of Cecilia's voice, Nica forced a smile. "Nothing's wrong."

Cecilia dropped to one knee and studied her mother's pained face, then asked her father, "What's going on?"

Antonio took a deep breath. Before he could answer, Carmen spoke up. "I'll tell you what's going on. Your stubborn mother insists on going on the route tomorrow. I told her that you and I will handle it, but . . ."

"No, Mom, the route is grueling!" Cecilia insisted. "You have to stay home!"

"I know what I'm doing," Nica replied in a low, determined voice. "I want to thank everyone who came to the kermés. They were there for me. I want to be there for them as well."

"Don't worry," Antonio said, "I'll ask for time off to help with the route."

Nica shook her head. "You have to start on the coffin, remember?"

The word "coffin" struck Cecilia in the chest like a dagger. "Dad's making the coffin?"

Antonio gave a quick nod.

"Well, we know that Nica is as hard headed as a mule," Carmen injected. "Why waste our time arguing with her? It's pointless." She fixed her gaze on Nica. "So, this is what I propose. I go do the cooking for tomorrow while you go rest. I stop by at four o'clock tomorrow morning to pick Cecilia up to go buy supplies to set up the truck and then we swing by to pick you up at five-thirty. Okay? You can then drive, cook, greet people or do whatever you insist on doing."

After a brief moment, Nica nodded. "Okay, thank you." She gave Carmen and Cecilia a warm smile.

"Now that we're all set," Carmen said, "I can go start on the beans."

"Do you want me to come help you?" Cecilia asked as she followed Carmen down the building's hallway.

Carmen called back over her shoulder, "No, you better get some sleep."

When Cecilia got back to her apartment, she found her father had helped Nica into bed.

"Are you sure you're okay helping Carmen tomorrow?" Nica sat up against the headboard.

"Yes, but I wish you would stay home to rest."

"I'll be fine." Nica rubbed her eyes. "And I want to hear everything about the *kermés*, but . . ."

"No, go to sleep. We'll talk tomorrow." Cecilia leaned over to kiss her mother on the forehead.

"Wait. First, let's say a little prayer for Micaela," Nica extended her hands to take Cecilia's hand in one and Antonio's in the other.

Antonio began the prayer by invoking Micaela's guardian angel and Saint Michael the Archangel to guide her to her new home in heaven. He finished with, "Micaela, we love you very much."

Antonio then led Cecilia out of the room and back to the kitchen, where father and daughter sat down to face each other.

"*M'ija*, are you really okay going on the route tomorrow?"

"Yes, Daddy."

"You're worried about your school work, is that right? About falling behind?"

Cecilia rubbed her forehead. She couldn't lie. Besides her schoolwork, she was worried about the stillbirth and her mother's health. She had already missed school to help her mom with the taco truck and now would be absent again. And then there was the upcoming trip to Mexico to bury her sister.

"I *am* worried," Cecilia replied. "But I want to help you and Mom. I'm also worried about my science project. I don't even have a clue about what to do."

"I thought that you and your friends were going to investigate something about the spirit world. Isn't that what I heard?"

"Oh, that's such a crazy, stupid idea. And anyway, Dad . . ."

"Yes?"

"How in the world do you go about testing the spiritual? Huh?" Cecilia muttered. "And what about what you said earlier? That we could study you? Do we then wait for some guy to call you to ask you to find his tequila bottle?"

"Cecilia! Like I've told you before: I do more than find lost things like tequila bottles with my *don*."

"Like what, Dad? And don't tell me that I have to wait, that it'll take time for me to understand, because if you're really serious about not wanting me to worry about my science project and all the school I'm missing, you'll tell me this very minute. I'm serious!"

"But it's midnight. You have to get up in less than four hours."

"I'll worry all night if you don't tell me. So come on, tell me."

Antonio held his chin in thought and said. "Okay. Let's see. . . . Well, take the prayer I just said for Micaela's soul to find its way to heaven. That's one example of not simply finding lost things like tequila bottles."

"But how do you prove that her soul really got to heaven?"

"It takes a soul nine days to get to heaven, right?" He peered into Cecilia's eyes.

"That's what you all say. But how do you know? Isn't the soul invisible? And where's heaven, anyway?"

"You would make a good lawyer . . . or *don* tester?"

"*Don* tester, what's that?"

"It's someone with the gift for testing whether those claiming specific *dons* actually have them or are just saying so."

"What?!" Cecilia was stunned to hear that her so-called *don* was actually going to be tested.

"Yes, after a person announces that she or he has been given a particular *don*, they're tested. 'Cause, how can the community benefit from a *don* that's faked or just wishful thinking?"

"But . . . wait. Who's the tester? And how do they test it?"

"One never knows. It's a secret." Antonio stood up and headed for his bedroom.

"Wait!" Cecilia jumped to her feet. "Please don't do this!"

"Do what?"

"Be all mysterious and secretive. Like I said before, I don't want to worry about getting behind in school while doing the apprenticeship. So I need to learn about this spiritual stuff in a way that makes sense to me."

Antonio nodded. "Okay, but only if you promise to go to sleep. It's past midnight. Okay?"

"Okay."

"First of all, I wasn't trying to be mysterious or secretive about the *don* testers. Testers are supposed to be secretive because the person being tested isn't supposed to know she or he is being tested. Let me tell you my *don* story. You'll discover that everyone with a true gift has their own *don* story."

"Antonio!" Nica's voice boomed from the bedroom.

"I'm coming!" Antonio answered. He bolted to his feet and dashed down the hallway, Cecilia at his heels.

"What's wrong?" he asked as they tore into the bedroom.

"Nothing's wrong," Nica said. "I just woke up and was wondering where you were."

Antonio nodded and his lips curved into a slight smile. "I was just making sure Cecilia went to bed."

"*M'ija*, it's late, really late. Go to sleep. Carmen will be coming for you soon." Nica blew Cecilia a kiss.

"Okay." Cecilia blew her a kiss back. "But . . . ," she began, then looked at her father.

"We'll talk later, I promise."

CHAPTER 23

"Good morning!" Antonio switched on Cecilia's bedside lamp and patted her on the arm. "I brought you a cup of coffee."

"What time is it?" asked Cecilia as she rubbed her eyes.

"Three forty-five." Antonio placed the steaming cup on her nightstand.

"What?" Cecilia was startled before she suddenly remembered that this wasn't her usual school day. "Oh, right . . . the taco truck."

She sat up and reached for the cup of coffee. She lifted it to her nose and inhaled. It smelled good and felt nice and warm in her cold hand. But it was too early to drink coffee, especially since her stomach was still asleep.

"Sorry, *m'ija*." Antonio sat down at the foot of her bed. "It's so early and cold. I put the heater on in the bathroom, though."

"It's okay." Cecilia took a sip of coffee and almost gagged. *Whoa, it's too strong.* Then she remembered. "So tell me your *don* story, the one you were going to tell me last night."

Antonio got to his feet and glanced at the clock on the night table. "Carmen will be here in fifteen minutes. I don't have time."

"I'm already dressed. See?" Cecilia threw back the covers. "I slept in my sweats, so I only need to put on my sneakers, like I'm doing right now. I'll wash up in a jiffy, and then I'll have ten minutes to hear your story."

Antonio tossed his head back and let out a short laugh. "You're something else. Okay, I'll start."

"Talk fast so I can hear the whole story." Cecilia went to the bathroom to splash water on her face. She left the door open to hear him.

Antonio sat back down on the bed and started. "The earliest thing I can remember—at the age of about four—is the delicious smell of *pan dulce*, of *conchas* baking in my mother's oven. My mother made the most amazing chocolate-topped *conchas*. People back then didn't simply go to the bakery like they do today. Anyway—and let me hurry—I remember one morning racing to the kitchen, all excited to eat a *concha*. But my mother shook her head and said she was really sorry, but that that batch of *conchas* was for my godfather Antonio because he was trying to help a man who was dying.

"You can imagine how this went over with my four-year-old self. I wanted a *concha* and I wanted it right then. Of course, I cried and hollered. I demanded my *concha*.

"Just as my mother was promising to make another batch for me, we heard knocking at the front door. It was my *padrino* Antonio, who rushed in, looking all concerned, and he asked if I had hurt myself. My mother told him what was going on, which caused him to roar with laughter. Then he lifted me up in the air and said to my mother, 'Let him come with me to visit Paco. I think it's time to train him.'

"'But he's only four years old!' my mother said. I stopped crying. I sensed something was going on, and that that something was about me.

"My godfather reassured my mother, promising to take good care of me. That's when I asked, 'Can I have a *concha*?' He laughed and said, 'Yes, if you come with me.' I wrapped my arms around his neck, turned to my mother and said, 'I want to go with my *padrino*.'

"My mother hesitated, then took a deep breath and nodded. Next, she filled a white paper bag with the *conchas*.

"To make a long story shorter—since you really have to go—I put on some warm clothes and went with my *padrino* in his big Chevy truck. We drove until we reached the front of a tiny, clapboard house. We went in and found this man named Paco slumped at the kitchen table, his head on the table and his arms over his head. His wife Blanca, who had let us in, explained that Paco couldn't sleep, and when he did, had the most terrible nightmares. Blanca said her husband spent most of his time passed out on the table. My *padrino* went over and gave Paco a gentle tap on the back and said he had brought Paco's favorite treat: chocolate-topped *conchas*, fresh from the oven.

"My *padrino* opened the bag and started placing one, two, three, four . . . all twelve *conchas* in a semi-circle around Paco's head. 'Where's mine?' I said, alarmed when I saw the empty bag. He raised a finger to his lips to silence me, and then I heard a strange rustling sound. It was the jerking of Paco's arms. Paco raised his head and revealed the face of a demon with a grisly beard and black bags under his bloodshot eyes. Suddenly, his purplish face broke into a huge, crooked smile and exposed blackish teeth. Terrified, I dashed behind my godfather and watched as the monster snatched a *concha* and devoured it in three humongous bites. Then another and another. I was getting really angry. Where was my *concha*?

"'He hasn't eaten for days,' Blanca said. She stared at her husband with disbelief. That's when I rushed over, grabbed one of the two remaining *conchas* and started to devour it as fast as Paco scarfed his own down.

"I heard my godfather and Blanca gasp. Paco glared at me with devilish eyes. As I took the last bite of my *concha*, I chewed as fast as I could and backed away from him. Paco grabbed the last one and wolfed it down. Then he smiled and looked like the happiest man on the planet. Next, he lunged at me, like he would eat me too. I froze. Paco then stretched out his arm and shook my hand. He said, 'You like *conchas*? Chocolate ones?'

"'Yes!' I said, and he replied, 'Good.' He turned around and saw Blanca. 'Blanca, is that you?' He shuffled to her and they embraced. Then they started crying with happiness.

"'He's going to be okay,' my *padrino* said to Blanca. That's the last thing I remember about that strange experience. I had totally forgotten it until ten years later, when my *padrino* came to see me holding a bag of twelve *conchas* and served them the way he had that day. That's when it hit me, that memory of Paco's house, as I inhaled the mouthwatering smell of the freshly baked *conchas*. 'I remember a man named Paco . . . ' I began, but my *padrino* cut me off and said, 'Now sit down because I've come to have a little *plática* with you.'"

"What did he say?" Cecilia pressed her father.

"It's too late," Antonio said, when he heard a light knock at the front door. "Carmen's already here."

He got up and went to let Carmen in. Cecilia was right behind him.

"Ready to go?" Carmen asked.

Cecilia nodded with a big yawn and replied, "Dad was telling me his *don* story."

"I'll finish telling it later, when you get back." He gestured for his daughter to leave with Carmen.

"Here." Carmen took out her cellphone and handed it to Cecilia. "While we're traveling in the taco truck or waiting for customers, you can call your father to hear the rest of the story."

"That's a great idea," Antonio responded, wrapping an arm around his daughter's shoulder, "especially since your Confirmation is just around the corner."

Carmen was quick to agree. "Hearing your father's *don* story will make my job a lot easier. But now, we really have to get going." She turned and practically ran out the door and down the hallway to the stairs.

Before Cecilia could run after her, Antonio said, "I'll be waiting for your call. Don't worry about your science project. I have a hunch it's all going to work out."

CHAPTER 24

Carmen and Cecilia travelled many miles in total darkness before the van suddenly swerved and jolted Cecilia awake.

"How about a cup of hot chocolate?" Carmen asked as she drove toward a shimmering sea of lights.

"Uh . . . sure." Cecilia grabbed the dashboard to steady herself as her eyes popped wide open.

"We'll make a pot of it right away . . . to take the edge off this icy cold morning."

Cecilia looked out the windshield. The moon and stars were still out, the city still seemed fast asleep, houses and apartment buildings were pitch black, but the taco truck park was a rip-roaring carnival. There were two, twenty, forty—more than eighty lit-up taco trucks, all parked side by side. Their radios blared, their pots popped, their grills sizzled, their motors revved and laughter and shouted conversations echoed from the people who worked inside them across the park.

Carmen pulled the van alongside Nica's taco truck, which was parked at its assigned spot. She turned off the engine and said, "Okay, I'll unlock the taco truck so we can take the food inside."

Cecilia leapt out, then quickly wrapped her arms around herself to guard against a sudden gust of cold air. She wrenched open the van's side door, grabbed a stack of food containers and handed them to Carmen.

Once all the food was transferred, Cecilia looked at her watch. 4:30 a.m. She locked the van and climbed back into the taco truck.

After she set a stainless-steel pot down on the hot grill, Carmen waved Cecilia over. "Can you make the hot chocolate this morning?" She placed several brown disks and a *molinillo* on the counter by the grill.

As she peered into the pot, Cecilia tried to remember what her mother had taught her about making chocolate, but couldn't remember much of anything. Thankfully, she found her mother's tattered recipe book on a shelf. She looked for "Hot Chocolate."

"The second the water is about to start simmering," she read, "add the chocolate disks. Use the *molinillo* to break and dissolve the disks. Twirl back and forth to froth the chocolate."

Carmen popped out of the truck and raised the two side panels.

Cecilia saw her aunt counting the bottles and other drink containers inside the ice chest, before doing the same to the bags and packages of chips, pastries, peanuts and other snacks on the shelf above.

Suddenly, the water erupted in the pot. Cecilia flipped off the burner and tossed in the chocolate disks. Next, she grabbed the *molinillo* and started breaking the disks into smaller and smaller pieces until they dissolved completely. The water was soon transformed into delicious-smelling chocolate.

I can't wait to taste it, thought Cecilia as she twirled the *molinillo* between her hands to froth the chocolate. *I wonder what I will do with Doña Faustina later.* She groaned, thinking of how tired she'd be by the end of the day. She watched Carmen continue with the inventory and remembered she had promised to call her dad. *Bang!* Cecilia flinched at the sound. She turned and saw Carmen climb over the driver's seat.

"*Ah,* it smells so good!" Carmen hurried over and peered into the pot. "And full of bubbles too—just like your mother makes it." Then she cleared her throat and added, "And if it tastes as good as your mom's . . . well, perhaps you got her *don* too. Wouldn't that be wonderful?"

"What?" Cecilia said, her face dropping. "I'm going to be a . . . a . . ."

"A cook?" Carmen raised an eyebrow at Cecilia.

Oh, no! thought Cecilia. She shook her head vigorously. *Here I go again. And it's not even five o'clock in the morning.* "Carmen," she said, trying to keep her voice calm and steady, "I didn't . . . well, you know what a terrible cook I am."

Carmen gave her head a brisk shake. "Look, the last thing I want is for you to think that this is just about cooking, that the reason your mother—who just lost a child—insists on going on the route is that she simply can't wait to start cooking again."

"Are you mad at me? Gosh, I'm sorry . . ."

"This has nothing to do with me, with my feelings," Carmen hissed. "This is about you, your life and—"

"And what?" Cecilia asked.

"Why? It won't make any sense to you. It's something you have to experience."

"Tell me anyway," Cecilia insisted.

Carmen glanced at her watch. "Come on, we've got lots to do."

"So tell me quickly."

Carmen stared at Cecilia for a long, awkward moment. Then she began. "A person's *don* is not only a talent to be discovered and nurtured so it can be shared with one's family and community—although that is important too. It is also the portal to a person's own divinity inside them."

Baffled, Cecilia waited to hear more, but Carmen turned abruptly and ladled the hot chocolate into a Styrofoam cup. "Here." She handed the steaming cup to Cecilia. "I told you that you wouldn't understand."

After she let out a heavy sigh, Cecilia started towards the front of the truck to call her dad.

"Your mother's chocolate is better," she heard Carmen say, "but yours is good too."

Cecilia sat down in the passenger seat and waited for her dad to answer. "Hey, Dad?"

She asked after her mother, and her father assured her that she was still fast asleep. Then Cecilia told her father about their trip to the taco truck park, that they were drinking hot chocolate to stay warm and that Carmen insisted she take a break to call him.

"I think she's mad at me," Cecilia whispered into the phone.

"Why?"

Cecilia told him, then added how much she admired her mother for being a cook, but that . . .

Antonio chuckled.

"What's so funny?" Cecilia asked.

"It reminds me of when I was your age and I told my *padrino* that I had absolutely no desire to have San Antonio's *don,* because I didn't want to spend the rest of my life being a stupid lost-and-found box."

She was relieved that she could finally talk openly with someone without fear that her thoughts were disrespectful or even profane. "But, Dad, you stayed with your same saint, right? Saint Anthony?"

"Yes, and this is an important part of my *don* story. So let me finish telling it so Carmen can let you off the hook."

Cecilia listened intently to her father tell her how, when he looked back at the visit he and his *padrino* had made to Paco's house, what stuck with him was the realization that what Paco had found was not a lost bag of *conchas,* but something far more important.

"It turned out that what Paco had lost was his soul. The horrible killings and cruelties he had witnessed as a soldier during the war made life a living hell for him afterwards. He was haunted by his memories, in his walking thoughts and his dreams, until his soul fled his body and left Paco an empty shell.

"So I asked my *padrino* why we had brought the *conchas.* 'They transported Paco back to a happy time when he was just a kid,' my godfather said, 'a time when he loved nothing more than his mother's homemade *conchas.*' His wife even had his mother's handwritten recipe for them. He asked my mother to make *conchas* with the same recipe.

"The smell and taste of those *conchas* sparked Paco's memories of his boyhood. He was reminded of the joy and warmth of his family and community, of a time when his soul was happy and strong.

"That's when I realized," Antonio continued, "that San Antonio's *don* pertained not only to finding lost things, but to helping people with spiritual losses as well, like Paco losing his soul."

Cecilia bit her lower lip.

"But what about the testers?" Cecilia said in a rush. Carmen was tapping her watch and waving at Cecilia.

"The *don* testers? Okay, okay," her father said. "Well, because I had been finding lost things since I was a little kid, even when I didn't want to, I had the sinking feeling my *don* could only be exactly that: finding lost things. After my Confirmation *pláticas*, however, I saw things differently. I wondered if my gift also included the finding of spiritual things, which was my godfather's *don*, so he began giving me trials to find out. One was to see if I could help an orphan boy who was being shuttled from relative to relative, and, as a result, had started to wet his bed and sleepwalk. I'll tell you the whole story later, but I passed this test and that made me feel incredibly happy.

"But a harder trial followed: one regarding a young man, the first in his family to graduate from college, who could no longer relate to his parents. I finally passed this test, too. Again, I was so happy, and this convinced me to choose San Antonio to be my Confirmation patron saint, and to have my *padrino* as my sponsor.

"Then, at my Confirmation, my parents hosted a big celebration with food, music and laughter. I overheard my *padrino* mention something about my *don* being tested, but, because I thought he was referring to the trials he had already put me through, I didn't pay attention. I didn't realize that a test would take place that very day . . . at the fiesta.

"I was being fussed over by the entire family—*tíos, tías, abuelos, primos*. Everyone patted me on the back, said how happy and proud of me they were, when the festivities suddenly came to a halt at the sound of a soul-wrenching scream. Next, all the lights cut off and everything was pitched into total darkness. We stood there, outside in the moonless night, stunned, and wondered what was going on as the screaming got increasingly louder and more wretched. Then I froze; I heard my name called.

"Initially, I thought they were calling my *padrino*, but, no, it was me—Antonio Guerra, not Antonio García. My legs gave way and I fell to the ground, but I jumped back up and dashed towards the voice, as if by instinct.

"*What's going on?* I kept asking myself while I stumbled through the crowd of people with my heart racing. Suddenly, I stopped. I couldn't believe it; it was Lucinda, our barrio's *loquita*—that's what we affectionately called her. *What's our 'little crazy one' doing here?* I stared at her in bewilderment. Then she dropped to the ground and writhed in the dirt and snatched at me with her gnarled fingers while she yelled out my name—over and over again.

"Desperate, I looked around and wondered what to do. Lucinda had gone crazy ten years earlier, after she woke up one morning to find her husband had left with their only child. He'd left a note saying that he didn't love her anymore. My *padrino* knelt next to Lucinda and sighed.

"*This can't be*, I thought. I felt my stomach drop. The *don* testers are testing me now? And with Lucinda, who, even my *padrino*, after perfecting his *don* for thirty years hasn't been able to cure? This is madness!

"I felt everyone's eyes bore into me, even in the darkness; they had followed the noise and were now gathered around Lucinda, who still cried out and clawed at me. *This is not happening*, I told myself as I fell on one knee and patted Lucinda on the head. I brushed back her tangled gray hair from her brow, just like my mother used to do when I would wake up in hysterics from a nightmare. I did this because I had no idea what else to do.

"And you know what? She fell fast asleep. The moment she closed her eyes, the lights flickered back on as if by magic and everyone gasped. I felt their eyes on me again, but this time they looked at me with wonder rather than shock and confusion.

"And that's my *don* story." Antonio clicked his tongue. "I bet you have a ton of questions, but we can talk later."

Cecilia said goodbye reluctantly, snapped the phone shut, leapt off the seat and joined Carmen in the back.

"Did your father tell you the rest of his *don* story?"

"Sort of." Cecilia followed Carmen out of the truck.

"Sort of?"

"He gave me the main points," Cecilia said as she wrapped her arms around herself. "It's so *cold*." She shivered and bounced on her toes to fight the icy wind.

"Didn't the chocolate warm you up?" Carmen asked. They walked towards the warehouse.

"A bit," said Cecilia. She hurried after Carmen, walking past truck after taco truck getting ready to serve food across the San Francisco Bay Area.

Carmen grabbed a metal cart from the front of the warehouse and had Cecilia push it through the wide-open entrance. At the cash register was an Asian woman punching keys as she quickly counted the bottles, boxes and sacks heaped inside a cart.

Cecilia and Carmen hurried along, getting all the items on the list: *tortillas*, cheese, juices and more. Every turn got increasingly harder to clear for Cecilia as the items rose higher inside the rattling cart. Eventually, it got to where Cecilia could not see in front of her and had to crane her neck to the side to avoid a crash.

When Carmen stuck the pencil into the spiral of her notebook and dashed off, Cecilia rubbed her aching arms before she took a deep breath and started after her. At the register, the cashier swiftly scanned their purchases and gave them the total. Carmen took a wad of bills from her pocket, paid, then wrapped the long receipt around the remaining bills and stuck it back into her pocket. Next, she grabbed the front of the cart and began to pull while Cecilia pushed it through the exit, past the jumble of empty carts and onto the pocked, rutted asphalt outside. The cart rattled while its rusty wheels rumbled over the gravely ground. Cecilia felt her teeth, cheeks, hands, arms—her entire body—rattle, too.

They reached their taco truck and began unloading the supplies for the week's route. Carmen then put the rest in the van. *How strange*, Cecilia thought. Her whole body felt like it was still vibrating even though she was no longer pushing the cart.

Cecilia was brought back to reality when a young man appeared and set down a wheelbarrow of ice next to her and hurried off without a word. She called out to Carmen. "Someone just left a wheelbarrow full of ice. Do you want me to toss it into the ice chest?"

"Yes, but be careful," Carmen said. "The shovel might be too heavy for you."

"I'll manage," Cecilia said. She grabbed the shovel's handle with both hands. She pulled hard, then harder, and finally yanked it out of the ice mound. *Wow*, she thought, *this shovel is heavy*. She took a deep breath, grasped the shovel's handle with her right hand, the shaft with her left, raised the shovel in the air, and jammed it into the ice as hard as she could. After another deep breath, she tried to lift the shovel back out, but it wouldn't budge. She leaned her weight into it and tried again and again.

Suddenly the shovel popped out, with only the thinnest layer of ice on it. Frustrated, Cecilia swung the shovel around with its pathetic bit of ice and flung it toward the ice chest. She groaned when the ice struck the truck's tire.

She sighed heavily before she gave it another go, then another and still another, until she had finally emptied the wheelbarrow and filled the ice chest. She leaned against the truck and wiped the sweat off her face with the sleeve of her sweatshirt. She was totally spent.

"Nice job!" Carmen said as she jumped out of the truck. "How about a cup of coffee?" She filled a Styrofoam cup from the dispenser next to the ice chest and handed it to Cecilia. "You're sweating."

Cecilia nodded. She felt her arms throb with soreness. "That was really hard!"

"Ready to go pick up your mom?"

Cecilia shook her head. "Not really. This work is too hard for her right now."

"Well, she insists on coming," Carmen countered. "You saw how angry she got when we tried to convince her to stay home and rest." Carmen drained her coffee cup. "Another thing: pay close attention to everything that happens on the route today. You've already heard your father's *don* story, and now you'll get to see your mother practicing hers. This is worth ten *pláticas*, but only if you pay attention. So let's get going."

Back inside the truck, they soon joined the long caravan that exited the park like an Army convoy headed for battle.

Nica, with Antonio's help, slid into the driver's seat to join Cecilia and Carmen. They waved goodbye and drove off.

"How are you feeling?" Cecilia asked her mother.

"I'm okay," Nica said. "Did you get all the supplies?"

"Yes, lots of chips, candy bars and sodas."

"It's terrible how much junk food they buy," said Nica. "That's why I like to offer healthy dishes from home."

Carmen changed the subject. "I told my godchild that she would get to witness you practice your *don* today, that you're more than just a talented cook."

As Carmen talked, Cecilia felt her stomach lurch. She worried that Carmen was going to mention that she didn't want to have her mother's *don* because she didn't want to be a cook.

"And Antonio told her his *don* story this morning. So I advised Cecilia that, if she pays attention, I won't have to give her ten *pláticas.*"

Nica nodded, then glanced at Cecilia and asked, "Have you selected your Confirmation saint?"

"Uh . . . no."

"Don't forget that she's also starting her apprenticeship with Doña Faustina, right after the route," Carmen said with a grin.

"Yes," Nica said. "That'll be memorable."

"Sure will," Carmen agreed.

"What are you both getting at?" Cecilia raised her voice over the rumblings of the truck.

Nica and Carmen exchanged a quick look, then Nica replied, "Just do what Carmen said and pay close attention."

Without warning, Nica pulled off the road and killed the ignition. "Our first stop!"

It was exactly like the day Cecilia had missed school and helped her mother: customers greeted Nica, had their first hot drink and ate their breakfast. Nica chatted with them, thanked them for coming to the *kermés* and for their sympathies for Micaela. Meanwhile, Cecilia straightened and replenished the snacks and did whatever else was needed to help Nica or Carmen.

Soon, they dashed down the highway to the second stop. After a while, Cecilia looked at her mother and said, "This is just like the last time. So what is it that I'm supposed to be paying attention to?"

"Where are you with the *pláticas*?" Nica asked.

"Oof . . . she's barely at the beginning," Carmen said with a groan.

Nica jerked her head towards Cecilia. "Remember that young woman—Barbara—who pulled up in a car and ordered two breakfast tacos?"

"Yes," Cecilia said.

"And do you remember recently reading about the wildfires close to Santa Barbara, the ones that were raging uncontrollably?"

"Yeah . . . ," Cecilia answered.

"Well, that's a good example of someone with a true *don*," Nica said.

"But doesn't she live on the second floor and work at Wal-Mart?"

Carmen suddenly expelled a gust of air through her teeth and raised her voice: "I told you, Nica, your daughter is still at the very beginning of her spiritual training. And her Confirmation is only a few weeks away!"

Nica shook her head and swerved into the exit lane.

"Why is Barbara such a good example of what I'm still so clueless and stupid about? Huh?"

While Nica drove the truck up one street and down another, Carmen fixed her eyes on Cecilia and asked, "Okay, my godchild, tell me what *don* Santa Barbara is associated with?"

Cecilia scrutinized Carmen's expression and wondered if she was playing with her or seriously responding to her question. "I don't know," Cecilia finally said.

"Fires. And lightning . . . which is often the cause of wild-fires," Carmen answered. "As for Santa Barbara's *don* story: she lived during the seventh century and wanted to devote her life to Christ, but her father insisted she marry. When she refused, he killed her. Then, shortly afterwards, he was struck and killed by lightning."

The truck came to a halt and this indicated they were at their second stop.

Cecilia scrambled out of the truck and raised the side panels. Nica stuck her head over the counter and waved at three young men who were headed towards them.

"Just like before," Cecilia said to herself as she climbed back into the truck.

"A cup of coffee and a plate of *chilaquiles*," Cecilia heard one of them say. He exchanged greetings with Nica. Carmen grabbed an egg from the carton and cracked it open onto the hot grill.

While she reached for another, Cecilia tapped Carmen on the back and asked, "So what's the rest of Barbara's story?"

Carmen glanced at Cecilia and smiled as she cracked a third egg.

"An order of *chorizo con huevos* for Jaime," Nica called out to Carmen. "And an order of *huevos rancheros* for Gilberto."

Carmen bobbed her head, cracked egg after egg, then spiced the eggs and added diced tomatoes, onions and chili peppers. She turned to Cecilia and asked, "Are you paying attention?"

"I'm trying."

"Well, Barbara was born on December 4th, on Saint Barbara's feast day, which explains why she was named Barbara. For her Confirmation, she picked the same saint, feeling she had a similar *don*: that of protecting against fires and lightning," Carmen said. "There was a terrible lightning storm years ago in Santa Cecilia. It started at dusk and continued for hours. At three o'clock in the morning, Barbara's parents heard a loud knock at the front door. Her father opened the door and found an old woman completely drenched in water." Carmen paused to scoop the food she had prepared onto a plate and handed it to Nica. "He was stunned because he had never seen this woman before, and everyone knew everyone in Santa Cecilia back then. He stared at her until Barbara's mother hurried over and, although she was startled and confused as well, asked the woman to come inside from the storm.

"They shut the door and asked how they could help her, but the old woman just stood there as if in a trance. Then she raised a finger and said, 'Barbara . . . Barbara . . . where is Barbara?'

"Stunned, Barbara's parents looked at each other. They wondered what to do while the woman kept asking for their daughter as the storm raged. *Was she mad?*

"'Why do you want her?' Barbara's mother finally asked, desperate to protect her daughter. She then ran to Barbara's bedroom to make sure she was safe, but discovered that her daughter had left her room and was headed towards the old woman with her eyes shut."

"Two bean burritos," Nica called out to Carmen.

"Then what happened?" Cecilia handed Carmen two flour tortillas, which she tossed onto the grill.

"What happened was that Barbara, still asleep, walked straight up to the old woman and extended her hand. In a panic, her parents grabbed her and tried to pull her back, but she kicked them off. The moment the old woman took Barbara's hand, the girl woke up and screamed at the top of her lungs. While her parents tried to drag her away and calm her, the old woman pitched forward and peered at Barbara with blazing eyes."

Carmen paused to spoon refried beans onto the tortillas and fold them into burritos. Cecilia waited in suspense.

"'I need Barbara to talk to the lightning,' the old woman said in a low, raspy voice. 'She needs to tell it to stop, to stop, to stop.'"

"And what happened?" Cecilia asked breathlessly.

"Ah, you like this little *plática*, huh? Maybe I should've shaped them all into scary stories for you. Well," Carmen continued, "Barbara's mother eventually realized what the old woman was talking about when she saw her point out the window at the furious storm.

"'Who are you?' she asked the old woman, trying to sound calm for the sake of her daughter, who trembled in her arms. 'Where did you come from?' But the old woman just stared at Barbara and repeated: 'Tell it to stop, tell the lightning to stop.'

"Frantic for the old woman to leave, Barbara's mother suddenly thought of something. Perhaps, if she coaxed her daughter to tell the lightning to stop and the woman saw that nothing happened, she'd finally go away. So the mother cupped her hand over Barbara's ear and whispered for her to repeat the following words: 'I ask you, storm and lightning, to stop in the name of the Lord. Stop right now, this very instant.'

"After she stared at her mother for a long, tense moment, the girl repeated the words in a barely audible voice. Instantly, the storm stopped. Then they heard the door slam shut. The old woman was no longer there. They looked out the window, opened the door and looked up and down the road, across the sky, everywhere. But it was as if the old woman had simply vanished."

"Wow," Cecilia said, stunned. "So is this why you say Barbara's got a true *don*?"

"Not exactly," Carmen said. She handed Nica a steaming plate of scrambled eggs with thick cuts of bacon. "Remember: she was just a young kid then. She hadn't even made her First Communion. Years later, at fifteen, while preparing for her Confirmation, she announced she was sticking with Santa Barbara for her patron saint. Then four years after her Confirmation, she answered the front door and was handed an envelope with a letter inside signed by 'Your *don* testers,' along with some money. The letter directed her to use her *don* to quell the wild fires raging in the Santa Barbara area, and that the money was to cover her expenses.

"Confused, she called her godmother right away to ask if the letter was real, but the phone went dead at the other end. Barbara thought the connection had been interrupted. Her *madrina*, however, who realized what was happening, had been shocked into silence. Why were the testers— whoever they were, since their identity was a secret to her too—subjecting Barbara to such a brutal test? The fires had blazed for weeks, in spite of the firefighters who fought them with helicopters and modern technology. And now what? A ninteen-year-old girl had been asked to do the impossible? Barbara's godmother rushed over to see her, to examine the letter. 'It's the real thing,' she told Barbara. 'A person's *don* gets tested, remember? But I've never heard of such a hopeless test, or for one so young.'

"Barbara couldn't believe it either. The out-of-control fires had been constantly on the news. Desperate, Barbara asked for advice from all her family members, then remembered the lightning storm years earlier. She asked her mother to repeat the exact words that had stopped the raging storm, when the strange old woman had come to their house. Two days later, Barbara took a bus to Santa Barbara, followed by a taxi to its Mission church, where she asked her patron saint to stop the fires."

"Then what happened?" Cecilia clutched the counter with both hands.

"It worked," Carmen handed Nica a plate of *machacado con huevo*, beef jerky scrambled with eggs.

"What worked?"

"The fires stopped," Carmen concluded.

"What?" Cecilia shook her head. "But I read that the fire-fighters had finally put out the fires."

"That's what the papers said, the radio and TV, what everyone believes, but . . ."

"But what?"

"Take the hurricane that recently hit the East Coast—Hurricane Sandy."

"That was a disaster. Julie lost her home and—"

"But it could have been worse . . . much, much worse," Carmen said, "if we hadn't called Michael the Archangel for help, as well as our mission saints."

"Mission saints?"

"Those associated with the Franciscan missions founded many years ago along the California coast by Junípero Serra. This was before there was even a United States or a Mexico. That's why our community came here, to California, in the first place, because of its spiritual roots."

Cecilia watched Carmen cook order after order and remembered studying the California missions in school, but this was the first time she had ever heard that her community was somehow connected to them. As for the story she had just heard about Barbara and her *don*, well, that was unbelievable, on so many levels.

Cecilia stepped closer to Carmen, who cracked three eggs onto the grill.

"What?" Carmen asked with a snort. "You're only now realizing how much you missed by avoiding our *pláticas*?"

"Well . . ."

"You'll just have to pay attention to what happens at Doña Faustina's later today," Carmen said. "And you can ask me questions anytime."

"What about Mom?" Cecilia gestured towards her mother, who chatted with the customers. "You said I would see her practicing her *don*, and . . ."

"And what?"

"And that today's route would seem different from the one I witnessed before."

"So, keep watching."

"*Buenos días*, Toribio!" Carmen waved to a silver-haired man who ate his breakfast.

"*Buenos días*, Carmen," Toribio beamed up at her.

"How are the *chilaquiles*?"

"Good, very good," Toribio replied with a nod.

"But not as good as Nica's, right?"

"Ah, these are good, Carmen." Toribio quickly glanced at Nica. "But . . . to be honest, Nica's cooking is really very special. It makes me feel like a kid eating my mother's cooking."

Carmen let out a loud laugh and said, "I know. Nica's cooking is magical, while mine, well, tastes good enough."

The next moment Carmen startled Cecilia with a touch to her shoulder. "Toribio, this is my godchild Cecilia, Nica's daughter. She's preparing for her Confirmation, so I've told her about *dons*. Can you tell her about your *don*, and how when you ate Nica's magical food, everything clicked for you?"

Toribio put his fork down, looked straight at Cecilia, and said, "I would be happy to." He began. "My name is Toribio . . . named after San Toribio, the patron saint for undocumented immigrants. My gift allows me to ask San Toribio to help those crossing the border. He appeared to me when I got lost on my way here, when I ran out of water and went crazy in the hot sun. He was wearing a cowboy hat and boots and showed me the way through the desert, to water.

"As for your mother's *don* of cooking . . . well, see, I came to California from Santa Cecilia to help my family back home. But I couldn't find work for weeks and I became homesick and depressed. Then one day I got a job at a construction site. I did whatever they asked me to do—dug holes, moved dirt with a wheelbarrow, carried pipes. Then I saw a food truck pull up. All the workers dropped whatever they were doing and dashed over to it. When I heard them call out orders for tacos, *menudo*, burritos, *carne asada* and other foods from home. I couldn't believe it.

"That's when I first met your mother. She greeted me with the biggest smile. Then, while I enjoyed her delicious *carnitas* that tasted like home, she asked me about my family, my name and whether I had any connection to San Toribio. I told her about how he had saved my life in the desert. Later, she asked me whether I had had any more experiences involving my patron saint. I told her I was recently asked by a co-worker who had a relative crossing back to Mexico to pray to San Toribio on his behalf, to ask the saint to guide and protect him throughout his journey, since they had started to arrest people going back too. Well, the man arrived there safely. One day, your mother introduced me to Father Ramón, and I've helped him with those who cross the border since then." He ended and gave Cecilia a slight bow of his head.

"Thank you, Toribio," Carmen said.

"Yes, thank you," Cecilia said with a quick smile.

"You should thank your mother," Toribio said, "because it's thanks to her and her amazing cooking that I was able to find myself and my community again."

Later, on their way to their final stop in the taco truck, Nica and Carmen dropped Cecilia off at Doña Faustina's house. As she approached the front door, Cecilia looked around and wondered where her friends were. She knew they would chicken out. She felt very much alone. *What friends!* She clenched her fists in anger.

CHAPTER 26

Cecilia dragged her feet up to Doña Faustina's door and wondered what she would encounter inside. She stared at the front door for a long, long time before she forced herself to raise her hand to knock. Before she could, the door flew open, which caused her to jump back and almost fall.

"I've been expecting you," a gravelly voice called out, followed by a rolling riot of giggles.

Cecilia gasped. "Is that you . . . Doña Faustina?"

"Yes, come in."

Cecilia stepped into the doorway, baffled by the shrill giggles she had heard. *Was Doña Faustina laughing at her?*

"Boo!" someone shouted and caused Cecilia to leap into the air. All of a sudden, Julie and Lebna popped out from behind the door. They giggled wildly and pointed at Cecilia's shocked expression.

Doña Faustina peered at her with a fox-like grin.

Cecilia fixed her stern gaze on the two girls and said in a sharp tone, "What's so funny?" Then, ignoring them, she greeted Doña Faustina and followed her to the kitchen.

Doña Faustina gestured for the girls to sit at the table in the middle of the room while she shuffled over to the sink and filled a glass with water. Then she plunked the glass down on the table, pulled out a chair and dropped into it with a loud thud.

"This is the beginning of his first miracle," Doña Faustina said, and locked her eyes on Cecilia's while she pointed at the glass with a long, bony finger.

Cecilia leaned forward and stared at the glass as Julie and Lebna looked on in wonder.

After a few moments of awkward silence, Cecilia cleared her throat and said, "Doña Faustina . . . I'm confused. What are you saying?"

The old woman looked at the girls' puzzled faces, then focused on Cecilia and said, even louder, "What was his very first miracle?"

Cecilia tilted her head slightly and caught a glimpse of the purplish hue of the setting sun outside, which suddenly triggered her memory. "Wine," she said and sat up in her chair. "Christ turned water into wine—at a wedding—at his mother's request. That was his first miracle."

"Yes," Doña Faustina said with a slight nod. "And what does this mean?"

Cecilia couldn't believe that, for her apprenticeship, she would be grilled on New Testament stories, stories she hadn't thought about for the longest time. *This is a total waste of time.* She was getting even more anxious about the science project she had not started. Then, as she caught sight of her friends' bewildered expressions, she thought, *Well, there's a silver lining to all this confusion. It will finally convince them that their science project idea—that we should go around investigating the ins and outs of the spiritual world—is utterly stupid.*

Cecilia flinched and felt her shirt yanked. When she raised her eyes, she found Doña Faustina staring at her.

"What were you thinking that was making you grin?"

"Eh . . . I'm sorry . . . I have no idea what it means—turning water into wine."

Doña Faustina then focused her penetrating gaze on Julie and Lebna, and this made them lean back from the table. *Good,* Cecilia smiled to herself, *they're worried Doña Faustina is going to quiz them next, and I'm all for it!*

After she got nothing but blank stares from Julie and Lebna, Doña Faustina shuffled over to the sink, where she filled a kettle with water and put it on the stove to boil before she shuffled back.

The girls sat stiffly and deathly quiet, observing Doña Faustina's every move, every gesture, to see what she would do or say next. But Doña Faustina just stared back at them until the kettle started to whistle. With this, she got back on her feet, and then the girls watched her make a pot of coffee using a jar of roasted coffee beans like those they had raffled off at the *kermés.*

After Doña Faustina had filled four cups, Cecilia jumped up and insisted on carrying them to the table.

Doña Faustina took a deep drink of her coffee and gestured for the girls to do the same. Cecilia inhaled its rich aroma and quickly drained her cup. She waved at her friends to hurry up and do the same. Once done, the girls stared wide-eyed at Doña Faustina.

Doña Faustina simply leaned back in her chair and fixed her gaze on Cecilia.

Cecilia felt the old woman's eyes bore straight into her. She gave her head a firm shake as if trying to free herself from a spell. "Doña Faustina, why are you staring at me?"

"I'm still waiting to hear your answer as to what the first miracle showed you."

"What?" Cecilia said with a groan. "I'm sorry, but I still have no idea."

"What about you? Do you know?" Doña Faustina looked from Julie to Lebna.

Julie gasped, then shook her head vigorously, while Lebna sat up straight and said, "No."

Cecilia smiled when she saw that her friends felt the heat too.

Doña Faustina weaved her hands together and said, "Here's the first lesson: Just as Mary asked her son to turn water into wine at the wedding feast, we can also ask our *don* to be revealed to us, since Christ works in ordinary things, too, not just in cosmic ones. Do you understand what I'm saying?"

Cecilia hesitated. Then she whispered, "I . . . I think so."

Doña Faustina nodded and continued. "So what *don* did you ask for?" After Cecilia stared blankly at her, she added: "Or what *don* did you pray to be revealed to you?"

Oh, no, thought Cecilia, *she's testing my words like the* don *testers will eventually test whatever gift I claim.*

Cecilia flinched when she felt her shirt yanked again. Doña Faustina was still waiting for her answer.

Cecilia averted her eyes and said in a low, plaintive tone, "I don't know anything about my *don* . . . not sure I have one . . . or even believe in them." She looked at Doña Faustina and expected her to be angry or disappointed for having selected her to be her apprentice.

Instead, Doña Faustina smiled broadly at her. She pitched forward in her chair and said in her gravelly voice, "Now it's time to tell you *my don* story."

Cecilia relaxed in her chair. She figured this story would be a long one.

"It was early Christmas morning, many years ago, when I was five years old and known as Clarita. I woke up after attending midnight Mass, just a few hours earlier, and heard loud noises coming from the kitchen. Wanting to go back to sleep, I pulled the blanket over my head, but then I heard my mother talking louder and louder, sounding more and more agitated. Fearing something terrible had happened to my father, I jumped out of bed and ran to the kitchen, shouting, 'Where's *Papá*? What happened to *Papá*?' But there he was, sitting at the kitchen table and staring straight ahead as if in a daze, while my mother shouted at the priest who, just hours ago, I had seen put Baby Jesus in the manger during Mass.

"'Clarita!' my mother said when she caught sight of me. She looked totally surprised.

"I went to her, wrapped my arms around her and started to whimper. She picked me up and asked what was wrong. My father began rubbing my back, trying to calm me down. Even the priest patted me on the head. After sniffling a bit longer, I quieted down and told them I was scared, thinking something bad had happened to *Papá*.

"My father assured me he was fine. He said that Father Gómez (who, incidentally, was related to Santa Cecilia's current Father Gómez) had simply stopped by to talk about the *don* party. 'Yes,' the priest said, going down on one knee to look me in the eye, 'I came to ask your mother the great favor of baking a special cake—a *pan de rosca*—for the occasion.' Then he asked if I had kissed the Baby Jesus at Mass. I nodded yes.

"For some reason, I suddenly scowled and yelled out, 'Why were you fighting with my mother?'

"'Oh, I need your mother's help,' he explained. 'I need your help too.'

"I looked at my mother, not understanding, but she looked confused too. 'Help with what?' I asked.

"'I need you to help your mother,' he said.

"'But how?' I raised my voice.

"'With the coffee. Help make the coffee,' the priest said, 'to go with the *pan de rosca*. Okay?'

"'Okay,' I shrugged. I didn't really understand what I had agreed to." Doña Faustina paused to take a deep breath.

Cecilia took the opportunity to ask, "But why was your mother so upset about simply baking a cake?"

"Well, later, on the fifth of January," Doña Faustina continued, "I found my mother in the kitchen, making a *pan de rosca* with eggs, butter, flour and all kinds of bright, candied fruit. I loved Mamá's *pan de rosca* and felt so excited to eat a big slice of it the next day for the Epiphany. I also dreamt I'd find the tiny, porcelain Baby Jesus she always hid inside the cake. I loved how my mother was always so happy when she baked this special cake, as if it was something celestial she did with the help of a hundred cheery angels.

"But Mamá looked incredibly sad, almost on the verge of tears. I asked her what was wrong, but she forced a smile and insisted everything was fine. Then, as if she suddenly remembered, she bent down towards me and asked, 'Do you remember what you promised Father Gómez?'

"I nodded. 'To help you make coffee,' I said.

"'Right.' She took me by the hand and led me to the sink, where she had me wash my hands. While I washed, I turned to her and asked, 'Why were you crying? I thought you liked making our *pan de rosca*.'

My mother didn't answer, just cracked more eggs into a bowl. She then said, 'Oh, Clarita, I'm sorry, but this *pan de rosca* is not for you, not for our family. It's for some special people.'

"'No!' I screamed. 'It's mine!' I grabbed her bowl and dashed off."

Cecilia thought of her father's *don* story, about how he cried and hollered when his mother told him that her *conchas* were for his godfather, not for him. Doña Faustina's words then brought Cecilia back to the present.

"My mother chased me through the kitchen, out the front door and finally caught me halfway down the street. I had no idea where I was running. My only thought was to steal the bowl to save the *pan de rosca* from the others who would eat it, regardless of how special they might be.

"I remember sobbing as my mother pried the bowl that sloshed with eggs from my hands. Then she pulled me back home as I kicked and screamed. But what happened? We ran straight into Father Gómez. 'What's the matter?' he said. I'll never forget his face, two inches from mine. His eyes bulged.

"'I'm so glad we ran into you.' My mother released her grip on me.

"'Did she fall?' he asked and looked me over from head to toe.

"'No, she's fine . . . not hurt at all. But she ran off with this bowl,' she said, raising it in the air, 'the moment I told her the *pan de rosca* I was making was not for her.'

"Father Gómez let out a loud horselaugh before he caught himself, when he saw my tear-stricken face.

"'And,' my mother added, 'I reminded her about her promise to you, the promise that she would make the coffee, but . . .'

"'I see.' He patted me on the head, smiled and said, 'How about you help your mother make some coffee, while I go get you a great, big *pan de rosca*? Okay?'

"I shook my head vigorously and said, 'No! I want Mamá's. Take yours to the other people.'

"Father Gómez straightened up, scratched his head and said, 'What a clever child you are.'

"He exchanged a quick glance with my mother, then said to me, 'Clarita, you have a very special mother . . . with a very special *don*. That's why she's preparing this *pan de rosca* for a very special occasion. I know this is hard for you to understand—perhaps impossible at your age—but one day you will. So if you want to help your mother, to make her happy, please help her make the coffee. And I'll be right back with a big, beautiful *pan de rosca* just for you. Okay? Please?'

"I finally nodded after my mother added that this would surely make me happy. No more than fifteen minutes later, Father Gómez knocked on the door with the biggest *pan de rosca* I had ever seen. I was thrilled, then confused after seeing that my mother's *pan de rosca* was not only much smaller but also less decorated with candied fruit than the one the priest had brought. *Why does Father Gómez insist on* giving the special people my mother's pan de rosca, I wondered, when they would be more dazzled by the cake he got at the bakery?

"The don party was held at our church, and everyone who had been confirmed and had passed their don test carried a stone that had been presented to them as a symbol of the talent they had been given. The stone also commemorated the gift Mary had presented to the Three Kings who came to see the Divine Baby. Before they returned to their kingdoms, we were told that Mary had given the Magi a small box. Later, on the way home, they had opened the box and were surprised and disappointed to find a rather ordinary-looking stone inside. Because they thought it was ridiculous to carry a useless stone, they tossed it away. Then they were astonished to see a blaze of fire shoot up to the sky from the very spot where the stone had struck the ground. They hurried to it and felt utterly humbled by this wondrous miracle, for the brilliant flame seemed to connect with the very heavens above. Awestruck, they each lit a torch with the flame and took them back to their kingdoms, where the perpetually burning torches were safeguarded as divine miracles.

"The stone symbolized Mary's faith in realizing her don . . . Mary is also the patron saint of dons, since she exemplifies the trust, faith and hope needed for a person's gift to actually emerge. Remember, she was not yet married to Joseph when Gabriel the Archangel appeared to her and announced that she had been chosen to give birth to Christ. Can you imagine being pregnant and not married at that time, in that society? Imagine how this must've affected her relationship with Joseph. But she had faith. And then what happened? An angel appeared to Joseph and asked him to accept Mary as his wife, even though she was already with child.

"At the *don* party four young people were introduced, who turned out to be the special people Father Gómez had been talking about. I looked them over, carefully, and found absolutely nothing special about them. They looked like typical teenagers: pimply and gangly, two boys and two girls. What was different about them, however, was that they looked spooked—all four of them—with slumped shoulders and dead-fish eyes.

"Standing between my parents, I stared at Mamá's *pan de rosca*, which had been set on a small table in front of the so-called special four. Then I tugged on my mother's sleeve and asked her what was so special about these pimply teenagers who were about to eat my *pan de rosca*.

"My mother was embarrassed, since the people who stood near us had overheard, and she shot me a stern look while she shushed me. Just then, Father Gómez stepped in front of the *pan de rosca* and asked us to say a special prayer for the four young people who had not been able to pass their *don* tests.

"All four dropped their heads and stared at the floor. *If they failed their tests, why are they special?* I wondered. *Why do they get to eat my* pan de rosca? I watched as the four stepped up to the table and, one by one, sliced off a big piece of my *pan de rosca* with a fancy silver knife.

"Unable to bear it any longer, I stomped my foot and yelled out, 'It's mine!' and dashed towards the cake.

"My father plucked me up as I was about to grab the cake and whisked me outside. He set me down on the crackling, frozen grass and pointed up to the sky. It was ablaze with the brightest, bluest stars.

"'Why can't I have a piece of the *pan de rosca*?' I whined.

He took my hand and said in a gentle, hushed voice, "'Because it's like a secret, one I promise to tell you someday. Okay?'"

"I hesitated for a moment, then nodded since I liked secrets. He led me back inside and said, 'It's time to help your mother make the coffee. This is part of the secret.'

"I was all excited and quickened my pace. Everyone's eyes were on me as they were served small slices of the *pan de rosca*. Next, Papá led me into the kitchen, where I caught sight of the four teenagers who, instead of being happy because they got special prayers and ate my *pan de rosca*, were crying. Papá pulled me towards my mother and said, 'Here she is, ready to help make the coffee.'

"'Okay, fill this with water.' She handed me a kettle. 'Then set it on the stove.'

"I sighed as the kettle got heavier and heavier with water, and wondered why I had to make coffee for these sad teenagers who were slumped at a table and staring at an invisible spot on the wall. *Why don't they make their own coffee? What could be so secret about any of this?*

"My mother tapped me on the shoulder and whispered, 'While preparing the coffee, please pray that they discover their true *dons*.' Then, as she helped me set the heavy kettle on the stove and grind the coffee, she told me why the four people were special.

"'They were tested by the *don* testers and failed.'

"'Why are they special if they failed?' I asked her.

"'Sometimes,' she said, 'Satan intervenes, or his demons. On the other hand, a person might have sincerely believed he had been given a particular *don*, but it never really bloomed. That's why I want you to pray for them while making their coffee. Ask Mary to pray for them too.'

"'But why did they eat my *pan de rosca*?'

"'I used Holy Water to make it,' she said.

"I remember it as if it happened yesterday." Doña Faustina's eyes brightened. "I turned to my mother and said, 'I want to make the coffee with Holy Water too!'

"She looked at me, astonished, then dashed out of the kitchen and returned with a pitcher of water. She said it was Holy Water. I refilled the kettle with the Holy Water and prayed silently while my mother guided me as I made the pot of coffee. We asked Mary and their guardian angels to help them find their true *dons*.

"While I scooped the ground coffee into the pot, my mother whispered that the teenagers were especially saddened because they had announced that they had received the *don* that the entire community had gathered specially to pray for—the *don needed* to defeat the terrifying dark forces that had attacked the town.

"When the townspeople heard that the *don* they had all been fervently praying and fasting for had finally been given to not only one, but to four members of their community, the town rejoiced. They celebrated with a week-long fiesta of processions, festive foods and fireworks. No one criticized the lavishness of the fiesta, since they knew that the four would direct their talents—even put their lives at risk—to fight their darkest enemy. They had not even waited for the *don* testers to confirm their gifts before the celebration began because no one in their right mind, they thought, would want a *don* that would make them fight demons, or especially Satan himself. But the townspeople's joy soon turned to despair when the evil attacks against the town continued. People lost hope and some even took their own lives.

"I trembled as my mother told me this story. I poured the coffee into the four cups on the table. As the teens started drinking, I imagined a ring of light that protected them from evil. As they continued to sip their coffee, I noticed their eyes start to brighten. Then, after they emptied their cups, they suddenly looked at each other as if they had just awakened from a spell and crossed the room to shake my mother's hand and thank her. They told her how much better they felt. My mother smiled, then pointed at me and said that I had brewed the coffee. They patted me on the back and thanked me, too.

"I stepped back, looked straight at them and said in a loud, demanding voice, 'So now tell us your real *don!*'

"The four stared at me, two with gaping mouths. The very next moment, I found myself being whisked up into the air again and carried out of the room by my father. 'Wait! Bring her back!' the four young people pleaded with him. Then they bent down towards me and asked me to repeat my question.

"As I stood there, I wondered if they were angry at me for embarrassing them. But they looked sincere and again asked me to repeat my question, which I did.

"That's when one of them stammered, 'I-I feel I have the *don* of lost causes. I remember . . . as a young boy . . . I felt I could heal this dog . . . a dog that lay on the road . . . dying.

I had passed it on my way home from school. Everyone had run past it . . . scared . . . as if it would bring bad luck. I ran back to the dog. It was still twitching . . . moaning with pain. I knelt next to it . . . stroked its head . . . "'No! It's rabid!'" . . . I heard people yell. "'Get away from it!'" But I continued patting the dog . . . talking to it . . . saying I was going to heal him. . . . Then, an old man appeared . . . jumped out of his wagon . . . picked the dog up . . . put him in his wagon. He then looked at me with tears in his eyes. He said it was his dog . . . that he would take him home. A week later, the old man knocked on my door . . . with his dog . . . to thank me. He said they would have shot it . . . that I had saved his dog's life.'

"The second teenager followed, then the third. Each recalled something about their childhood before they announced what they believed their *real don* was. Father Gómez witnessed all three stories. But the last of the four, a slight, pale girl, remained silent, with her head bowed. I went up to her with the boldness of a five-year-old, tapped her on the shoulder, and told her, 'You're the one who got the *don* right?' The girl started to cry. My father was about to whisk me off again, when the girl grabbed his arm and said that I was right, that losing battle after battle had exhausted her to the point she couldn't even get out of bed anymore.

"Father Gómez placed his arm around the girl's shoulder and said he would help her, because having her *don* could be terrifying. He also said that he had prayed for this gift to be given to him, but realized how hard it would be to understand, to grow and, especially, to use such a *don*."

Doña Faustina now leaned back in her chair, folded her hands on her lap and looked right at Cecilia, who flinched at the directness of her stare.

"Uh . . . Doña Faustina, are you going on with your story?"

"That *was* my *don* story. Now tell me about yours!"

Cecilia hesitated and then said, barely audible, "Well, one thing that struck me about your story is how you discovered your *don* as if by accident. I mean . . . you thought you were just making coffee, right? But, after you learned about the four, you prayed for them and used Holy Water to prepare the coffee and asked Mary to help. And they found their true *dons*. Right?"

"That's the first lesson," Doña Faustina said. "Don't forget that Mary is the patron saint of *dons*. Tomorrow I will give you the second lesson."

Just then, there was a knock at the door. Carmen let herself in, ready to take the girls home. On the ride back to the apartment, the girls sat quietly in the van until Carmen's laughter shattered the silence.

"It must have been quite a lesson," Carmen said, "since the three of you have never, *ever* been so quiet. What kind of spell did Doña Faustina cast on you?"

"Well, she told us her *don* story," Cecilia said.

"And how's your science project going?" Carmen asked. "Are you still spies?"

Cecilia groaned. Doña Faustina's story had allowed her to forget about schoolwork. It was as though it had transported her to another realm. Now her mind raced again and she was filled with a sense of dread.

Cecilia remained silent, so Carmen asked, "Since Doña Faustina has stunned Cecilia into silence, what do you two think?"

"I still think our idea for the science project is great!" Julie exclaimed.

"I do too," Lebna seconded. "Don't you, Cecilia?"

"What's so great about it, huh?" Cecilia spat out.

"Ah, well . . . let's see . . . ah . . . ," Julie sputtered.

"Exactly," Cecilia said. "You have no idea."

"Wait!" Julie raised her palm to silence Cecilia. "I . . . I do have an idea."

"Really?" Cecilia asked in a sarcastic tone.

"Come on, give Julie a chance to talk," Carmen boomed. "Go on," she added, "what's your idea?"

"Well," Julie said, "the *don* stories . . . those I've heard . . . mention that a person is recognized upon passing their *don* test, right?"

"Yes, go on," Carmen encouraged her.

Julie swallowed hard and continued, "They were given a stone, right? To commemorate their passing the test? So why don't we interview the people who have stones . . . and ask them how they've used their *dons* to help the community? We should find out who in our apartment building has a stone, and—"

"And how do you see us proposing this insane project to Ms. Bellows?" Cecilia said in a cutting tone. "We want to ask people about their rocks?"

"Let her finish!" Carmen admonished Cecilia.

"Well," Julie added, "how about the four people that Doña Faustina mentioned? The ones who, after drinking her coffee, found their real *dons*? We could talk to them."

"No!" Cecilia interrupted. "If they're still alive, they're in Santa Cecilia . . . in Mexico."

"But you're going there, right? For the burial?" Julie asked.

"Yes, but—"

"I wish I could go too," Julie interrupted.

"Go where?" Cecilia said.

"To Santa Cecilia."

"Me too," Lebna said with a slight nod.

"What in the world for?" Cecilia asked.

"To attend the burial and experience the town," Julie said. They arrived at the apartment building's garage and got out of the van. As they headed for the stairwell, she added, "It sounds so amazingly magical there."

"Oh, yes," Lebna piped in.

"And you could do some interviews there, like three little spies," said Carmen.

"That's bonkers!" Cecilia stopped and grabbed Carmen by the arm to see if she was joking.

"What's bonkers?" Carmen hurried on again.

"For Julie and Lebna to go with us to Santa Cecilia."

"Only if you make it so," Carmen grunted.

After climbing up to Lebna's apartment door, Lebna turned to Carmen and said, "I had an amazing time. Thank you so much for arranging everything." She then turned to Cecilia, "I really hope we can do the science project together . . . as a team."

Next, on their way to Julie's apartment, Julie tapped Cecilia and said, "If it's okay with you, I'll draft a quick proposal for the science project."

Cecilia averted her eyes and kept walking, resentful of her friend's presumptuousness. But then she thought that, if Julie wrote the proposal, she would finally realize how stupid and hokey it was, especially since their teacher was incredibly strict and believed that science was the font of all human progress. Surely she would scoff at the proposal and insist that science was about facts, only facts. *So why worry about this? Julie will never finish once she starts writing and discovers how stupid her idea really is.* When she said good-night to Julie at her door, Cecilia told her to go right ahead and write up the proposal.

Carmen grabbed Cecilia's arm once they finally reached her apartment. "Don't forget that Doña Faustina discovered her *don* while she helped her mother with something that seemed totally unrelated." As Cecilia unlocked the door, Carmen added, "The funeral is tomorrow. The second rosary, the next day. Then you'll fly out for the burial in Santa Cecilia. All new experiences." Overwhelmed, Cecilia went in and headed straight for bed.

Early the next morning, there was a knock on Cecilia's bed-room door. "Julie's on the phone for you," Cecilia's father announced. He handed her the phone and a cup of coffee.

"What's up? Why are you calling so early? I didn't expect to hear from you today . . . because of the funeral."

"That's why I'm calling," Julie said and her voice dropped.

"What's wrong?"

"Nothing's wrong. Except . . . except . . ."

"Except what? I don't have all day."

"It's . . . my mother."

"Yes?" Cecilia asked as she tried to stay calm.

"She . . . she wants to come to the funeral!"

"Why?"

"Will it be a problem?" Julie asked in a tentative tone.

"No . . . I don't think so." Cecilia wondered why a deeply depressed person would want to attend a funeral. "Don't tell me she feels obligated to come."

"It's not that. She's Episcopalian, and I can't recall the last time she attended a church service. And I'm not sure she even believes in God. It's just that, well, remember the jar of coffee that I won?"

"Yes."

"I've been making her a cup of it every day. And it cheers her right up. She's even started to tell me stories. I've told her stories too, about my experiences with you and your family. The coffee is making her feel better than she's felt in a long, long time."

"So what you're saying is that your mother wants to come to the funeral because Doña Faustina's coffee has made her feel better?"

"It's a start, right?" Julie said.

"A start to what?"

"To her feeling interested in life again." Julie sounded excited. "She's intrigued by my stories about your culture and community. Am I making any sense?"

Cecilia winced. The funeral was going to be sad, especially for her parents. Now she had to contend with Julie's mother, a stranger to her religion and traditions.

"Can she come? Please. You know how desperate I am to help her."

"Okay, as long as you're there to look after her."

"Yes, of course, and . . ."

"And what? Come on, my parents are waiting for me."

"Lebna wants to come too!" Julie said in a burst.

"Fine." Cecilia rubbed the back of her neck, frantic to get off the phone. "It's at the funeral home right next to the church, the church where we met for the *kermés*. The viewing starts at three."

❧   ❧   ❧

When Carmen showed up at Cecilia's apartment, the family was having breakfast. Carmen took a seat at the table and Antonio poured her a cup of coffee.

Carmen folded her arms over her chest. "I just got a call from Doña Faustina. She's coming to the funeral and wants me to pick her up. And," she added, pointing her chin at Cecilia, "she wants *you* to prepare the coffee for the reception after the rosary. You need to blend Lebna's coffee with the coffee Julie won at the *kermés*. This, she says, is the second lesson of your apprenticeship."

"Julie's also bringing her mother to the funeral. What do we do with her while—"

"So that's what Doña Faustina probably meant," Carmen interrupted, "when she said something about bringing the three mothers together."

"But Lebna's mother is not coming." Cecilia looked puzzled.

"I don't think she was referring to your mother or Lebna's," Carmen clarified.

"So who are the other two mothers, aside from Julie's?"

"*M'ija*, you have to figure this out for yourself. It's part of your journey." Nica gave Cecilia's hand a gentle squeeze.

Cecilia turned and looked directly at Carmen. "So you don't know either?"

Carmen shrugged. "No, not exactly. But like your mother said, this is about you, not us."

After she hesitated for a moment, Cecilia said, as calmly as she could, "And what exactly does that mean, that it's about me, not you?"

"It simply means that you're the apprentice, not us," Carmen retorted.

Cecilia fell back in her chair. *It's pointless to ask any more questions.*

"Well," Carmen said, "now that that's settled, I have something to give you." She took out a thick envelope from her pocket and placed it in front of Nica and Antonio.

Nica gave her sister a warm smile. "Thank you so much."

Antonio added, "Yes, and we'll thank everyone at the rosary."

Cecilia shifted in her chair. Finally, curiosity got the better of her and she blurted out, "What's that?"

"It's the money raised at the kermés," Carmen said.

Her father leaned towards Cecilia and said, "It's to fly Micaela's body to—"

"Why can't we just bury her here?" Cecilia asked. "There are cemeteries here. We live here . . . and she died here."

"Here, drink this," Carmen ordered.

Cecilia took a sip of strong coffee and hung her head. She felt emotionally spent.

"Keep going. Drink it all down," Carmen added.

Cecilia quickly downed the rest of the coffee and said, "Sorry. I shouldn't have said anything."

"Don't worry, you'll understand." Her mother gave Cecilia a warm pat on the back.

The telephone rang. Antonio answered it and conversed with someone quietly. He soon hung up.

"That was José López," Antonio said.

Cecilia thought to herself, *How dare he call Dad at such a time to ask to go find something.*

"She's ready." Antonio gave Nica a slight nod.

"Who's ready?" Cecilia asked.

"Micaela is ready," Nica said softly.

Oh, I see. Mr. López is the funeral home director. Now we can go for the viewing.

"I can drive you there so you don't have to worry about traffic." Carmen placed her hand on Nica's shoulder.

Antonio and Nica gave her a quick nod. Then Carmen asked Cecilia, "Do you want to come too?"

"Yes, I'll go."

⁂

When they arrived at the funeral home, Cecilia felt tense. She wondered what the body would look like. Or would the coffin be closed in this case because she had not even been born? *Why are they making such a big deal about this stillbirth? All of this is like intentionally stretching out a nightmare.*

"It'll all connect, you'll see," Carmen said to Cecilia. "Just be patient."

Inside, a tall man shook hands with Cecilia's parents and talked quietly with them. "That's José López," Carmen said to Cecilia in a whisper as they got closer to two arched wooden doors. Mr. López turned to face them, bowed his head slightly and opened the door for the mourners.

Cecilia stiffened when she spotted a tiny, white box on a marble table propped open at the far end of the chapel-like room. She wrapped her arms around herself and forced herself to follow her parents down the center aisle in between two sections of pews. The intense scent of flowers shocked the air with the smell of a totally other world, a world without time. *Is this the smell and feel of death?* She watched her parents walk slowly, their heads bowed.

Cecilia gasped when her mother suddenly rushed towards the coffin with her father right behind her. Her heart raced as her parents peered into the casket and then reached inside. Cecilia stopped, but Carmen took her by the elbow and pulled her forward. She felt as if death had swept her along, like a rushing river.

Cecilia took a deep breath, stood next to her mother and forced herself to look inside the coffin. She was stunned. It was a baby! A tiny baby wearing the white dress she was to be baptized in and a satin bonnet. She looked up and found her parents and Carmen looking at her with compassion. Her father wrapped his arm around her while her mother gave her a warm, understanding smile.

Carmen hurried over and whispered something to Mr. López—something that caused him to nod and quickly exit the room.

Carmen hurried back over to them and said in a soft voice, "He's bringing the rocking chair in case anyone wants to hold her."

"Hold the baby?!" Cecilia exclaimed.

"Yes," Carmen answered, "since you didn't get a chance last time."

Cecilia stepped away from the coffin, startled. Suddenly the door opened and Mr. López carried in the rocker.

Cecilia stifled a gasp as her mother reached inside the coffin and raised the dead body to her breast. Then she lowered herself into the chair and began to rock slowly while she gazed lovingly at the tiny form.

Before Cecilia had a chance to process the jarring image, the door swung open again and in strode a young man with spiky hair. He clutched a laptop computer in one hand and a camera in the other. A small spiral notebook and several pens poked out of his shirt pocket. He hurried over to José and started to whisper while he gestured towards Nica, who continued to rock the baby.

Is he the press? Cecilia's stomach tied itself in a knot as she imagined a front-page picture of her mother rocking a dead baby in tomorrow's *San Jose Mercury News,* with the banner headline: "The Bizarre Ways of Mexican Immigrants." Then she gasped and thought about how unspeakably awful school would be for her.

Stepping over to Carmen, Cecilia cupped her hand by her mouth and whispered, "Who's he?"

"Carlos," Carmen said in a casual tone before she gave him a little wave.

"And who in the world is Carlos?"

Carmen shrugged and reproached her, "This goes to show that you've missed all the recent funerals too."

Cecilia grimaced. "Yes, but it's because I've been—"

"Too busy with school?" Carmen interrupted.

"Yes," Cecilia admitted. "But who's Carlos? Don't tell me he's the media."

"The media? Well, yes, I guess you could call him that."

"Well, he better not take any pictures!"

"That's why he's here—to take pictures," Carmen said with a slight grin.

"I can't believe this. This is terrible!"

"What's terrible?"

Cecilia swallowed hard and forced herself to stay calm. "Look, he's going to write an article," she said, "about how *Mamá* rocked a dead body . . . he's going to make us all look like a strange, backward group of morbid people. We can't let him do that!"

"What? Would you rather have dead babies just thrown into dumpsters like you read about in the paper?" Carmen tossed her head back. Cecilia felt overwhelmed. "Don't worry. Carlos is doing media for Santa Cecilia." She raised a finger to her lips so Cecilia would keep her voice down.

Not realizing she had been talking loudly, Cecilia glanced around, surprised to see José and Carlos staring at her. Her parents were looking at her, too, as if wondering what was troubling her. Cecilia forced herself to flash them a slight smile, then waved her hand. She sighed with relief, seeing them all nod and return to what they were doing.

Next, she turned back to Carmen and whispered, "What do you mean he's doing media for Santa Cecilia?"

"He runs an internet site where he posts news, stories and pictures concerning the Santa Cecilia community—both here and at home in Mexico. This will be the first time that we try to coordinate the rosary in both places at the same time."

"But how?"

"Skype." Carmen took Cecilia by the elbow and pulled her towards her mother. As they got closer, she added, "It's your turn."

"My turn for what?"

"To hold her." They stopped in front of the rocking chair.

Stricken, Cecilia stared wide-eyed at her mother. *Gosh, she looks so calm and peaceful.*

Nica looked up at Cecilia and asked, "Do you want to hold her?"

Cecilia stared blankly at her mother for a few moments, then nodded and slowly extended her arms to take the body. Feeling its slight weight settle into her arms, her heart raced as she forced herself to look at it, surprised to see a face with tiny, closed eyes, as well as a button nose and mouth, and even tiny fingers with the tiniest of fingernails. *Wow, she is a baby!* Suddenly she felt a rush of hot emotion shoot through her.

Her mother got to her feet and gestured for Cecilia to sit down in the rocking chair. Cecilia hesitated, then lowered herself into it and rocked the baby back and forth while she peered at her little face. Distracted for a moment, she heard Carlos whisper to her parents. She looked up as he wheeled around and snapped a picture of her, then several others. He said that he would post them right away, before the rosary started. Then he dashed out the door.

Cecilia turned to her father and said, "You can hold her now, Dad."

She gently handed him the baby and got to her feet. After her father rocked the baby, Mr. López placed her back inside the coffin.

Cecilia felt a tap on her back.

"I'm going to pick up Doña Faustina," Carmen said in a voice loud enough to cause her parents to look up and nod. "Do you want to come along, Cecilia?"

Cecilia realized that before she had held the baby, she would have jumped at any chance to escape this macabre, crazy world, which had turned a stillbirth into the death of a beloved family member. But now she felt differently.

"I think I'll stay," Cecilia said.

Carmen gave a quick nod and smiled. "Good, I thought you would."

Cecilia leaned back and caught her father's eye. He beamed at her. Her mother's eyes were closed in prayer.

After a while, Cecilia heard the door open. She turned to see Julie and Lebna rush over to her. Doña Faustina trailed behind, leaning on Carmen's arm. Cecilia jumped to her feet.

"Mom's coming later," Julie whispered to Cecilia midway up the aisle. She lifted the jar of coffee she had won at the raffle.

"And I've brought my coffee, as Doña Faustina requested." Lebna pointed to the straw basket hooked on her arm.

Then Julie directed her gaze towards the casket. "Have . . . have you seen . . . ?" She paused suddenly, as if she did not know how to put the question.

"The baby? Yes. I even rocked her in the chair," Cecilia said.

"What?!" Julie and Lebna asked in unison. They looked astonished .

"You're kidding . . . right?" Julie added.

"No, she's not," Carmen declared. She startled Cecilia's friends as she led Doña Faustina into their circle. "And now she feels quite differently about the whole thing. Right, Cecilia?"

Cecilia changed the subject before her friends were weirded-out any further. "Doña Faustina, it's so good to see you," she said, shaking her hand.

Doña Faustina gestured toward the casket and said in her raspy voice, "Let's go see her."

Cecilia nodded, then wrapped Doña Faustina's arm around hers and led her up the aisle. With a toss of her head, she signaled for her friends to come along. They followed, but stopped a few yards away from Micaela.

At the casket, Doña Faustina crossed herself and gazed warmly at the baby. Then, after a few moments, she took Cecilia's arm again and started towards Cecilia's parents. They stood up and embraced *Doña* Faustina.

Cecilia turned to Julie and Lebna and asked, "Want to see her?"

Lebna nodded. Julie turned and stared at the coffin, her face drained of color.

"What's the matter?" Cecilia said. "You're as white as a ghost."

"The matter?" Julie flinched before she gave her head a vigorous shake as if to snap out of a spell. "I'm . . . well . . . I've never seen a dead body before."

"What?" Lebna asked with an incredulous look.

Cecilia stifled her frustration, grabbed Lebna by the elbow and pulled her towards the casket. They left Julie staring at her feet. A minute later, Julie forced herself to look up and was surprised to see Lebna smile as she gazed into the coffin. *What is there to smile at? No one smiles at death.* Then Julie took a deep breath and joined her friends. In front of the casket, she took another deep breath and forced herself to look.

Gosh, she looks just like a sleeping baby! "She's darling," she whispered and felt her heart melt.

Cecilia tapped Julie gently on the back after she noticed Doña Faustina wave her over. The girls then followed Doña Faustina and Carmen to the reception room and left Nica and Antonio alone with the baby.

In the reception room, Carmen helped Doña Faustina into a chair and began to fan her vigorously with her hand. Cecilia had a sick feeling: *Oh, no, is Doña Faustina having a stroke?!* She looked at the old woman's slumped posture, closed eyes and the paleness of her skin.

"What's wrong?" Cecilia asked. "Should I call 911?"

Registering Cecilia's stricken look, Carmen said, "Get her a glass of water—hurry." She fanned Doña Faustina even faster.

Cecilia dashed across the room, filled a glass of water at the sink and returned to hand it to Carmen.

"She looks so weak," whispered Cecilia. "Is she going to be okay?"

Carmen brought the glass to Doña Faustina's lips and said in a soothing tone, "Here, drink this."

After several moments of silence, during which Cecilia felt her chest tighten with the fear that Doña Faustina had died, she flinched when the old lady slowly opened her eyes, then blinked rapidly as if she had been in a deep sleep and now found herself in a strange place. The three girls stared, wide-eyed and riveted. Doña Faustina clutched the glass with both hands and took a drink before she handed the glass back to Carmen and said in a grave voice, "It's back, it's back."

Cecilia froze when she saw the words strike Carmen like a dagger through her heart.

What's back? wondered Cecilia. It had to be something unspeakably terrible to cause Carmen—who seemed to take everything in stride—to be so shaken. Doña Faustina suddenly grabbed Carmen's arm and pulled herself to her feet, then shuffled towards the sink. Cecilia quickly joined

Carmen and took Doña Faustina's other arm to help steady her.

"What's back?" Cecilia silently mouthed to Carmen.

Carmen darted her eyes towards Doña Faustina as if to say, "Ask her yourself." Cecilia tightened her hold on Doña Faustina, who kept veering wildly from side to side as she stepped stiffly and slowly along. It was as though she hadn't taken a step for years and had forgotten how to walk.

The old woman grabbed the edge of the sink and switched on the faucet. Then, after washing and drying her hands, she turned around and faced Cecilia and her friends, who'd joined them by that point, with an intense look in her eyes.

"Why are you staring at me?" Doña Faustina said, narrowing her eyes at them.

Startled, Cecilia swallowed hard and said, "We . . . we are not staring at you."

With a short laugh, Carmen put an arm around Doña Faustina and said, "They want to know why you said 'it's back.' Right, Cecilia?"

Cecilia nodded.

"Let's get started," Doña Faustina turned towards the counter. "We have a lot to do before the rosary."

After the girls exchanged puzzled looks, Cecilia asked, "How can we help?"

"Yes," said Julie and Lebna. "How can we help?"

Carmen chuckled because the girls did not dare badger Doña Faustina with their burning question. Then she thought about Doña Faustina's comment for herself until she caught sight of Cecilia's imploring stare.

Carmen nodded at Cecilia, placed her hand on Doña Faustina's shoulder, and said in a soft, casual tone, "When you said, 'It's back,' were you referring to . . . Satan?"

The girls spun around and gaped at Carmen before they turned their fear-filled eyes towards Doña Faustina, who, shockingly, nodded with a grave look in her eyes.

Cecilia forced herself to lean towards Doña Faustina and ask, "Did you hear what Carmen said?"

Doña Faustina nodded again, then started to fill a kettle with water.

When Cecilia realized that Doña Faustina was not going to elaborate and that she was using the edge of the counter to steady herself, she hurried towards Carmen, who was standing next to the round table in the center of the room, and said, "What's going on?"

"What do you mean?"

"You know exactly what I mean," Cecilia said, her eyes ablaze with frustration. "If this is the second lesson," she continued, "and I'm supposed to be Doña Faustina's apprentice, then I need to know what's going on. Otherwise . . ."

"You'll quit?" Carmen said with a snort.

"It can't be . . . right? That I'm undergoing this training . . . this apprenticeship . . . in order to fight Satan?" Cecilia shook her head vigorously. *It had to be a joke, right?* But, when she scrutinized Carmen's expression and saw it become even more serious, a sense of dread overcame her.

Carmen saw the shocked look in Cecilia's eyes and said, "Don't worry. This is not about you alone fighting the evil one, but about strengthening the community to do so."

"To fight Satan?" Cecilia asked as she turned her back to Doña Faustina and her friends so as not to reveal her anxiety.

"You don't believe he exists?" Carmen asked in a half-mocking tone.

"Look, Carmen," she said, "this is a difficult time . . . with the funeral . . ."

Carmen suddenly grabbed Cecilia by the wrist and pulled her out of the room, waving to Doña Faustina and saying that they would be right back, that Cecilia's friends would stay there to help her. Julie and Lebna exchanged baffled looks. They wondered what was going on and why Cecilia looked thunderstruck.

"**W**here are you taking me?" Cecilia asked as Carmen dragged her out of the funeral home and into a court-yard with a spouting fountain at its center.

"Look, don't think I'm making things seem mysterious just to play with you," Carmen replied as she plopped down onto a cement bench and pulled Cecilia down to sit beside her. "No, this is serious business."

"Fine, so tell me what's going on."

"When I went to pick up Doña Faustina, I knocked and knocked, but there was no answer. I had called earlier to remind her that I would swing by to pick her up at one and she was fine. That's why I worried when she didn't open the door. I called her on my cellphone and heard her telephone ring and ring inside. But she didn't answer. So I ran to the back and banged on her door. Still nothing. Worried she had had a heart attack, I was ready to dial 911 and break the win-dow to get in. Then I peered through the window and saw her slumped on the kitchen table with her arms over her head. *Oh my god,* she's dead, I thought, and I looked around for a rock to smash the window. Then noticed her arms start to twitch. I watched as she slowly lifted her head from the table. I screamed out her name, banging on the window and waving frantically at her. She leaned back and started to rub her eyes.

"When she finally saw me, she got to her feet and opened the back door. After I gave her a big hug and helped her back to the chair, I noticed that something was wrong, *really* wrong."

"What?"

"Doña Faustina trembled terribly. I rushed over to the sink and poured her a glass of water. I thought she might have suffered a stroke. Then, after I gave her several sips of water, I asked her if I should take her to the emergency room. She shook her head before she raised her quivering hands and stared at them.

"After she took another sip of water, she pressed her open hands flat on the table to still them and whispered, 'It's back: the hurricane . . . the shooting . . . and now another great evil approaches.'

"I waited for her to say more, to explain, but she just sat there and stared at her hands until they finally shook no more. That's when she pushed off the table with one hand, got to her feet and said, 'Let's hurry.' She started towards the door, and I jumped up to help her with her coat. We got into the van and talked on the way over to pick up Julie and Lebna."

Carmen paused and fixed her blank gaze on the fountain as she mulled this over. After a long silence, Cecilia tugged on Carmen's sleeve and asked, "What did Doña Faustina tell you in the van?"

"Well, she said that after she returns to us from these trances she has mysterious knowledge that, however crazy it sounds, often turns out to be true."

"Like what?"

"Years ago, back in Santa Cecilia, she had a vision where a man dressed like a Franciscan monk appeared to her and told her to go to California, that he had planted seeds for a spiritual awakening there.

"When Doña Faustina awoke, she had no idea what the vision meant. So she went to Martín, an old man reputed to have the *don* of mysterious knowledge, just like his patron saint San Martín de Porres.

"It took a whole week before Martín knocked on Doña Faustina's door to announce that the man in her vision was Junípero Serra, a Spanish Franciscan friar who founded a chain of missions along the California coast during the 1700s, and who needed one more miracle to be declared a saint.

"To make a long story short," Carmen added, glancing at her watch, "she had more visions, which finally persuaded her and others in the community to move here. Since then, they regularly visit Junípero Serra's grave at the second mission he founded—the Carmel mission in Monterey—to ask for his guidance. The women who lead tonight's rosary are members of that mission's prayer group."

"Wait!" Cecilia said. "You still haven't told me what Doña Faustina's latest vision means."

"She told me that Satan and his demons caused Hurricane Sandy to veer onto the East Coast, and that he was at Sandy Hook, the elementary school where twenty children were shot. She warned that, if we don't all come together as one community, the Earth is doomed—from an asteroid or a plague—because the souls in heaven can no longer protect us."

"What?" Cecilia asked. "You don't really believe this, do you?"

"Oh, so you think Doña Faustina's crazy?" Carmen asked.

"Uh, no . . . not really . . . ," Cecilia said with some hesitation.

Carmen got up to walk back to the funeral home. "You do know that an asteroid struck Earth millions of years ago, near the Yucatán Peninsula, and that that led to the extinction of the dinosaurs, right?"

Cecilia rolled her eyes.

"Look, you don't have to help or train with Doña Faustina if you don't want to. And if that's the case, go join your parents at the chapel." Carmen then started towards the reception room.

Cecilia took a deep breath. She could not put out of her mind what Doña Faustina had told Carmen about the hurricane and the school shooting. *Is Doña Faustina for real?* she wondered. *Or just delusional like Don Quixote?* Various characters from *Don Quixote* popped into her mind, and how they had played along with the mad old man. *Okay,* she told herself, hurrying after Carmen, *I'll play along too, at least until I don't feel so confused.*

Cecilia found Julie and Lebna in the reception room. They noticed that Cecilia was stressed, but, before they could speak to her, Julie's mother walked in. Julie introduced her to Doña Faustina and Carmen.

While Marie chatted with them, Cecilia leaned close to Julie's ear and whispered, "The rosary doesn't start till four. Why is your mom here so early?"

"Doña Faustina told me to call her. She's the third mother," Julie whispered back.

"So who are the other two?"

"I have no idea," Julie said.

Doña Faustina directed Julie and Lebna to set the pots of the coffee they had just brewed on the table. Then she motioned to Marie to sit down. Marie hesitated, wondering why Doña Faustina had asked only her to sit at the table. Everyone, except Carmen, looked as confused as she felt. She shrugged and took a chair.

Cecilia now took hold of Doña Faustina's arm and helped steady her as she approached the table. Mid-way there, she bent towards Doña Faustina and asked, "About the three mothers you mentioned earlier . . . if Marie is one, who are the other two?"

Doña Faustina suddenly stopped shuffling and pointed towards the table. "The two pots of coffee," she said, then sat down beside Marie.

How crazy is that? Cecilia thought. *And how stupid could a science project get? This is all just a colossal piece of non-sense!*

Marie shifted in her chair uneasily. Cecilia put her hand on Doña Faustina's shoulder and asked, "Can I help with something?"

"Bring me a cup from the cupboard," Doña Faustina replied as she removed the lid from Lebna's pot.

After Cecilia set the cup on the table, Doña Faustina pointed to Julie's pot. "Now pour that into this one." She gestured towards Lebna's.

Cecilia lifted Julie's pot, then slowly tilted it and drained it into Lebna's. Putting the empty pot down, Cecilia waited for further instructions.

"Now, swirl it, slowly." Doña Faustina gently tapped Lebna's pot.

With a quick nod, Cecilia took the pot by the neck and raised it. It felt heavy and warm, its belly hot. When she glanced up, she registered her friends' stares and Marie's puzzled look. She swirled the pot, around and around, until Doña Faustina directed her to stop and set it down.

Cecilia watched Doña Faustina place the cup next to Lebna's pot. "Fill the cup."

Cecilia did, inhaling the rich aroma of the freshly brewed coffee. Suddenly, she was surprised to catch sight of Marie's tense face as Doña Faustina whisked the steaming cup over to her and said in her low, raspy voice, "Okay, you can drink it now."

Marie pushed back on the table and asked Julie in a weak voice, "She . . . she wants me to drink this? What is it?"

Red with embarrassment, Julie bent towards her mother and said in a half-whisper, "Mom, it's just coffee. I made it using the coffee you love, the one that makes you feel . . ."

"But what about that other pot?" Marie gestured towards Lebna.

Lebna stepped up. "I made that coffee." She flashed Marie a slight smile. "It's Ethiopian, from where I was born."

Marie gave Lebna a blank look, then blinked her eyes rapidly. She looked bewildered, like a cornered animal.

"Marie, don't worry," Cecilia said after an awkward silence. She felt she had to say something to break the tension. "You don't have to do anything you don't feel comfortable doing. Right, Doña Faustina?" She turned towards her, and saw Doña Faustina watching Marie with a steady, penetrating gaze. Cecilia continued in a reassuring tone, "Doña Faustina simply wants you to feel better. But, if you don't want to drink this, don't."

After another awkward silence, during which Marie only looked more anxious and confused, Cecilia tapped Doña Faustina on the arm and asked jokingly, "How about I drink it? Marie thinks you're trying to poison her."

"What?" Marie said and shot Cecilia a sharp look. "I said no such thing." She grabbed the cup and drank it straight down.

Doña Faustina bobbed her head in approval while Carmen chuckled and the others looked startled.

"There!" Marie plunked the empty cup down on the table. "I drank it, poison or not!"

Astonished, Julie tossed an arm around her mother's shoulders and said excitedly, "Go, Mom! How do you feel?"

Marie tilted her head back and let out a short laugh as tears poured down her cheeks. Then—*Boom!*—everyone flinched at the sound of a thunderclap, everyone except Doña Faustina and Carmen, who exchanged knowing looks, then broke into the biggest, radiant smiles.

"What's wrong? Why are you crying?" Julie asked.

Carmen handed Marie a tissue and she started to wipe the tears from her face.

"Mom?! Say something. What's going on?" Julie pleaded.

Cecilia took everything in and rubbed her head. She wondered why Doña Faustina and Carmen seemed so pleased, when a thought suddenly popped into her head— something she had overheard her parents or Carmen say. It was that the universe often recognizes a reunion of what had previously been separated or fractured with a sudden clap of thunder. She went to the window, pulled back the curtains and found not a single cloud in the sky. The sun still shone brightly. She turned around and Doña Faustina waved her over, while Marie told Julie that nothing was wrong, that she actually felt better than she had in a very long time.

"Can I possibly have a second cup?" Marie smiled at Doña Faustina.

Doña Faustina nodded and motioned for Cecilia to pour her another cup. Then she asked the girls to bring cups for everyone so Lebna could perform her coffee ceremony.

Immediately, Lebna arranged six cups in a circle around her long-necked Ethiopian pot. Next, she raised her hands and held them over her pot and the six cups.

Breaking into a broad smile, she beckoned softly, "Please sit."

Now, squaring her shoulders, Lebna said, "I had a *plática*, a talk with Doña Faustina this morning on our way here. She asked me about my mother country of Ethiopia, where I was born. I was surprised that she knew about the Ethiopian coffee ceremony. We also discussed stories that my mother had told me: how coffee had been discovered in Ethiopia, and legend tells us that it was discovered by a shepherd who one day noticed his goats acting unusually excited and happy while nibbling on red berries, berries that turned out to be coffee beans.

"It turns out that, not only was my mother born in Ethiopia, but everyone's mother originated there." She paused when she noticed her friend's perplexed looks, but the adults seemed to follow what she had said. "Yes, it turns out that we are all descended from the same Ethiopian mother. In other words, every single person on this planet can trace their DNA back to her."

Cecilia and Julie exchanged startled looks.

After a brief pause, Lebna pointed at her pot and continued. "As for the coffee ceremony, it's still practiced today. It's a spiritual moment where a group gathers to witness the ritual of roasting, grinding and brewing coffee in a pot just like this one." She tapped the neck of the pot. "Then the hot coffee is poured into small cups and sipped by the group for purposes of nourishing and strengthening the community. Also," she pointed her index finger in the air, "it's served with popcorn."

Oh, thought Cecilia, *I remember the delicious popcorn from the* kermés.

Doña Faustina then cupped Julie on the shoulder and said, "Now tell us how you made your coffee."

Julie looked surprised, licked her lips and said in a low, thin voice, "Uh, well . . . I first ground the coffee beans I won at the *kermés*. Then I brewed the coffee—while thinking good thoughts!" She looked at Doña Faustina to confirm she had said enough.

Doña Faustina gave her a slight nod.

Cecilia rubbed her forehead. She saw how Lebna's coffee represented one mother, since it came from Ethiopia, where supposedly everyone's mother originated. But she still didn't get how Julie's coffee could possibly constitute the second mother.

Cecilia leaned towards Doña Faustina. "Is Julie's coffee the second mother?"

Doña Faustina nodded.

Cecilia realized she had to plumb this further. So, she took a deep breath and added, "I don't understand how . . . or why. Can you please explain this?"

"The Holy Water." Doña Faustina waved her hand and narrowed her eyes at Cecilia.

Cecilia gave her head a brisk shake. "I . . . I still don't understand."

"Water into wine, remember?" Cecilia heard Carmen mutter from across the table.

Cecilia looked at Carmen, expecting her to continue, but Carmen just plopped her head on her hands and stared back.

Why does this have to be so hard? Cecilia fell back in her chair with a heavy sigh. Then, all of a sudden, she jerked forward. "Is making coffee with good intentions like Jesus's first miracle, when he turned water into wine at his mother's request?"

Carmen and Doña Faustina nodded.

"But how is Marie the third mother?"

After exchanging a quick look with Carmen, Doña Faustina rapped Cecilia on the arm and demanded, "Pour the coffee." She swept her hand over the cups.

Cecilia hated to be ignored. She stifled a groan of frustration. Snatching the Ethiopian pot by the neck, she filled the cups. Finished, she began to drop back into her chair, but Doña Faustina stopped her. "Now give everyone a cup."

Cecilia handed the cups around. Then, following Doña Faustina's example, everyone raised their cup to their lips and took a sip, then another, until the cup was empty.

Wow, thought Cecilia as she set her cup down, *that was good coffee, even if it's just coffee.* Then she heard the door open, and she jumped to her feet when a surge of women in black dress clothes rushed into the room.

The group huddled around Doña Faustina. They hugged and kissed her on the cheek, fussed over her and said that it had been ages since they'd last seen her.

Cecilia leaned close to Carmen's ear and whispered, "Who are they?"

"The prayer group committee," Carmen said. "First Carlos the photographer, now the prayer group ladies. Don't you know who anyone in our community is anymore?"

"But the rosary doesn't start for over an hour!"

Carmen explained. "Doña Faustina wants them to drink her coffee before the rosary. It's connected to the vision she had."

"But there's hardly any left," Cecilia said. "I poured it all out."

"We need to make more for them and for after the wake," Carmen said. She started to scoop grounds into the funeral home's stainless-steel coffeemaker. "See those thermoses?" she asked the three girls. "Bring them over."

Just as the girls were headed towards the thermoses, the door opened slowly and in walked the oldest woman Cecilia had ever seen. The woman was stooped over, draped in black and carried a thick, heavy book in her arms. The prayer group ladies hurried to greet her and help her to the table. Carmen pulled a chair out for her, and she dropped her book onto the table before she sat next to Doña Faustina.

The women hovered around the table expectantly, soon joined by Cecilia and her friends. Marie watched wide-eyed from across the room, not wanting to intrude. Cecilia stood on her toes and peered over the head of the woman in front of her. She saw the ancient woman open the thick tome to reveal a hodgepodge of strange shapes and images on its pages: ovals and arrows with markings and scribbling on the sides. The woman turned to the end of the book and laid it open on the table. Then one of the prayer ladies handed her what looked like an antique fountain pen. She grasped the pen in her gnarled fingers and held it over the book, then, with her other hand, she gestured to Doña Faustina. Doña Faustina gave a slight nod and in her gravelly voice she described the vision she had had. The ancient woman recorded it in the book.

Carmen whispered to Cecilia, "The coffee's ready. Come help me."

Cecilia hesitated. She didn't want to miss anything, but then she whispered to Lebna, "Help me with the coffee. We'll get Julie to tell us what happens."

Lebna nodded and followed Cecilia. Julie was so focused she didn't notice them walk away.

"Who is that old woman? And what is that book?" Cecilia asked as she handed Carmen a thermos.

"That's Benedicta, one of our ancient elephants, like Doña Faustina."

"Ancient elephants?" Cecilia furrowed her brow. She thought she must've heard wrong.

Carmen glanced at the clock on the wall and said, "We really have to hurry. I'll explain more later. But those of my generation and older refer to the eldest and wisest women in our community as 'ancient elephants.' Why? Because, in nature, the oldest female elephants keep their community together. They are the ones who lead the others to water during a drought. But today, unfortunately, our younger generations are becoming too Americanized, something we are increasingly worried about. Why? Because it means the eventual death of our culture—our stories, rituals and traditions."

Moments later, Carmen told Cecilia and Lebna that Benedicta, as the leader of the prayer group, had inherited the ancient-looking book from the previous leader. And, as for the ovals and other strange symbols that Cecilia had noticed in the book, those were the recordings of the true ancients, who had originally etched their thoughts and visions on quartz and stones.

"And who were the true ancients?" Cecilia asked.

"The shamans of long ago," Carmen said, taking out twelve cups. "Please start filling them, but only halfway."

"Do you want me to help too?" asked Lebna.

"This is something that Cecilia has to do herself," Carmen replied. She gave Lebna a quick smile. "You already did your magic by preparing the coffee that Cecilia added to the thermoses."

"It all seems so weird," Cecilia remarked. "True ancients . . . etching visions on stone." Cecilia poured the coffee.

"You make it sound so crazy," Carmen interjected. "Hurry, we're running out of time."

"Why are the prayer group ladies having coffee? Do they do this before every rosary?" Lebna asked.

"No. Actually, this is the first time they will do this," Carmen answered.

"What? So why . . . ," Cecilia began.

"Because we need a miracle. That's why," Carmen said with a heavy sigh.

"But why?"

"Look, we have to hurry," Carmen insisted as she gestured towards the empty cups.

"Okay, but tell me while I hurry."

"It concerns Doña Faustina's vision. The ladies are here because our community needs a new *don* to be given to someone who can help us defeat this dark evil force. Don't ask for details. You'll just have to watch what happens. Now, let's finish up so the prayer group ladies can have their coffee."

They carried the trays of cups to the table and placed them in front of the ladies. Then Benedicta raised her cup and, as the others followed, she cleared her throat and said in a deep, somber voice, "We need a miracle—a big, powerful one—so let us now ask and pray for one, one strong enough to defeat the evil Doña Faustina has seen."

They all shut their eyes and prayed silently. Then Benedicta slowly opened her eyes and cleared her throat, which prompted the other ladies to open their eyes as well. Benedicta announced that, after they had finished their coffee, the group would select the patron saint for the miracle they desperately needed.

"So who will be the patron saint?" Benedicta asked as she swept her intense gaze across the ladies' faces.

Almost as one, they dropped their heads in thought. After a minute of dead silence, all the ladies opened their eyes at the same time and smiled slightly.

"So?" Benedicta said and studied their faces.

"How about we jot our selections down on slips of paper?" a woman with short, silver hair suggested.

"Good," Benedicta responded. "Let's do that."

After taking out pieces of paper, pens and pencils from their pockets and purses, they scribbled down their choices, then folded their papers and handed them to Benedicta.

Carmen glanced at the clock on the wall and announced, "The rosary is scheduled to begin in fifteen minutes."

All of the prayer ladies got to their feet and helped Benedicta and Doña Faustina out of their chairs. They filed out of the room.

"What just happened?" Cecilia asked.

"That," said Carmen, "is a ritual to select the patron saint most suited to help us carry out our mission. Each woman wrote down the choice that was revealed to her in prayer. At the rosary, Benedicta will ask those who've been confirmed to do the same, to jot down their choices."

"Oh," said Cecilia, still a little puzzled.

"And," Carmen continued, "it'll help explain what you might see at the rosary. Spiritual things often occur or reveal themselves at these rituals, things that those not trained to watch for will miss entirely or simply dismiss as coincidences."

"Carmen!" Cecilia said in a half-stifled gasp as she glanced at Marie, embarrassed that Carmen was talking so bluntly.

"What?" Carmen tossed her head back with a chuckle. "I wasn't referring to anyone but you, Cecilia. You're the one who thinks all this is weird!"

CHAPTER 29

*W*ow, *it's so crowded*, thought Cecilia as she stepped into the funeral home's chapel.

Julie leaned close to her and said, "Go up front and sit with your parents. Don't worry about us. We'll be fine."

Cecilia nodded, then weaved through the people who were in line to give her parents in the front pew their condolences. Soon Father Ramón stepped forward and announced that they would start the rosary, and that he had spoken with Padre Gómez in Santa Cecilia, where the rosary was about to start too.

People dashed back to their seats or found a place to stand and took out their rosaries. Cecilia sat with her parents. Carmen sat beside Cecilia. Benedicta positioned herself next to the coffin, while the prayer group ladies gathered behind it. After she cleared her throat, Benedicta announced in a grave tone that everyone who had been confirmed should pray for a revelation as to the best patron saint to select for an important miracle they needed. She then crossed herself and officially started the rosary.

As Benedicta began reciting the first "Our Father," Carmen reached into her pocket and extracted two rosaries. She handed one to Cecilia.

While praying the second decade of the rosary, Carmen leaned over and whispered, "Remember what I told you earlier, try reciting these prayers to send you off, to have your own personal *plática* with the divine."

Cecilia didn't have a clue what Carmen was talking about, since the prayers just sounded like the buzzing of bees. Benedicta started every "Our Father" or "Hail Mary" and the group finished it off. Soon, Cecilia's mind began to wander, and she wondered what Marie and her friends thought of the rosary. She looked at her parents, who were praying with bowed heads. *Are they actually having a* plática *with the divine—whatever the divine means? And the others?*

As Cecilia followed along, mouthing the words she had learned for her First Communion, she stared at the open casket and thought of how she would never be able to help Micaela learn her first prayers.

After Benedicta finished the last part of the rosary, she swept her eyes across the room and asked everyone for their petitions. Cecilia cocked her head to one side, wondering what this meant. She was surprised to see everyone's eyes lock on her parents.

"That she, my beloved daughter Micaela," Cecilia now heard her mother say in a soft, halting voice, "helps to protect and strengthen our community, both here and in Santa Cecilia."

Her father cleared his throat, leaned forward and said, "I pray that she feels our love and that she helps deepen our sense of community, the community that Junípero Serra and his fellow Franciscan friars planted along the California coast."

Suddenly, Cecilia noticed everyone looking directly at her.

"Say your petition," Carmen urged her.

Cecilia swallowed hard and blurted out the first thing that came to her mind: "Uh, I pray that she helps us all."

Others voiced their petitions: "That she helps bring peace and hope to those plagued by illness, poverty, drugs, violence . . . to those who are separated from their families . . . to the dying . . . and to the soul of this divided, polarized country and world."

Cecilia added another one silently: "Plus don't forget to help me with that friggin' science project!"

Once the petitions were over, Benedicta officially ended the rosary. She then raised her hands high in the air and asked everyone who had received a revelation to stay behind while the others proceeded to the reception area. After people filed out, she lifted a package of colored markers to be used for writing a note to Micaela on slips of paper or even directly on the casket.

As Carmen and Cecilia headed for the reception room, Cecilia noticed one of the prayer group ladies draw a huge, red heart on the casket while Benedicta collected slips of paper from a knot of people. Once there, Cecilia recruited Lebna to help her and Doña Faustina serve the coffee.

Cecilia noticed tears had pooled in Marie's bloodshot eyes. She stood next to her and asked softly, "Are you all right? Can I get you some water?"

"I'm fine . . . fine," Marie said and dabbed at her eyes with a tissue. "I was just moved by all this." She patted Cecilia on the shoulder. "Go on. I'll stay here with Julie."

Cecilia and Lebna made their way across the reception area through the crowd, over to Carmen.

"Look around the room and tell me what's missing," Carmen said.

Cecilia looked around and observed that people served coffee from the thermoses, drank it, talked in huddles and thanked Doña Faustina.

"What do you think is missing?" Cecilia asked Lebna.

"I have no idea, except that we seem to be the only teenagers here."

"You're right." Cecilia then turned to Carmen and with a slight grin said, "What's missing is that no one's drinking tea because everyone's drinking coffee."

Carmen shot Cecilia a reproachful look before asking Lebna. "What do you think is missing?"

Lebna's eyes widened, surprised that Carmen had asked her. "Uh . . . well . . . I told Cecilia that we seem to be the only teenagers here. But of course this can't be what you're referring to."

Carmen clapped Lebna on the back. "That's exactly right!"

"But why does that matter?" Cecilia asked.

"Because you appear to be our only hope. Teenagers nowadays are not interested in learning about our culture," Carmen said with disgust.

After she let out a heavy sigh of frustration, Cecilia cupped her hand over Lebna's ear and whispered, "Carmen has no idea how many of us are pressured and even bullied to act 'American.' I bet that's why they're not here."

"Cecilia! Come here!" Doña Faustina called.

Doña Faustina lifted Cecilia's arm in the air and announced, "Let me now introduce you to my apprentice."

Cecilia was instantly surrounded by those present. They grabbed her hands, petted her on the back and on the head and said that they were going to pray extra-hard for her.

They wished for her to be given Doña Faustina's *don*. Cecilia forced herself to smile, but she felt like a carnival freak.

Later, after the coffee had been consumed and everyone had offered their best wishes to Cecilia, Carmen approached the girls and told them that she would take Doña Faustina home and that they should catch a ride back to the apartment with Marie.

"What about my parents?" Cecilia asked.

"They're talking with Father Ramón," Carmen replied. "He'll give them a lift home."

Cecilia and Lebna went to the chapel, where they were surprised to see Julie and Marie scribble directly on the coffin while Cecilia's parents and Father Ramón stood next to them. Cecilia and Lebna rushed down the aisle to the casket. It was ablaze with images of stars, hearts, angels and words of love in gem-like colors.

Julie gestured for Cecilia and Lebna to follow her out the door. As they exited the chapel, Julie announced excitedly, "It's Juniper . . . Juniper Serra . . . and . . ."

"Who's Juniper?" Cecilia interrupted.

"The patron saint for the miracle," Julie said. "Benedicta announced it after the prayer ladies finished counting all the slips of paper."

"Do you mean *Junípero* Serra, the founder of the California missions?" Cecilia asked.

"Okay, yes! And—"

"But that can't be . . . he's not even a saint." Cecilia shook her head firmly.

"That's what your parents are discussing with Father Ramón right now . . . that and an idea for the second rosary."

"What do you mean? It's taking place tomorrow at home . . . before we fly out to Santa Cecilia," Cecilia said.

"No," Julie said, her face flushed with irritation. She raised her voice, "Benedicta doesn't want to hold the second rosary at your apartment, but at the Santa Clara Mission. She wants a procession to start here, at the San Jose church, and to travel to the mission in order to bring the two communities together, to strengthen their spiritual bond . . . something like that."

"So what are my parents talking to Father Ramón about?" Cecilia asked.

"Well," said Julie, "I only picked up that, when Benedicta announced the saint for the much needed miracle —Junípero Serra—Father Ramón shook his head and said that he was not a saint . . . that he had been beatified by Pope John Paul II . . . but not yet canonized. And that's when it got really interesting."

"Come on, hurry," Cecilia said impatiently.

"Okay . . . well . . . Benedicta told Father Ramón that Junípero Serra was perhaps even better suited for the miracle because he was a saint-wannabe, desperate for the one more miracle he needed to make him a full saint," Julie said. "Her prayer group had already talked to the mission's prayer group and arranged it all, to have the second rosary there . . . and the mission even has a relic of Junípero Serra." Now turning to her mother, she added, "And there's more. Right, Mom?"

"Uh," Marie started, "well . . . please forgive me, Cecilia, if you find this presumptuous of me. See, I was so moved by the rosary—especially when people started voicing the petitions, asking the baby for help—that I began to weep, remembering that I once had a miscarriage, and that my ex-husband told the nurses to 'dispose of the remains,' before I could see him. He told me it didn't matter, I should focus on him and Julie, and that I could always have another. Julie was only a year old at the time. And then he left us. After the rosary, I went up to Benedicta . . . just to say how touched I was . . . and she asked me why I had been crying. I didn't know what to say. Then, all of a sudden, I broke down sobbing . . . and told her. She just stood there and rubbed my back. When I was done crying, she looked me squarely in the eyes and told me that I should come to Santa Cecilia for the burial. She said I should stay there for the Day of the Dead festivities to reconnect with my . . . my little one. . . . Well, that's the gist of it," she added with a long sigh.

Cecilia gave Marie a warm, sympathetic hug.

Julie broke into a smile, reached into her purse and pulled out her iPhone. "Read this!" she said, excitedly.

Cecilia and Lebna leaned over and squinted as they tried to read a news update about a $3 million prize given annually for discoveries that cured diseases previously thought to be incurable and prolonged human life.

"I don't get it," Cecilia said.

"And I don't either," Lebna seconded.

"Don't you see? It's perfect," Julie said in a gush of excitement. "We might even win a million bucks each!"

"I can't believe this," Cecilia said, exasperated.

"Come on, ladies," Marie said, "let me get you all home."

"But, Mom," Julie said hurriedly as she grabbed her arm, "I haven't finished explaining."

"You can do it in the car." Marie took the car keys from her purse and hurried out the door.

The moment the car backed out of the parking space, Julie picked up where she had left off. "Ms. Bellows will just love it. And . . . we could even win a Breakthrough Award! Since I'm volunteering to write up the proposal, I'll need you two to sign off on it." Her eyes darted from Cecilia to Lebna. "I want to submit it to Ms. Bellows first thing tomorrow morning. What do you think? Can you summarize it for me so I know I got it . . . so I can write it up?"

Cecilia began in a singsong, tired rhythm: "Okay, so let's see . . . the proposal for our science project is . . . that we four—you, your mom, Lebna and I—fly down to Santa Cecilia to observe the burial of Micaela. . . . to investigate if there's proof that her soul makes it up to heaven in nine days. And we investigate the existence of *dons* . . . by listening to people tell their gift stories. Now, all this constitutes not only the perfect science project, but might also win us a fabulous award . . . while your mother"—here Cecilia spoke in a whisper, after she made sure Marie was not listening— "connects with her dead baby. Is this what you're proposing? Is this the gist of it?"

"Gosh, Cecilia, you make it sound so absurd!" Julie protested.

Cecilia grinned, "Really? What do you think, Lebna?"

"Ah, well," Lebna said, "I don't get—at least not yet— how this project will help cure an incurable disease or lengthen life."

"Exactly!" Cecilia said.

"Wait! Let me explain this further before you nix the whole thing," Julie almost shouted.

"Okay, I'm listening," Cecilia said in a thin, weary voice.

"Well, let's see. As for the first question, how will the project cure an incurable disease—it's like those illnesses you, Cecilia, have mentioned, that you say Western medicine doesn't even recognize: *susto* and *espanto.* Your community considers these to be illnesses of the soul. Right? And as to the second question, how the project will increase life . . . Well, what if the soldiers suffering from PTSD and committing suicide—aren't twenty-two of them killing themselves every day?—what if they're suffering from *susto*? Curing them would certainly prolong their lives. Right? And—"

"We're here," Marie announced. She turned off the car engine and got out.

Then Julie added in a whisper as they followed behind Marie, "That's another example: my mother. I haven't seen her so hopeful since . . ." She buried her face in her hands.

"Okay." Cecilia touched Julie on the elbow kindly. "Go ahead and write the proposal. Lebna and I will stop by your apartment early tomorrow to look it over. Okay?"

Julie gave a slight nod, and the girls parted ways.

❦   ❦   ❦

Very early the next morning, the three girls sat around Julie's kitchen table and drank coffee that Julie had made using Doña Faustina's coffee beans. Cecilia and Lebna read and reread Julie's science project proposal.

The moment Julie left the table to use the bathroom, Cecilia whispered, "Julie's dreaming if she thinks Ms. Bellows will sign off on this."

"But it's a big waste of time," explained Lebna, "to even try to convince Julie. She's so desperate to lift her mother's spirits. Do you think she served us Doña Faustina's coffee because she's hoping for a miracle?"

Julie returned and sat down between the two. After she took a sip of coffee, she said, "Mom's so excited. She's looking into where we'll be staying. And she's reading all these articles about the Day of the Dead."

"So what do you think, Lebna?" Cecilia asked as she held the proposal in the air.

Lebna hesitated for a moment, then drew in a long breath and nodded.

"Okay, we're in. Where do we sign?" Cecilia asked.

"You mean it?" Julie beamed.

"But this doesn't mean Ms. Bellows will sign off on it," Cecilia cautioned, "or that . . ."

"Or that what?" Julie asked with a frown.

"Or that any of this will help your mother . . . even *if* Ms. Bellows approves the project."

"But it's still worth a try. Already she's like a changed person. I've never seen her so excited."

"And, of course, it doesn't guarantee we'll win that award," Lebna warned.

"I know that, but I'm so excited," Julie said.

"What about our other school work?" Cecilia felt her stomach knot with tension. "How can we ever catch up?"

"Mom's taking care of that, too. See, after Ms. Bellows approves our proposal—well, let's assume that she does—Mom's going to arrange with our teachers and principal to homeschool us, to keep us on track with Skype. It's really cheap. Plus, her brother just sent her some money that she wants to use to find us a nice hotel—one with Wi-Fi and a place to study."

Astonished, Cecilia shook her head to help clear her mind and told herself nothing would happen if Ms. Bellows didn't okay the proposal. *So why worry?* She turned to Lebna. "What about you? Will you be able to come?"

Lebna whispered, "I need to talk to you in private."

The two girls stepped outside. Lebna drew Cecilia close and said, "I haven't even mentioned this to my mother."

"Because you don't think the proposal has the slightest chance of getting approved, right?"

"You're starting to read minds . . . just like Carmen."

"No, it's just that I'm thinking the same thing," Cecilia said. "And I guess we're both going along with this so as not to hurt Julie's feelings?"

"Right. But what if the proposal's shot down and Julie and her mother still want to go to Santa Cecilia?"

"There are so many 'ifs,' I don't even want to think about them." Cecilia sounded exasperated. "So for now, let's just wait and see what happens with the first 'if'—convincing Ms. Bellows to sign off on the proposal."

"What if Ms. Bellows has questions for us about the project, since we're supposed to be a team?"

"I don't think it'll get that far, so let's not worry about that now," replied Cecilia.

Lebna nodded and followed Cecilia back inside, where they quickly signed the proposal.

The girls returned home, then Cecilia raced to see Carmen. "I have to talk to you."

"What? You're in need of my *pláticas* now?" Carmen gave a short laugh as she led Cecilia down the hallway to the kitchen.

After she fell into a chair, Cecilia rubbed her face as if to wake herself from a bad dream, then told Carmen about how they'd signed off on Julie's absurd proposal, and how excited Julie and Marie were.

"So?"

"This is insane!" Cecilia almost shouted. "Is it true that the second rosary will be held at Santa Clara Mission—not at home? And that there's even going to be a procession?"

"Drink this. It'll soothe you," Carmen poured her a cup of steaming tea.

After she forced herself to swallow a mouthful, Cecilia set her cup down and said, as steadily as she could, "Why are we—all of a sudden—having the second rosary at Santa Clara, huh?"

"Because Junípero Serra was chosen to be the sponsor of a miracle. You see, back when he founded Santa Clara Mission in 1777, there was a big feud between the town of San Jose and the mission. The dispute was finally resolved when they built a road that joined the town and the mission. So, the procession from San Jose to the mission for Micaela's second rosary will lay the foundation for the miracle we need by connecting the physical with the spiritual."

Cecilia sighed heavily. "This makes no sense, no sense at all."

"You're right," Carmen said, "no sense on a linear level, but this concerns the spiritual dimension." Then she abruptly changed the subject: "Did you hear what Benedicta told Marie to do?"

"About attending the burial in Santa Cecilia and staying for the Day of the Dead?"

"No!" Carmen said and rapped the table with her hand.

"That's what Marie said!" Cecilia challenged.

"Yes, but I bet she didn't mention that Benedicta also instructed her to take her kitchen dishes for a drive in her car. Did she?"

"What craziness is that?" Cecilia blurted out.

"Yep," Carmen raised her cup as if to give a toast.

"That can't be! You mean that Benedicta told Marie—who knows nothing about our community or culture—to load all her cups, plates and soup bowls into her car and take them for a drive? Really?!"

"Yes. And I think you should do the same," Carmen said.

"And why would Marie—or I or *anybody*, for that matter—want to do such a stupid and ridiculous thing as that?"

"Because it'll help you understand why the procession and the second rosary at the mission will help bring about the miracle we need. You will see that doing things that are out of the ordinary influences ordinary events . . . how prayer, for instance, affects people."

"But taking *the dishes* for a drive?" Cecilia said, sarcastically. "How can that possibly change anything, other than to convince Marie—or others like her—that we're strange and superstitious people. It'll just prove the stereotypes about us from books, magazines and TV. No wonder we get bullied at school!"

"It works because it shakes people up and snaps them out of their self-absorbed bubbles," Carmen declared.

Cecilia hung her head and uttered, "So what time does the procession start?"

"We'll gather at the San Jose church at four."

Cecilia nodded, rose to her feet and headed to the front door, then she turned and asked, "But what does the drive with her dishes do for Marie? I mean—"

"Your science project, that's what," Carmen said and opened the door. "See, during her talk with Benedicta, Marie mentioned your science project. She described what you and your friends proposed to do and asked how she might help get it approved. That's when Benedicta told her to take her dishes for a drive."

Cecilia sighed and waved goodbye as she hurried off to her apartment.

🐝 🐝 🐝

"Oh my god!" Julie gushed over the telephone.

"What?" Cecilia said, impatiently.

"It's a go!" Julie shrieked.

"What's a go?"

"Our science project! Ms. Bellows signed off on it!"

Cecilia felt her heart race as she tried to stay calm. She was stunned.

"It was like she was under a spell," Julie continued. "I walked to her classroom, all nervous and sweaty. I thought about all the things you said she would say . . . like 'this is the craziest, most stupid proposal I've ever seen' . . . or that she would take a quick glance at it and laugh in my face.

"I forced myself to march into her room. She sat at her desk and glanced up from her book. I totally froze. Then she smiled at me. When have you seen her crack even a hint of a smile? Never! Then she said, 'Good morning, Julie. And what do you have there? Your proposal?'

"I was dumbstruck. How did she know? I wondered. *They aren't due for another week!* I felt sick as I got closer to her desk. I handed her the proposal and stepped back, terrified. She looked it over and started to nod her head. Then she said: 'I love it! I love it!'"

Cecilia dropped to the floor, propped herself up against the wall and asked, "She actually signed off on the project?"

"Yes!" Julie squealed. "But when I told my mother that Ms. Bellows had approved the proposal, she said the craziest thing, " she added in a worried tone.

"Yeah? What?"

"She said that she took our kitchen dishes for a drive, and that's why Ms. Bellows approved our proposal. I think she's worse!"

"Don't worry," Cecilia chuckled. "Benedicta told her to do it, to take the dishes for a drive."

"Why?"

"I warned you," Cecilia said, "that this project would take you—us—to another crazy world."

❧ ❧ ❧

Cecilia, her parents and Carmen stood in the portico of the Cathedral Basilica of Saint Joseph, waiting for the hearse that carried Micaela's body to arrive from the funeral home so the procession could begin.

"Uh, Carmen?" Cecilia said, "About what Benedicta told Marie to do . . ."

"About the dishes, you mean?" Carmen said. "Did it work?"

Cecilia pressed her lips into a line and nodded.

"See?" Carmen said. "And I bet now you wonder how the procession will help induce the miracle. Right?"

Startled at Carmen's uncanny ability to read her mind once again, Cecilia wondered if, aside from being a *curandera*, she had a second *don* that allowed her to read people's minds.

"You know," Carmen explained, "this church served as San Jose's first parish. The procession will take Micaela to the mission that was not only founded by the sponsor of our miracle, but also contains a relic of his."

"And that will help Micaela get to heaven, where she'll then work the miracle?"

Carmen gave a quick shrug before she went down the stairs to meet the hearse.

Just then, Julie waved, called out, "Cecilia!" and hurried over with Lebna and Marie close behind her. Cecilia waved to them and headed towards the hearse, now parked in front of the church. People gathered around and looked through the car window at the coffin. Cecilia forced herself to glance inside. To her surprise, she saw that the coffin lid was bejeweled with what looked like glazed fruit—the loving words and drawings people had inscribed on it.

"It looks like a cake!" Julie said and pressed her nose against the window.

"Let's start the procession!" Carmen's voice boomed from the church's portico. Then she ordered everyone to get in their cars and to line up behind the hearse.

Once Cecilia, her parents, Carmen and Benedicta were seated inside the hearse, José López got behind the wheel and headed down Market Street, while a long line of cars followed in procession. Soon, they were on El Camino Real, the so-called King's Highway that had once connected the twenty-one California missions founded by Junípero Serra and his fellow Franciscan friars. They then got off the highway to enter the Santa Clara University campus, where the Mission Santa Clara de Asís is located.

The hearse parked in front of the mission's double doors. Everyone got out, and Cecilia's father and uncle went to the back of the vehicle to carefully remove the coffin and carry it into the church. Suddenly, the mission doors swung open and Cecilia, her mother and Carmen followed her father and uncle as they carried the coffin inside. Carlos flitted about like a hummingbird, recording everything and coordinating with the people in Santa Cecilia.

Cecilia gasped, deeply moved by the beauty of the church's interior. They proceeded up the center aisle towards the front altar, which sparkled with light that came through the stained glass and featured a statue of Santa Clara at its very center.

After the casket was placed on a small, marble-topped table at the altar, Cecilia joined her parents in the front pew, then watched Carmen lead Benedicta over to the ancient elephants huddled near the altar. Cecilia spotted her two friends and Marie sitting a few pews behind her. Julie gave her a quick wave.

A few minutes later, Benedicta and another elderly woman shuffled over to the coffin, where they crossed themselves and started the second rosary.

After it ended, Carmen turned to Cecilia and said, "Get your friends. I want to show you something." She led them over to a side chapel and pointed at a speck in a gold-framed glass case. "That's the relic of Junípero Serra."

"What is it?" Cecilia asked.

"A piece of his leg bone," Carmen said and then pointed at a painting. "And that's an image of him."

"Wow," said Julie, "this stuff looks really old."

Not very impressed, Cecilia changed the subject. "So what happens next, Carmen?"

"You fly to Santa Cecilia for the burial and complete the rest of the nine rosaries, then wait for the return," Carmen said with a slight smile.

"The return? What's that?" Cecilia said.

"The Day of the Dead, when they—including Micaela—will return for a visit."

CHAPTER 30

On the flight to Mexico, Cecilia finally had time to relax and think things over. *If Micaela's soul really exists, and it takes nine days for it to get to heaven, and then it returns on the Day of the Dead, we could set up the project to verify this. We could make that our hypothesis for the project. And, when we investigate, we might actually debunk this entire "soul belief." Well, it'll certainly take us out of the running for those awards Julie was raving about. But that was all pie-in-the-sky anyway.*

Cecilia slumped back in her seat and smiled inwardly. The project, however strange, might finally allow her to stand up to Carmen and the others who insisted that she spend more time trying to learn about her Mexican culture. Now, when they complained about how Americanized she was, she could simply point to the results of their experiment, which would prove that a soul does not ascend to heaven in nine days and then return to visit on the Day of the Dead. She let out a sigh of relief, shifted in her seat and felt lighter and freer. After this, she could just be herself and not some servant living her life apprenticing for the benefit of her entire community. She took a deep breath, leaned her head against the window and dozed off.

At the Oaxacan airport, Cecilia and her parents stepped through a smoked glass door and encountered a crowd of people standing behind a metal rail. They smiled and waved at their friends and family.

"Dad, where's the coffin?" Cecilia tugged at her father's arm.

"Don't worry," her father said, "José López arranged for it to be delivered to your *abuelitos'* house."

"What?" Cecilia said. "The coffin is going to their *house?*"

"That's the custom here," her father answered.

Just then, they spotted Nica's parents, and Cecilia ran over to her grandmother and gave her a big hug.

After the greetings, hugs and kisses, they headed to Santa Cecilia in her grandparents' car. They soon pulled up to a small, white-stuccoed house near the town plaza and only a block away from the parish church. After they settled in, they gathered at the kitchen table for cups of frothy hot chocolate and freshly steamed *tamales*. While Cecilia unwrapped her second *tamal*, there was a knock at the front door. She followed her mother and grandparents. The coffin had arrived and was promptly taken inside and placed on top of a small table in the living room.

Jeez, I just hope they don't open it again, Cecilia thought as she watched her grandparents cross themselves before they touched the tiny casket. A few moments later, while she sat on a chair and stared at the floor, Cecilia felt a hand on her shoulder. It was her grandfather Abel.

"This must be hard for you," he sympathized.

Cecilia gave a quick nod and sat up straight.

"Come with me. I want to show you something." He led her to the room where her grandmother had put Cecilia's suitcase.

Grandfather Abel crossed the room and pointed at two oval-framed photographs of sleeping babies.

Cecilia studied the photos and asked, "Is that my mother and Aunt Carmen?"

"No, those are their baby sisters."

"But I thought they were the only girls," Cecilia said. Then she caught herself and realized that the two children had died somehow. "And this was my mother's and Carmen's bedroom?"

Abel responded with a quick nod.

Cecilia looked around the room. She imagined her mother's and Carmen's early childhood in this room decorated with pictures of their dead baby sisters, the same room where she would spend the night.

Before she had time to process this thought, there was another knock. Her grandfather explained that people were coming to offer their condolences and went to answer the door. Cecilia found her grandmother in the kitchen making a fresh pot of hot chocolate.

Her grandmother smiled and gave Cecilia a handful of chocolate disks, which she whipped into frothy chocolate the way she had been taught by her mother and Carmen. While she did this, her grandmother greeted and thanked people who stepped into the kitchen, carrying dishes filled with soups, stews and other delicious-smelling foods to nourish the family during this difficult time. But, the more people her grandmother introduced her to, the more confused Cecilia became. Once they knew she was Nica's daughter, they suddenly lit up and asked her if she was the *new* Cecilia, the one who was supposed to finally bring them all together.

When the first person asked her this, Cecilia thought she had simply heard wrong, because she had always thought that Saint Cecilia was the patron saint of music. She had never heard anything about her bringing people together. *Does the saint have a second don?* So Cecilia had just nodded politely because she didn't know how to respond. One of the well-wishers mentioned that the first Cecilia had lived only seven years, but that she, the second Cecilia, would be able to do even more.

As the platters, pots and baskets of food, fruit and confections began to pile up on the counter, then the table and even the chairs, Cecilia walked over to the far end of the kitchen, where she found her grandmother Andrea placing translucent green pebbles of copal in a three-legged ceramic bowl.

Cecilia took the opportunity to ask her, "What do people mean when they ask me if I'm going to continue the work of the *first* Cecilia?"

Her grandmother gave Cecilia a surprised look, took her by the elbow and led her out the back door to the stone bread oven in the backyard.

"*M'ija*, I thought you knew this already. Your godmother should've told you this long ago. It's something that should be learned from your godmother, not your grandmother."

"Well, I . . . I haven't heard about this from Carmen . . . at least not yet."

"I can't believe my daughter has been neglecting her duties. . . ."

"She tried! Really she did!" Cecilia said anxiously. "I was just too busy to listen to her."

"So, I guess you haven't heard about *El Diablo* either?"

"You mean, Satan?"

"Yes."

"What about Satan?"

Suddenly, Cecilia's grandmother reached down, lit the green copal pebbles with a match, then picked up the three-legged bowl and began to walk around and around Cecilia, engulfing her from head to toe in a cloud of smoke. After she put the bowl back down, she brought her finger to her lips to silence Cecilia.

Then, in a voice edged with urgency, Grandmother Andrea said, "One day, many years ago, a handsome young man appeared in Santa Cecilia. While he walked past a woman who sat on her porch and rocked her baby, he suddenly stopped, smiled at her with the whitest teeth and said, 'What a beautiful baby you have. Too bad she won't last the day.' Then he hurried off and left the mother stunned.

"Next, a farmer's son, whose father plowed a field, saw the same man and heard him say, 'The plow will be the end of him.' Later that same day, a boy had breakfast with his grandmother at a café and noticed the stranger walk in and stare at her, and, just then, she started to choke to death. At the exact same moment, the baby convulsed and died in her mother's arms. And the farmer's plow flipped over and killed him.

"That evening, when the priest summoned the town to church for a communal rosary, they realized the enormity of the evil that had attacked them. A total of twelve people had died that day. They were cursed—but why? Through-out the nine days of rosaries, they petitioned their dead, once they got to heaven, to reveal to them how to break the curse.

"After the last rosary, a little barefoot girl walked into the church as the prayer group ladies tidied up. They rushed to her, thinking she was hurt or needed help. Then they noticed that her eyes were shut. She was sleepwalking. One of them guided her towards a chair when, all at once, the lit-tle girl opened her eyes and shouted, 'He killed them all, all twelve of them!' After they finally managed to calm her down, one of the ladies recognized her as a neighbor's daughter, a girl named Cecilia. They took her home, where her mother thanked them and insisted they stay for a cup of coffee.

"They drank their strong coffee and stared at the moth-er with the child on her lap as she gave the girl sips from her cup. After the sixth sip, the child pushed the cup away and said, 'The same man was there . . . with every person who died. El Diablo. He killed them all . . . because of Faustina's coffee.' Then she fell asleep in her mother's arms.

"Stunned, the prayer ladies left to investigate whether the twelve people who had died had indeed been seen in the man's company. They were. By the wee hours of the morning, the ladies were back at the church. Filled with dread, they wondered why El Diablo had attacked them. 'The child said that it was because of Faustina's coffee,' one of them uttered. But what could that possibly mean? they wondered. Then another said in a hushed voice, 'Faustina's don is very special, as we all know. Her coffee can awaken people's souls to their true dons. I believe her gift has alarmed *El Diablo*. It threatens his grasp on the world. Our community has many awakened souls thanks to her, and we can work as a bridge between Heaven and Earth. After he lost the battle in Heaven, the Devil has gotten used to his power on Earth. I think that's why he wants to destroy us.'

"The prayer ladies felt sick and hopeless. They knew that they could not possibly fight the Devil himself. Then, they almost died from shock when the church's heavy front door suddenly flew open. They huddled together because they expected the Devil to fly in. The next moment they almost fainted with relief when they saw that it was Little Cecilia, instead. Again, she was sleepwalking, but this time she didn't scream when she opened her eyes. They gathered around her and were astonished when she announced that she would help them. They took her home to her mother. Soon after, the little girl developed a raging fever and was constantly retching. Then, in three days, she went from being a lively, healthy child to the ghost of one.

"Little Cecilia died on the evening of the third day, and, after her ninth day of rosaries, the town awoke freed of the curse. They thanked the little girl Cecilia for this. Soon afterwards, the community gathered together to honor the miracle child and to proclaim her the town's patron saint."

With that, Grandmother Andrea went back inside to resume her funeral duties. And Cecilia felt she needed to talk to Carmen, and she needed to talk to her *now!*

CHAPTER 31

Cecilia telephoned Carmen and cut to the chase: What could she do to avoid winding up dead like Little Cecilia?

Taken aback, Carmen said wearily, "No one knows if you're in actual danger. And no one knows what will happen after Micaela's ninth rosary. Our best hope is to destroy the curse before then." She added that she hadn't told her the story of the first Cecilia because she didn't want to scare her unnecessarily, especially since she thought the curses had ended. But after Doña Faustina's latest vision . . . well . . .

"But how?" Cecilia felt her pulse quicken.

"Well, by now you realize how serious the situation is, but I can't give you an answer yet. I need to consult with Benedicta. I'll call you back in ten minutes." Carmen clicked off.

Those were the longest ten minutes of Cecilia's life. This had turned out to be worse than she thought. She had expected Carmen to laugh the whole thing off, or at least to say that she had overreacted before reproaching her for missing her *pláticas.* But Carmen had not reacted that way at all—far from it.

Cecilia stared at the phone in her hand as her heart pounded and she wondered what had happened to Carmen. Fifteen minutes had already passed. She put the phone down on an end table. She was afraid of what she would discover when it finally rang—what if I have a *don* like Little Cecilia's?

She forced herself to breathe deeper and deeper. *I have to calm down.*

Finally, the cellphone rang. When Cecilia answered it, Carmen explained that this was the worst time ever to be subjected to the Devil's attack. The community was more divided than ever. Fewer and fewer people were returning to Santa Cecilia to honor their departed ones on the Day of the Dead.

"I talked to Benedicta. She agrees that something must be done before the ninth rosary. She says that she'll try to get hold of Junípero Serra's personal rosary, and the leader of the rosary group down there will ask Little Cecilia's mother for her daughter's rosary—the one she used for her First Communion. After that, they're going to pray for a *don* to be given to someone to destroy the curse. We will double our efforts. This is what we prayed for in San Jose when Benedicta had us conduct the coffee ceremony."

"So what can we do, Carmen?" Cecilia asked anxiously.

"Coffee, *m'ija.* You and your friends need to prepare and serve coffee after every rosary, and they will continue praying for the *don* to manifest in someone, either there in Santa Cecilia or here in San Jose."

CHAPTER 32

Julie, Lebna and Marie arrived at the church together. When Julie entered, she gasped at how beautiful it was. Lebna—feeling grateful that Marie had finally convinced her mother to let her come—nodded as she looked at the sparkling stained-glass windows, the glowing gold of the altar and the flickering radiance of the tall white candles. The church bells rang and everything and everyone in the church vibrated as one.

"Look, there's Cecilia and her parents in the front pew," Julie said as she led Marie and Lebna to a pew at the back of the church. "And look, that must be Isabel—Carlos' counterpart—taking pictures to post online for the community back in San Jose!" she added excitedly as she rapped Lebna on the knee and gestured towards the front.

After the funeral Mass ended, the priest walked over to the casket and sprinkled it with Holy Water. Then he gently swung the silver incense burner as he walked around it until the casket was enveloped in a cloud of wispy, white smoke, and he blessed it with the sign of the cross. Next, Cecilia's father and grandfather walked over, gently lifted the coffin and followed the priest down the aisle. Everyone, aisle-by-aisle, joined in a long procession out the church doors, where they were each handed a white calla lily. The mourners continued on foot up a long, winding road.

Julie, Lebna and Marie were at the very end of the procession. They held their calla lilies upright, and thought of Micaela's soul ascending higher and higher into heaven.

When she glanced at her mother, Julie saw tears streaming down her cheeks. "Mom, are you feeling sick? Do you want to sit down?"

Marie shook her head as the procession started to climb a grassy hill. "I was just thinking . . . about my past life." She hugged Julie close to her side and added, "But I'm so glad I have you."

Julie smiled and took her mother by the hand as they proceeded to climb higher and higher, until they came to a tall wrought iron gate, through which they entered the town's cemetery. They walked slowly past stone crosses, statues of winged angels, Christ Jesus and the Virgin Mary. The procession finally stopped beside a large, lovely tree where a small hole had been dug, a mound of fresh earth beside it.

"It's so beautiful and peaceful up here." Julie inhaled deeply while she took in the green fields and the charming, miniature-looking town of Santa Cecilia down below.

The priest stepped in front of the casket, which had been set on a small table, raised his hands and started to pray. Cecilia, who stood beside the coffin, felt an intense sinking feeling as she peered into the blackness of the hole. *That's the darkest darkness I've ever felt.* She clenched her jaw. By her side, her mother gazed at the casket with a look of deep sadness, and so did her father.

When the priest finished his prayer and had sprinkled the casket again with Holy Water, two men in white stepped forward, lifted the coffin and placed it on two belts that were suspended over the dark hole. With one on each side, they started slowly lowering the casket deeper and deeper into the darkness until Cecilia could no longer see any sign of it.

Then her parents and everyone carrying lilies stepped to the edge of the hole and gently tossed in their flowers. Cecilia thought her flower struck the casket with the sound of a bird taking flight, and that is precisely how she would always remember it. Next, the priest and everyone in the procession tossed a handful of dirt from the mound into the hole. With each toss, handful after handful, Cecilia felt hollowed out, bit by bit.

After everyone in the town had passed by the gravesite, the two workers filled in the hole and created a small mound, which other townspeople covered in flowers. Before the procession headed back to town, Cecilia noticed her grandfather smiling at her.

"Don't worry. She'll be in Heaven soon," he said softly.

Cecilia nodded. She wanted to believe this, even if it was only wishful thinking. As she glanced around, she couldn't deny the deep sense of peace it seemed to give those around her. But what if, upon reaching Heaven, Micaela helped her discover her true *don* and it was similar to Little Cecilia's? She shuddered at the thought.

On the way back, Cecilia asked her grandparents, "So what happens next?"

Her grandmother answered, "We'll gather at the house, have some food and tell stories before the next rosary starts."

"Is everyone staying for the rosary?"

"Not everyone, but the prayer group will be there, of course."

"Why do you ask?" her grandfather asked, studying her.

"Oh," Cecilia tried to sound casual, "I was just curious."

"You're worried about something," he said. "I know. But I also know that you'll ask if you need help. Right?"

"*M'ija*, I hope your parents retire here, like we did," her grandmother then added out of the blue, "as Nica told us she's dreaming of doing some day. And that you'll come too."

What? Cecilia stifled a gasp. She couldn't imagine living in a place like this—with no skyscrapers, highways, theatres. . . .

"Don't you want to come live here, near us?" her grandmother continued, weaving her arm around Cecilia's.

"Uh, *abuelita*," Cecilia tried not to be rude or insensitive, "but . . . but I was born in San Jose . . . in California."

Her grandparents exchanged a long look before they hurried home to prepare for the arrival of their guests.

CHAPTER 33

Her grandparents' house was a beehive of activity. The kitchen was abuzz with the clatter of bowls and platters being laid on the table and counters filled with steaming hot *tamales, moles, guisos* . . . roasted meats. Cecilia moved to the living room to wait for her friends to arrive. She watched as people entered and moved through the house like a rushing river. Then, the young woman named Isabel appeared and snapped a picture of her.

"Hey, Isabel," Cecilia said, "did you do that?" She gestured towards a photo of Micaela that was already framed amid the other family photos.

Isabel nodded, "I just added it to our site, along with photos from the burial."

Cecilia took a deep breath and tried to sound casual. "And who has access to the website?"

"Everyone." Isabel looked as if she did not understand the question.

"You mean everyone in the Santa Cecilia community— those here and in San Jose?"

"Yes, and everyone else," Isabel answered as she excused herself. She added that she wanted to take and post more pictures before the rosary began.

248

Oh no, just what I was afraid of, thought Cecilia, *everyone at school and the entire world can look at the Santa Cecilia website.*

"There she is!" Cecilia suddenly heard Julie say. She waved to her friends as they stepped through the front door.

"Are you okay?" Marie asked, placing her hand on Cecilia's shoulder with a look of concern.

Startled, Cecilia quickly said that she was.

"Mom cried through the whole thing, and Isabel took a picture of her," Julie said.

Cecilia sighed. "I just asked Isabel, and she said that the whole world has access to the website. Our school included."

"Don't worry." Lebna gave Cecilia's arm a gentle squeeze. "We have bigger fish to fry."

"You mean saving the life of *this* particular fish?" Cecilia asked as she pointed at herself.

"That's exactly what I mean," Lebna replied. "We just spoke to Carmen on the phone."

"To help with that—though I don't know how—Carmen wants us to make and serve coffee after every rosary." Cecilia led her friends into the kitchen, where people talked and shared pictures of their children and grandchildren, and talked about how excited they were about the Day of the Dead.

"What are you making for Micaela?" the prayer group leader asked Cecilia.

Cecilia had no idea what she was talking about. After a long silence, the words "Hot chocolate!" erupted from her mouth.

Just then, her grandmother hurried over and proudly said to Doña Mercedes, "And she's staying here for the Day of the Dead to make it for her. Right, *m'ija?*"

Cecilia nodded awkwardly and realized what they were all talking about: the special sweets and treats that they would offer the souls of the children who returned on the Day of the Dead.

Doña Mercedes gave Cecilia a warm smile and said that she knew about her conversation with Carmen. She added that she would talk to Little Cecilia's mother about the rosary and that Cecilia and her friends could start making the coffee.

During the rosary, people again petitioned for Micaela's intervention to destroy the curse, and stared at Cecilia, especially when she helped serve the coffee afterwards.

On their way to the car, Marie turned to Cecilia and asked whether she wanted to call Carmen at the hotel, where there was more privacy.

Cecilia nodded.

"What about?" Julie said as she darted to Cecilia's side and Lebna quickened her pace. They were both eager to hear.

Cecilia gave Julie a long look and wondered what she could say to pacify Julie's curiosity. She didn't want to reveal what she really needed to ask Carmen.

"Oh, no you don't!" Julie said sharply. "We're in this together. So scary or not, you have to tell us everything! Right, Lebna?"

Lebna shrugged slightly. She didn't want to say anything that might make things harder for her friend.

"Okay," Cecilia said as she climbed into the car. "If it's true, really true that it takes a soul nine days to get to heaven, I want to ask Carmen if there's actual proof that Little Cecilia's soul got there. And . . . what happened to *El Diablo*, the evil man she destroyed? Did he simply vanish or is he buried somewhere? And what happens on the Day of the Dead for demons like him? Do they return too?"

"Whoa," Julie exclaimed as the car swerved into the hotel's parking lot. "Can we be there when you talk to her?"

"Honey," Marie sighed, "let's let Cecilia come up and tell us afterwards, okay?"

"Thanks," Cecilia said, "I appreciate it."

Marie parked the car and the group went into the hotel.

❧ ❧ ❧

"Carmen, is there any hard evidence that Little Cecilia's soul actually got to heaven?"

"Well, *m'ija*," Carmen said, "I have heard stories of dying people seeing Little Cecilia as part of the committee welcoming them to their next life. The leaders of the prayer groups in San Jose and Santa Cecilia can confirm this, because they keep a book where they record all the spirits seen by those they pray for."

After drawing a deep breath, Cecilia bombarded Carmen with more questions. "Do Benedicta and Doña Mercedes both see spirits?"

"Sometimes," Carmen replied, "but at least one member of their group always does, those with the *don* that allows them to see spirits. Also, a dying person often talks to or mentions spirits in the room, like a person's late mother. Or the Virgin Mary."

"What about the man associated with the curse? Was he really the Devil? And what happened to him?"

"Ask your *abuelito* about that . . . when you visit the cemetery on the Day of the Dead."

"Is the man buried there?" Cecilia whispered. "Oh, and how is that even possible, if people thought he was the Devil? Huh?"

"It's called possession," Carmen said. "Remember when Jesus cleansed a man of his demons, which then possessed a pack of pigs that ran off a cliff? It's sort of like that."

Cecilia was not able to take in any more of this baffling information, so she wished her aunt a good night.

Later, up in the hotel suite, Julie sat pale and stunned as Cecilia relayed everything about the first Cecilia and the new curse, as well as what Carmen had said. Lebna was overcome with emotion, but she squeezed her hands underneath the table to appear calm. As for Marie, she nodded her head slightly, trying to be supportive of Cecilia's efforts to communicate something that was very confusing.

After a long pause, Julie pitched forward in her chair and asked, "So how can we use this . . . this new data to set up our science project?"

Lebna gave Julie a reproachful look.

"What?" Julie frowned at Lebna. "I didn't say anything wrong."

Marie took Julie's hand and said, "No, sweetie, you didn't say anything wrong. But the science project is not the most important thing at the moment—"

"Well, we need . . ." Julie interrupted.

"It's late," Marie said as she got to her feet and patted Cecilia on the shoulder, "so let us drive you back before your family starts to worry or you collapse from exhaustion."

Cecilia nodded and thought that they had no idea about the suffocating sense of dread she felt.

CHAPTER 34

Early the following morning, Cecilia said goodbye to her parents at the airport. Once again, they explained to her why it was important—even essential—for her to stay for the Day of the Dead. Her parents had grown up with this ritual and, though they wished they could stay, they couldn't miss more work.

Later that day, Cecilia went to the hotel to study with her friends. Once the girls settled down, Cecilia opened her email and quickly scanned the list of class assignments. Then, zipping open her backpack, she pulled out one of her schoolbooks, slapped it open on the table and started reading, trying to ignore all the questions she had about *dons*, the curse, Little Cecilia, and the fast approaching Day of the Dead rituals, during which she had to make a cup of hot chocolate for Micaela's soul.

The girls worked until lunchtime and then joined Marie at the restaurant downstairs. While they sat around a table by a sunlit window and enjoyed tacos and tall glasses of tamarind water, Marie and the girls were relieved to chat about school for a change. After lunch, Marie shooed the girls back up to the room to resume their schoolwork. She, too, was off to do her own homework, she said—to work on a project that Doña Faustina had assigned her.

"I bet she's taking a potted plant from the hotel for a car ride," Julie snickered to Cecilia and Lebna as they went up the stairs. She added that she wouldn't be at all surprised if her mother's *don*—if indeed she had one—turned out to be nothing more than to give silly things rides in her car. Cecilia and Lebna couldn't help but laugh. It occurred to Cecilia that she would feel so relieved to have such a safe *don*.

Back in the room, the girls were finally ready to confront their science project.

"Let's get cracking," Cecilia began, "otherwise, we'll be like stupid pinballs bouncing from one crazy thing to the next without the slightest clue of what's going on. So let's focus on our questions, what we plan to investigate. I can always call Carmen if we get stuck."

Julie's hand instantly shot up. "Oh, I have an idea!" she announced as she bounced in her chair with excitement. "Well, if souls do exist, and it takes them nine days to get to heaven . . . and Little Cecilia has appeared to dying people . . . let's get the prayer ladies to give us proof of this—just like Carmen suggested."

"But the people who saw her are dead," Lebna countered.

"I know that," Julie said sharply, "but we can ask if someone in the prayer group has seen her . . . those with the *don* of seeing spirits, like Carmen mentioned."

"But how does this fit with the science project?" Cecilia asked.

"And how is this going to win us one of those Breakthrough Awards you talked about?" Lebna added.

Julie glared at Lebna as she fell back in her chair and tried to think of what to say.

"It's so ridiculous to dream of winning one of those awards," Cecilia said. "There are—what?—two things required to win an award, right? It must cure an incurable disease and also prolong life. So, based on these two requirements, how do we set up our science project?

"Ideas?" She tapped her pen on a blank notebook page while she scrutinized her friends' expressions. "Oh, I get it," she added, "you don't want to say anything because you're worried that the project is about my life, right?

"So let's start there," Cecilia continued. "Let your thoughts fly without worrying about me. Otherwise, it makes no sense for either of you to be here. You can just go back to San Jose and resume your normal lives."

"Okay, we get it," Lebna said and raised her hand to stop Cecilia.

"So, if you get it," Cecilia replied, "prove it. I want to be bombarded with all your brilliant ideas."

After a long silence, Cecilia sat up and said, "Well, one can suppose that the incurable disease is the destruction of the entire planet, by an asteroid, plague or something else catastrophic, which of course includes the lives of everyone. So, stopping the curse will cure this incurable disease, and prolong everyone's life. Right?"

"What you're saying," Julie said "is that we should assume, as a hypothesis, that a curse is coming for us . . . a curse that will destroy everyone and everything . . . unless we—that is you, Lebna and I—stop it? That that should satisfy the award's two requirements. Is that right?"

"Bingo, Julie! So, what can we do about it?"

"Hold on!" Julie grabbed Cecilia's arm. "Are we also assuming—as a hypothetical—that the new curse is following a similar timeline as the first one—that something might happen after the ninth day of rosaries?"

"Yes," Cecilia answered.

Lebna leaned forward in her chair and said, "So what's the next step?"

"How about we take this table . . . ," Cecilia rapped the top, "for a ride in your mother's car?" She gave Julie a big smile.

Julie jumped out of her chair and glared at Cecilia. "Knock it off!"

"Julie, I have no idea why you're so upset . . . what do you want me to knock off? Please sit down and tell me, okay?"

Julie dropped her arms heavily by her side. "You're doing it again. You agreed to stop teasing me, to stop treating me like a baby."

"Hold on!" Lebna said. "Look, I've heard every single word that the two of you have said and, if we can't even talk to each other as close friends, we don't stand a chance of accomplishing anything."

"Okay, why don't you referee this?" Julie fell back into her chair.

"Fine," Lebna agreed. "And the sooner we learn to discuss things as a team, the less time we'll squander fighting like spooked cats. Okay?"

The three of them finally nodded.

"I wasn't baby-talking when I suggested taking the table for a ride," Cecilia said to Julie. "It's just that there seems to be a strange cause and effect connection between things. Like, who would have thought that a group in need of something could simply ask that a *don* be given to someone to fulfill the need?! Or that Ms. Bellows signed the proposal after your mom drove her dishes around?"

"Okay," Julie said, "so what do we do now?"

"Well," Cecilia said, "we can go ask the prayer ladies what *don* they're praying for, since it'll give us some insight about the curse . . . like what it'll take to stop it."

"No," Lebna said, "I actually think Doña Faustina is the person to ask. Besides, I believe she's trying to bring into being the needed *don* by encouraging the three of us to work together."

"Oh my god!" Julie squealed.

"Come on, Julie," Lebna said, "you can't have it both ways. You don't want to be treated like a kid, but then you pop off with your 'oh-my-gods' at the slightest thing. We don't have time."

"Okay! Okay!" Julie said. "It was just that, after hearing what you said about Doña Faustina preparing all three of us, I . . . I . . ."

"Out with it!" Lebna said impatiently.

Julie quickly glanced up at Cecilia, then hung her head.

"I think what Julie's trying to say," Cecilia clarified, "is that I'm not the only one in danger, that this might also involve the two of you. Am I right?"

Julie took a deep breath and nodded.

"Well, then, the three of us are the target . . . and we have the responsibility," said Cecilia. "And this means there's another rule that our team needs to follow: that however stupid, hard or embarrassing, we must always tell the others what we're thinking or feeling. Okay?"

Her two friends nodded in agreement.

Cecilia picked up her pen and said, "So let's start brainstorming. Is a colossal asteroid about to strike the Earth, like the one that struck close to the Yucatán Peninsula and caused the extinction of the dinosaurs? Or a plague?"

Lebna and Julie exchanged a baffled look and shrugged.

"You know," continued Cecilia, "instead of asking what the curse is, should we perhaps ask why? Why is the curse—El Diablo—striking us now?"

She paused, then added, "Didn't the first curse come right after Doña Faustina received the *don* of awakening other people's *dons* through her coffee ritual? And right after we started learning the coffee ritual. . . ." Cecilia's voice trailed off.

"Are you saying," Lebna tried to clarify, "that by learning the coffee ritual we are threatening the Devil so he might be casting a new curse?"

"Do you mean," Julie said, "that the Devil wants to destroy us—us three—because we're making coffee?"

"That sounds really bonkers, but that's the gist of it," Cecilia said. "And I could be completely wrong."

"But if it's true, what do we do?" Julie's eyes darted nervously around the room as if making sure the Devil wasn't lurking in some corner.

The three sat there in an uneasy silence and tried to think of something, anything that might work.

"Let's each of us ask Junípero Serra," Cecilia suggested, "in a kind of silent prayer. He's the patron saint of our much-needed miracle, so let's ask him to point us in the right direction. Here's paper and pens to write down ideas.

"But wait! Before we start writing," Cecilia added and held up her hand, "let's first agree that whatever idea we write down comes from our heart or soul, and not the head. Okay?"

"And whatever idea is picked," added Lebna, "regardless of how weird or wacky, hard or impossible . . . we commit to doing it. Agreed?"

Lebna extended her hand to the other two and, after hesitating, the trio executed a sort of triple handshake. Then the girls closed their eyes. After a moment of silence, Julie opened her eyes and started to scribble on her piece of paper. Cecilia shrugged, then started to write too. Lebna soon followed. When they finished and folded their papers, Julie jumped out of her chair and left the room. She returned a moment later with an empty flower vase.

"How about using this?" She tossed her paper into the vase.

Cecilia and Lebna followed suit.

"Now, Cecilia, go ahead and pick one." Julie raised the vase in the air.

Cecilia reached inside and withdrew one of the folded papers. She handed it to Lebna and said, "You read it."

Lebna swallowed hard, unfolded the paper and pursed her lips in thought.

"What does it say?" Julie asked as she tried to look over Lebna's shoulder.

"Okay, here it goes." Lebna waved the paper in the air. "It says, 'Go talk to the leader of the prayer group ladies.'" Then she folded the paper and stuffed it into her pants pocket.

"That's it?" Julie said.

"Yep!" Lebna said and shrugged.

"What now?" Julie asked.

"We go talk to the ladies, that's what," Cecilia said.

"But what do we tell them?" Julie asked. "I mean, we can't just go up to them and say, 'We're desperate! We need a miracle because we only have a couple of days to stop the curse . . . or the Devil will kill us!'"

"Julie!" Lebna cried as she grabbed her shoulders and gave her a firm shake. "We agreed, as a team, to follow through on whatever idea was picked. Right? And we asked for Junípero's help in picking the idea. So, perhaps the prayer ladies will be able to help us solve this puzzle."

"And remember that Carmen already spoke to their leader, Doña Mercedes, about the miracle we need," Cecilia stood up. "So let's get going. We don't have a minute to waste."

"Where does Doña Mercedes live?"

"I have no idea," Cecilia said, "which is why we're first stopping at my grandparents' house. They'll know."

Cecilia's grandfather was tending a wood fire, shoveling its silvery coals into the stone oven, while her grandmother stood next to a tray filled with balls of dough. They were in their backyard.

"We're baking bread," her grandmother said.

The girls greeted them warmly, and then Cecilia asked as casually as she could, "Where does Doña Mercedes live?"

"She lives with her daughter, near the *mercado*."

"She'll be here later, to lead the next rosary," her grandfather added. "Do you need her for something?"

Cecilia hesitated and wondered what to say.

Her grandfather then tossed his head back and let out a short laugh. "It's about her delicious grasshoppers, right? I bet your aunt Carmen just called you and asked you to buy her a big bag of them. Right? She loves those things."

Lebna stepped up next to Cecilia, flashed Cecilia's grandparents a warm smile and said: "Yes, you're right. Carmen wants us to buy her a bag of . . . grasshoppers."

"Yes," agreed Cecilia. "So how do we get to her house?"

"I'll take you," Cecilia's grandfather said and smiled at the anxious-looking girls, "but after we have a cup of coffee."

CHAPTER 35

"**Y**ou will always return to Santa Cecilia if you eat a *cha-pulín*, a grasshopper," Cecilia's grandfather said, chuck-ling at the three girls' startled faces as they stepped in front of baskets piled high with what looked like bright red chili peppers. But, on closer inspection, they turned out to be grasshoppers, with dotted eyes, curling antennae and spiky, wiry legs. Only after they heard Cecilia's grandfather greet Doña Mercedes did they realize that she was the woman sitting behind the heaping, creepy towers of insects.

The girls forced themselves to smile politely as they watched Doña Mercedes reach over and pick up the biggest, ugliest grasshopper they had ever seen and offer it to Cecilia. She repeated, "Whoever eats a *chapulín* always returns to Santa Cecilia."

Cecilia stared at the grasshopper and could not bring herself to say anything.

Doña Mercedes and her grandfather roared with laugh-ter.

Cecilia turned to Lebna and asked, "Want to give it a try?"

Lebna shook her head briskly. She directed a squeamish smile at Doña Mercedes and asked, "Will you please excuse us? I need to talk to Cecilia for a moment?"

The two adults exchanged a puzzled look and then nodded.

Lebna took Cecilia aside by the elbow and Julie followed. "Why do we have to eat those things?" she asked.

"Well, I'm afraid that we're not going to get to talk to her until we do." Cecilia shook her head. "Her daughter sells them at the *mercado*."

"Yeah," Julie interjected, "and eating it means you want to return . . . so refusing would be rude."

"Okay, but both of you have to eat one too," Cecilia insisted.

"But that thing looks like a . . . a . . . ," Lebna said, coughing into her hand.

"A giant roach!" Julie squealed.

"They're delicious," Cecilia's grandfather said loud enough for the girls to hear.

"What are you eating?" Cecilia asked her grandfather who chewed with gusto.

"*¡Chapulines!*" he said and gestured towards the three heaping baskets of grasshoppers. Then he took another large grasshopper that Doña Mercedes dangled in the air, popped it in his mouth and chewed with a look of intense delight.

Cecilia's grandfather swallowed and encouraged the girls. "*Chapulines* are a great source of protein." Then he chose one from the basket and offered it to Cecilia.

After hesitating a moment, Cecilia hooked her shoulders back and took the grasshopper by its curly antennae.

"Go on, just pop it in your mouth," her grandfather prompted her.

With a slight nod, she shut her eyes, tossed the grasshopper into her mouth and started chewing. She swallowed it quickly, barely tasting it. Then, Lebna and Julie forced themselves to select the tiniest *chapulines* in the basket and swallow them whole. Both girls had a coughing fit afterwards.

Her grandfather chuckled to himself and left them with Doña Mercedes to talk privately.

"Come sit over here," Doña Mercedes invited the girls. "What do you want to ask me?"

"Why . . . why do people always turn to stare at me," Cecilia began, " . . . during the petitions . . . when someone asks Micaela to help stop the new curse. And why do they mention Little Cecilia and the previous curse?"

"Yes, Carmen and I talked. I finally got Little Cecilia's rosary from her mother. I have been praying with it. And Doña Benedicta has been praying too, with Junípero Serra's rosary. And you girls are helping by making and serving coffee after the rosaries.

"But sometimes things stay a mystery for a long, long time—time that we don't have. The only advice I can give you right now is to go see Doña Jerónima at the bookstore at the plaza. And know that we're all praying—hard and often—about this. And for you." She then embraced the three girls in a long hug, adding that this was to help protect them.

CHAPTER 36

After consulting with Doña Mercedes, the girls felt the mystery of the curse would be even *more* impossible to crack.

"Come on, we have to hurry!" Cecilia said and dashed out of Doña Mercedes' house.

"Where to?" Lebna and Julie cried out in unison.

"To the *librería*, the bookshop in the plaza. To talk to Doña Jerónima."

"Was she at the rosary?" asked Julie. Her breath was heavy as she tried to catch up to her friend.

"I don't know," Cecilia called back.

"Why does Doña Mercedes want us going after reading material now, of all times?" Lebna asked.

"It might not be exactly a bookstore, so let's see what we find," Cecilia said.

"Great," Lebna groaned, "more mysteries—just what we need."

"Look, Lebna, these ancient elephants of our culture are revered because, according to Carmen, they hold its secrets, stories and rituals, which shape and sustain the community. But for how much longer? Who knows. I always thought Carmen was overreacting when she complained about the younger generation becoming too Americanized.

Now, I think she may be onto something. If it weren't for these ancient elephants, we wouldn't even know who to ask for help. And I'm not taking any chances—not with our lives on the line. Although my American side still thinks that this is all crazy nonsense.

"That one over there!" Cecilia then gestured as she headed towards a shop with the gold-lettered word "*Librería*" on its plate glass window.

Lebna caught up with Cecilia. "Whoa, it feels like I'm about to enter the wand shop in *Harry Potter*."

Julie's eyes were as big as saucers as they stepped through the shop's elaborately carved door.

"What? Are you looking for wizards now?" Cecilia rolled her eyes.

All of a sudden, long gnarled fingers waved them inside and all three girls got goosebumps. That's when they came face-to-face with Doña Jerónima, her amber eyes, hooked nose and crooked smile.

Cecilia tried to steady her nerves and muttered something of a greeting. Before she could even introduce herself, they found themselves hurried inside and led to a high-ceilinged, wood-paneled room, lined floor-to-ceiling with shelves filled with thick, black books. The old tomes were completely covered with dust, as if they hadn't been touched in decades.

Doña Jerónima slowed to a halt and turned to face her. "I know why you've come, girl," she croaked in Spanish. "You want information from my library."

"Uh, maybe," Cecilia muttered, also in Spanish. She no longer had to translate for her friends since they had been intensely studying Spanish, plus many people in Santa Cecilia spoke English.

"Yes," croaked the ancient one, "it is our community's *don* library . . . and you have questions."

"I don't understand," Cecilia said. "The books all look exactly alike."

"*Dons*. Each book contains the names of those having a specific *don* and how it was manifested. They also record the obstacles they confronted and overcame through the *don's* three stages."

"What are they? A *don's* three stages?" Cecilia blurted out.

"They correspond to the three virtues of faith, hope and charity," Doña Jerónima continued. "Faith is like when you immerse a seed in water and cause it to awaken and germinate. Hope is like when it grows, how the seed becomes a plant. And charity is how the *don's* fruit is shared. I'm saying this now because this is the time when your *don* grows. Picture a small plant breaking through the ground."

"Okay, I've grown, but . . . but . . . there's so much I don't . . ."

Doña Jerónima abruptly raised her bony hand and swept it across the spines of several books. "That one," she pointed directly at a tome on the fourth shelf. "Get that book for me."

Cecilia reached up, pulled it out and wiped the dust off the thick volume. On its cover, gilt letters spelled the word "Vocation."

"Now, bring it over to the table," Doña Jerónima ordered.

After she set the volume down, Cecilia watched Doña Jerónima carefully open it and point to an image of the Virgin Mary.

"The patron saint of *dons*," Doña Jerónima tapped her finger on the bright image.

Then she flipped to the back cover, and quickly swept her finger down an index of handwritten names with a page number next to each, before she stopped at a particular name and then turned to an image of a man in a friar's habit and the words "Junípero Serra" written right above it in calligraphy.

The three girls gasped with astonishment.

Doña Jerónima looked up at the ceiling and thought to herself, then turned the pages again. She pointed at what looked like some type of recipe. After she studied it for a few moments, she said, "*Chipotle.*" She then quickly shut the book and looked at Cecilia as if this was the answer to her question.

But what's the question? Cecilia stared blankly at Doña Jerónima.

Out of the blue, Lebna asked, "Are you saying that Junípero Serra added *chipotle* to his chocolate?"

What? Cecilia thought to herself. She began leaning toward Lebna to tell her to keep her mouth shut.

But Doña Jerónima gave Lebna a quick nod and said, "The shop across the plaza—the Shop of Chiles—has it. Go get it there." She turned and gestured towards the front door and added, "And hurry, so you can make it before the next rosary starts."

Cecilia was totally confused. Lebna shook Doña Jerónima's hand, thanked her and then hustled her friends out the door.

"What's going on?" Cecilia asked as Lebna dragged her across the plaza.

"We're going to buy *chipotle* . . . just like Doña Jerónima told us to do," Lebna ordered.

"But what does this have to do with our crisis?" Cecilia tripped on a cobblestone as she tried to keep up with Lebna's manic pace.

"How did you know what Doña Jerónima meant in the first place?" asked Julie.

"Come on, you two. I know because, while you two stared at books, Doña Jerónima whispered to me."

"She . . . did? What did she say?" Julie sputtered.

"Turns out, Junípero liked to spike his chocolate with *chipotle*. So that's why we need to buy some *chipotle* . . . so we can spike the chocolate we're making for him at your granny's," Lebna explained.

"But what does this have to do with the miracle we need?" Cecilia said.

"It will attract Junípero's soul, so we can ask him for help more directly," Lebna responded. She halted in front of a big, plate glass window that displayed pyramids of green, yellow, orange and red peppers, all shapes and sizes. "What kind of chile pepper is a *chipotle*, anyway?" she added as she pushed the shop door open.

Cecilia shrugged. She had never bothered to distinguish between the seemingly countless varieties of chiles that her mother cooked with—a chile was just a chile as far as she was concerned. But her mother and the generations before had a special name for every kind from *serrano* to *ancho* to *cascabel.*

The shop was neat and brightly lit. There were many baskets of fresh chiles, shelves with jars of pickled ones and strings of dried ones hung like garlands from the rafters. There didn't seem to be anyone around.

"Wow," Julie said, "I never realized there were so many different kinds of—"

Suddenly, there was a blast of laughter from the back room. A tiny, elfin man rolled out from the back in a wheelchair. His eyes were twinkling as he kept repeating, "*Chipotle! Chipotle! Chipotle!*" in between guffaws.

"I hear you girls want *chipotle!*" he finally announced as he rolled behind the counter and introduced himself as Don Diego.

Cecilia hesitated for a moment, then shook his hand, wondering how he knew. "Yes . . . we want to buy *chipotle.*"

"I know!" Don Diego said with a puckish grin. "Doña Jerónima just called me. That's why I turned on the shop lights."

"Gosh, I'm so sorry to disturb you," Cecilia said, all flustered as she realized that he was clad in red-striped flannel pajamas. "We'll run over to the *mercado* to get some . . . so you can go back to bed."

"The *mercado?*" Don Diego said, shaking his head. "You can't buy it there."

"But I saw heaps of chiles at the *mercado,*" Cecilia said, knitting her brow in confusion.

Don Diego let out another blast of laughter before he raised his hands high in the air and said, "Yes, of course you saw tons of chiles there, but those are for eating!"

"Yes?" Cecilia asked, confused once again.

"Those at the *mercado* are, like I said, for eating, for everyday living. But these here are for the working of *dons*. I'm telling you this," Don Diego said pointedly to Cecilia, "because your godmother Carmen told Doña Jerónima that we needed to complete all the *pláticas* you missed with her."

How could Carmen do this to me? Cecilia flushed with embarrassment.

"Don't worry," Don Diego said. "We all want to help you as much as we can, especially since you may have been intentionally kept away from your *pláticas* because your *don*—if you succeed in realizing it—is extremely needed. And this might also explain the difficult trials you've encountered so far . . . and the even harder ones to come."

Don Diego raised his hand and gestured towards the row of shelves below the shop window. "Go over there and bring me the jar that says *chipotle*."

With a quick nod, Cecilia, Julie and Lebna darted over to the shelves and scanned the labels on the rows upon rows of small glass jars.

"Is that it?" Julie asked as she pointed to one on the lower shelf.

Cecilia grabbed it and was surprised to find that it was a powder, richer in color than ground cinnamon.

"You seem confused about *chipotle*," Don Diego said, taking the jar and turning it over in the light like someone admiring a precious stone. "See, *chipotle* starts off as a green *jalapeño* pepper. When it's left on the plant to mature, it turns red. Then after it's smoked and dried, it becomes *chipotle*. Junípero Serra liked *chipotle* because *he* changed names too. And you, Cecilia," he added, placing the jar in her hand, "might also do the same . . . once you realize your *don*."

"How much is it?" Cecilia reached for her wallet.

Don Diego raised his open palms and said, "Nothing! Since it's for your *don*. I really hope it helps." Next, he bent over, opened a drawer, dropped something into a small paper bag and presented it to Cecilia. "And here's a little *pilón*, a little extra."

"Thank you so much." Cecilia bowed her head slightly.

"And you'll soon see that the *pilón* is for all three of you." Don Diego flashed the girls a bright smile.

"Oh, thank you," Julie and Lebna chimed in.

After they thanked him again, the girls hurried on.

"What's in the bag . . . candy?" Lebna asked as they crossed the plaza on their way to Cecilia's grandparents' house.

"One thing at a time. . . . Let's wait until after we make Junípero his cup of chocolate," Cecilia said.

❦　❦　❦

Cecilia poured the frothy hot chocolate she had just made into a cup for Junípero Serra.

"How much do I add?" asked Lebna, holding up the jar of *chipotle*.

"I don't know," Cecilia said as she filled three more cups, "but don't forget that we have to drink his cup afterwards."

"A pinch?" Lebna asked. She took a whiff of the open jar and quickly tossed her head back. "Gosh, it smells potent!"

"About a teaspoon," Cecilia said.

"I can't drink that much," Julie piped in.

"How hot is *chipotle* anyway?" asked Lebna.

"Look, I don't know, but we really don't want to screw this up," Cecilia said in an exasperated tone. "Think of this as trying to get Junípero's attention. So . . . the more, the better. That's why I think we need at least a teaspoon, especially since he lived such a rugged life, constantly traveling up and down the California coast, from San Diego to San Francisco—to establish his nine missions."

"Okay." Lebna scooped out a teaspoon, then stirred the *chipotle* powder into Junípero's chocolate.

"Whoa! It does smell potent." Cecilia sniffed the steam that rose from the cup. *One step at a time . . . one step at a time*, she reminded herself and sat in the chair in front of her cup. Julie and Lebna sat down in front of theirs. They left a chair empty in front of Junípero's cup.

"Let's start this *plática*," Cecilia said. She spoke directly to Junípero's cup and then to the empty seat where he was supposed to come sit. Then, after she remembered Doña Faustina and how she conducted her *pláticas*, Cecilia cleared her throat and said, "So . . . Junípero Serra . . . patron saint for our much needed miracle . . . we're asking for your help again."

Just then, the kitchen door flew open and Marie dashed in. "There you are!" she said with a big smile. "I see you're having some chocolate before the rosary begins." When she noticed the cup in front of the empty chair, she asked, "And who's the fourth lucky person?"

Cecilia exchanged a panicked look with Julie. Lebna jumped to her feet and exclaimed, "Please don't sit there!"

"Why?" Marie was startled.

"Sorry, Marie, I didn't mean to be rude. It's just that we're not simply having chocolate. We're actually conducting a sort of *plática* with Junípero Serra."

"The Franciscan friar who established the missions in California?"

"Yes, Mom," Julie piped up. "Instructions from Doña Mercedes. And Doña Jerónima, one of her friends."

"But why Junípero Serra, if I may ask?" Marie said.

Julie took the initiative and replied, "Because he's somehow connected to our science project."

"Oh . . . okay," Marie said, turning to leave.

"Wait!" Cecilia rushed after Marie. "Please join us," she added, catching Marie by the arm.

"Don't be silly," Marie shook her head. "I'm the one who intruded. You don't have to make nice with me."

"Look," Cecilia explained, "if there really are no coincidences—as we've been taught to believe here—then there might be something to you walking in at the exact moment I started asking for Junípero's help." She gestured towards the table. "Please sit down with us."

Marie nodded and joined the girls at the table.

Cecilia poured her a cup of chocolate. Then she sat down again, cleared her throat and focused on Junípero's cup. "Dear Junípero, turning to the big miracle we need. . . . We're asking for you to help us destroy this new curse. And now we'll drink our cups of chocolate—as well as yours—and wait for your guidance." Cecilia paused again and looked around the table at her companions. She whispered, "Want to add anything?"

After she blinked her eyes rapidly several times, Marie looked at the girls and said in a low, solemn tone, "Well, I sure hope I can be of some help to this team—whatever's going on—so please help me with that."

"Let's now drink to our bond," Cecilia said. She lifted her cup and took a big sip as she watched the others do the same.

They all proceeded to drain their cups and felt the hot chocolate electrify them. Cecilia then realized that Marie had to drink a quarter of Junípero's *chipotle*-spiked chocolate to successfully complete the ritual.

"Ah . . . Marie," Cecilia said, taking a deep breath, "as you may know, from your *pláticas* with Doña Faustina, part of the ritual is to drink the guest's cup. But let me warn you, we added a potent *chile* powder to Junípero's chocolate, since we were told that that's how he drank it. It's supposed to be a powerful way to get his attention. I hope this is okay with you."

Marie nodded and reached for Junípero's cup. "Okay, I'll go first." She brought the cup to her lips and its strong, sharp scent went straight up her nose, causing her to start coughing uncontrollably. When she finally stopped coughing, she forced herself to take a quick sip and almost spat it right out. It was *that* spicy!

Julie, Lebna and Marie stared at Cecilia as if they had been served poison. Cecilia flashed them a smile and forced herself to drink, trying her hardest not to react. Then she slid the cup over to Lebna.

Shifting in her chair, Lebna shuddered slightly and asked, "How does it taste?"

"I think it's part of Junípero's answer," Cecilia said.

"What do you mean?" Lebna asked.

"Drink your part and we'll compare notes," Cecilia said.

Sighing, Lebna grabbed the cup and took the tiniest sip. Then, she plunked the cup down and began to fan her open mouth rapidly. "Wow!" She clutched her throat. "It's hot!"

Julie followed suit and uttered the words the other girls had come to expect: "Oh my god!"

"I'll go again," Marie said and saw that the cup was still almost full.

The girls were astonished when Marie took a big gulp. She smiled, then drained the whole cup and said, "Wow, that was great!"

"Right," Cecilia said sarcastically. Her throat still burned. "So let's now have a *plática* about how Junípero's *chipotle* chocolate might help us."

"How about we write it down?" Lebna said.

Cecilia jumped up and went to get her backpack, out of which she handed each person a pen and a sheet of paper. All four quickly jotted down their thoughts and folded their slips. Lebna got up and brought a bowl to the table, and they tossed their papers in .

"Since it's your idea." Cecilia pushed the bowl over to Lebna, "why don't you do the honor of picking one?"

Lebna placed her open hands over the bowl and said, "Junípero, let the paper I pick provide a clue to help us break the curse." She shut her eyes and shook the bowl before she reached in and pulled one out.

The four of them stared at the folded slip, riveted.

"Look inside the *pilón* bag," Lebna read.

The girls had all but forgotten about the extra gift they were given at the chile shop.

Cecilia got to her feet and darted over to where she had hung her coat. After taking the *pilón* bag out of her coat pocket, she raced back. She expected to find an assortment of hard, bright candy inside. But, when she opened the bag, she was stunned to see a bunch of rocks instead.

"What's inside?" Julie asked. She almost danced in anticipation.

"Rocks," Cecilia announced as she pulled one out, looking disappointed.

Lebna seized the stone and turned it around in her fingers. "It's got something written on it," she said. "It's the name San Gabriel. Look!"

"And this one says San Capistrano!" Cecilia looked stumped.

Julie picked one up and read, "San Diego."

Marie read out the rest: "San Carlos . . . San Luis Obispo . . . Santa Clara . . . San Antonio . . . San Buenaventura . . . and this last one? Um, San Francisco."

"What does this mean?" Lebna asked and shook her head.

"These are the nine missions that Junípero Serra founded along the California coast," Marie said with a smile.

"But aren't there twenty-one, not nine, missions?" Lebna said.

"Yes, but I read that the others were founded after his death by his fellow friar Lasuén," replied Marie.

Cecilia nodded. She wondered how this all fit in. Suddenly, the door flew open and the prayer group ladies rushed in. The girls greeted them with smiles as they got busy making pots of coffee.

Shortly afterwards, everyone gathered in the living room for the rosary, which Doña Mercedes again began by lighting a candle and crossing herself. At the end of the rosary petitions, Cecilia fell back in her chair with a deep sense of relief, glad she hadn't heard anyone ask for Micaela to help her break the new curse, although she wondered how many had asked silently.

CHAPTER 37

On the day of the eighth rosary, as Cecilia poured coffee into a thermos in her *abuelitos'* kitchen, Lebna whispered to her, "We only have one more rosary."

Cecilia tensed up. "And?" She gave Lebna a hard look to signal that she shouldn't say anything in front of Marie, who was right behind them.

"What are you trying to hide from me?" Marie stepped between them. "I know you're keeping something from me, something really important." Then she took them by their hands and pulled them down the hallway into the room where Cecilia was staying. Julie followed them.

Marie shut the door and crossed her arms heavily over her chest. She looked them straight in the eye. "If we're truly a team, then tell me what's going on."

Cecilia hung her head and said, "It's nothing, just ridiculous nonsense, not worth . . ."

"Well, I want to hear it, regardless of how absurd it might sound," Marie insisted. She reminded them about the days she spent driving dishes and brooms and hotel plants around—proof of her absolute immunity to thinking anything was too crazy.

Cecilia, Julie and Lebna could not stop themselves from tittering with laughter as Marie went on about all the ludicrous things she had given car rides to, willingly and without judgment, fulfilling every last one of Doña Faustina's assignments.

Cecilia told her, as quickly as possible, the story of the first Cecilia and what they feared might happen after the ninth rosary: that, after Micaela reached heaven, she would intervene to crush the curse, and, for her to succeed, it might cost the lives of Cecilia and perhaps the entire team. Marie looked astonished, but didn't utter a word.

⚜ ⚜ ⚜

Later, when the prayer ladies, friends and family headed to the kitchen for a cup of coffee, and the room was almost empty, Lebna, Julia, Marie and Cecilia stayed behind.

Cecilia fell heavily into a chair in front of her team. "You know, I've been thinking that you don't have to stay for the last rosary."

"No way!" Marie quickly retorted. She turned to Lebna. "I told you she would do this, didn't I?"

Lebna nodded in agreement. But then she told the group, "Wait a second . . . it's probably nothing, but Marie just said something that made me think."

"What?" Marie interjected. "What did I say?"

"It's just a hunch, but when you warned me earlier, after Cecilia told you what had happened to Little Cecilia after the ninth rosary, that she would tell us to skip the last rosary and return home . . . I suddenly remembered that you've also predicted other things."

"She has? I didn't know that," Cecilia said.

"Yes, she has," Lebna continued. "But I didn't want to bother you about it. What I'm getting at is that Marie seems to have the uncanny ability to predict the future."

Lebna paused to study Marie's tight, pensive expression. When she glanced at Cecilia, she found her casting a worried look at Marie. "So, I was wondering," Lebna added, turning back towards Marie, "if you have any inkling about the new curse . . . ?"

"Yes, Mom," Julie raised her voice, "can you see what will happen . . . what we might expect?"

Marie looked stricken. She shook her head.

"Don't worry about it," Cecilia reassured her. Then she cast Lebna a sharp look.

"Yes, it was just a silly thought," Lebna said. She wondered whether she should have kept her big mouth shut. Maybe Marie's sudden paleness and faraway look were a sign that she was feeling depressed again.

"Okay, time for bed," Lebna announced. She pulled Marie to her feet, then helped her with her coat, before the four walked out to the car.

When Cecilia asked Marie if she was okay, Marie gave Cecilia a faint smile and shut the car door without saying a word. She sped away without giving the girls even a minute to say goodbye to each other.

The next morning, Cecilia raced over to the hotel earlier than usual. She was concerned about Marie.

"How's Marie?" Cecilia asked Julie at the door to their hotel room.

"She left super early this morning," Julie responded, waving her inside. "But don't worry, she looks okay. She spoke to Doña Faustina for a very long time."

Cecilia said that she had talked to Carmen for a long time too.

"What did Carmen say?"

"She said to do our schoolwork."

"How can we possibly . . . possibly concentrate on our schoolwork? The ninth rosary is today! Oh my god!" Julie said and slapped her hands over her face.

"Let's try, okay? Let's hit the books," Cecilia said and took her laptop out of her backpack just as Lebna joined them.

Lebna sighed and thought that she couldn't even pretend to do her schoolwork at a time like this. "Do you want some coffee?"

Cecilia and Julie both nodded. They realized this might help them release some of their nervous tension. After Lebna brought in the coffee, the girls worked until lunchtime. Then they met Marie in the hotel restaurant.

"I think I finally get this thing about the three mothers," Julie said. She bit into a *carnitas* taco.

"And what is it?" Marie asked.

"Well, I get that one of the three mothers is the Virgin Mary, the patron saint of *dons*. And that the second one is associated with the Ethiopian coffee ceremony . . . since we're all descended from the same mother who came from Ethiopia . . . where coffee was discovered."

"Go on," said Lebna with a smile on her face.

"*So who's the third mother?*" Julie continued. "That's what I kept asking myself, not wanting to believe that it was Mom, as we did last time, thinking that Doña Faustina and Cecilia were just being polite. But now I get it," she added as she turned and gave her mother a long wink before she leaned back in her chair.

Cecilia and Lebna traded startled looks. Marie squeezed Julie's arm and told her, "Given your friends' bewildered looks, I don't believe I'm the only one who doesn't think you've answered the question of the third mother. Right, girls?"

"It's really you, Mom!" Julie clapped Marie on the back.

"And why are you finally convinced that I am the third mother? Because you're dazzled at my *don* assignments, to be the chauffeur of brooms and dishes?" She gave a loud click with her tongue.

"Exactly!" Julie laughed. "No, seriously," she added, "it's because you really inspire me with your attitude and total focus on finding your *don* . . . especially since it's looking more and more like you're an Uber driver for household objects! It's so wacky . . . it's divine! You're like the perfect *don* seeker!"

Marie gave Julie a quick peck on the cheek before she swept her arms across the table and said, "Okay, team, listen up when the third mother speaks. Finish your tacos: that is an order. For the final rosary, we have to prepare the coffee ceremony . . . with the other two mothers. Not just make coffee like we've done for the other rosaries."

The girls nodded and polished off their lunches. Shortly afterwards, they climbed into the car and headed to Cecilia's grandparents' house.

As they passed the church, Cecilia thought of the first Cecilia and felt a chill shoot up her spine. There was no denying that today's rosary was the final one. She and her friends had laughed earlier, but it was to mask the fear they felt—and constantly talked about—because they had failed to destroy the curse before the ninth rosary. They were still clueless, for instance, about the meaning of the rocks they had found inside the *pilón* bag, except that they bore the names of Junípero Serra's nine missions. And each time her friends had expressed anxiety about the approaching final rosary, she had reminded them that the ancient ones—Doña Faustina, Doña Benedicta and Doña Mercedes—were still praying and working hard to protect them.

CHAPTER 38

"**Y**our *abuelito* is outside, making a fire for your coffee," Cecilia's grandmother said as she greeted Marie and the girls.

"Why?" Cecilia asked.

"Doña Mercedes stopped by and said that Carmen had called to tell her that the coffee you girls prepare for each rosary should be replaced by your special coffee ceremony for the ninth one. Carmen got the instruction to call Doña Mercedes from Doña Benedicta and Doña Faustina. We were told that we should start a fire."

After the girls shot Marie an astonished look, they walked through the house and out the back door to find that Cecilia's grandfather had made a roaring blaze. After he greeted them with a friendly smile, he rearranged the silvery logs as they shifted and crackled, and said, "The coals are ready. Where do you want me to put them?"

Lebna removed a round metal pan from her coffee bundle that she had brought from the hotel room. She said, "I need to roast the green coffee beans on this, over a fire."

Cecilia's grandfather gave a slight nod, then strode over to the side of the oven, grabbed some bricks piled there and stacked them on the ground in front of the oven. "This should work," he said. He took the metal pan and set it over the bricks. Then he shoveled and raked up a heap of reddish coals and placed them under the pan. "That should do it. And I'll keep the fire going in case you need more coals."

After they thanked him several times, Cecilia and Julie helped Lebna place her coffee items on the oven's ledge. Lebna took a cupful of green coffee beans from her sack and said, "I'll start roasting them now." She then poured them onto the hot pan with a clatter.

"Wow," Marie exclaimed as she watched Lebna stir the beans around and around with a metal spoon, "I've never seen this done before."

Julie explained that the ritual had begun. "We have to keep quiet and concentrate on sending good thoughts . . . because we want the coffee to attract the *don* we desperately need. It's not like we're at a barbeque or watching the Cooking Channel."

Cecilia and Lebna burst out laughing, unable to stop themselves despite their grim situation.

Marie flashed Lebna a sheepish look. Then she bowed her head slightly and wondered what kind of *don* could stop the curse. Suddenly, her thoughts shifted to what Lebna had said about her uncanny ability to predict what would happen. *What will happen?*

The earthy, sharp smell of roasted coffee beans caught Marie's attention. She noticed golden-brown, translucent specks rising from the pan and fluttering like miniature butterflies. *What in the world are those?* She was transfixed, not realizing that the flying flecks were the skins flaking off the roasted beans.

Julie and Cecilia looked on, mesmerized. Although they had witnessed the ceremony before, it somehow felt more enchanting and other-worldly here, in front of the crackling fire, under the open sky and luminous moon.

Cecilia watched the coffee skins ascend slowly into the night sky like tiny angels. She took a deep breath and filled her lungs with the pungent fragrance of the roasting beans. She wondered how the nine stones that Don Diego had given them might fit together to help them fight the curse. She had been staying up late at night to read everything she could find about Junípero Serra. What struck her most— beyond the childlike, irrepressible spirit that stirred him to do seemingly impossible things—was his dying the happy death he had always wished for.

Julie, on the other hand, struggled to conjure any good thoughts to project onto the ritual. *Good thoughts! Only good thoughts!* she chanted to herself. She pressed her eyes shut and clenched her fists until she finally got a glimpse in her mind of baby Micaela with angel wings in heaven next to Michael the Archangel. This allowed her to relax enough to turn her attention to the ritual.

Lebna moved the coffee beans continuously around the pan while she listened intently for the first pop. How proud she felt as she performed this sacred ritual of her mother-land—of everyone's motherland. Then, she gazed up at the star-studded night sky and felt illuminated by a thought: the curse could be destroyed if everyone had the awareness that we are all related, that evil was what separated us, one from the other, and even from our true selves.

Lebna finally heard a distinct pop and said, "Just a bit more . . . until the second pop." With that, she swirled the beans faster—their color now a rich, dark brown. When the sound of the second pop finally came, Lebna lifted the pan off the hot coals and poured the roasted beans into a metal colander Julie held.

"Shake it—vigorously," Lebna instructed, "while I roast the next batch."

And that's how it went for the next hour. Lebna roasted batch after batch of green coffee beans until they were the color of chocolate, while Julie shook them and cooled them off. At last, six bowlfuls sat on the oven ledge.

"Now, we can grind them."

"But how?" Cecilia asked Lebna. "Isn't the traditional way—based on what you've told us—using a wooden mortar and pestle?"

"We'll use a coffee grinder this time," Lebna said as she extracted one from her bundle. "All we need is an electric outlet."

They gathered the six bowls and went into the kitchen, where the girls made quick work of grounding the roasted beans. They would brew the coffee right after the rosary.

Twenty minutes later, Doña Mercedes began the ninth rosary for Micaela's final ascension into heaven the way she usually did, by crossing herself. But, this time, she paused and announced, "Today we will pray for Micaela's soul to enter through the gates of heaven. As soon as she does this, she will be able to intercede and help our community."

Doña Mercedes turned and fixed her gaze on Cecilia. So did everyone else. Stunned, Cecilia shifted nervously in her chair as a surge of heat shot up her spine and through her entire body. *Why is Doña Mercedes doing this?* Cecilia clenched her fists and stared at a blank spot on the wall.

"And we pray that Micaela, once in heaven," Doña Mercedes continued, "helps her sister Cecilia find her true *don and bring her gifts to fruition.*"

Cecilia dropped her head and looked out of the corner of her eye. Everyone she saw nodded and looked at her with concern—everyone except Lebna, Julie and Marie, who looked stricken.

Then the group began praying the rosary. They ended with petitions, and one was once again for Micaela to help her sister discover her *don,* "so she can help destroy the curse, like Little Cecilia did."

"Please stay in your seats while Cecilia and her friends prepare a special surprise for us," said Doña Mercedes.

Cecilia felt overwhelmed as she entered the kitchen, especially since she was the one most likely to be "gifted" with the curse-killing *don.* She spotted Lebna, who stood in front of the stove putting scoops of ground coffee beans into her Ethiopian coffee pot.

"How can we help?" Marie said.

"We need cups for everyone, plus a tray to carry them on," Lebna replied as she added water to the pot.

"What about the popcorn?" Julie asked and peeked inside Lebna's burlap bundle.

"Popcorn?" Marie shot Julie a stern look, trying to communicate that this was no time to be flippant.

"Yes, popcorn!" Julie insisted. "That's the tradition . . . right, Lebna? Serving popcorn with the coffee?"

Lebna lowered the flame under the pot and said, "Yes, but I wasn't sure. . . . well, what do you think, Cecilia? I did bring a bag of popcorn kernels. . . ."

"You sure think of everything," Cecilia said with a chuckle. "Why not? Especially since corn originated in Mexico."

After a few minutes, Marie inhaled the scent of the brewing coffee and the popping corn. "My, it smells so good."

As the coffee brewed, the girls loaded a tray with small, green-glazed cups. Marie cleared her throat and announced proudly, "Do you know that I have given these very cups a ride in my car? Twice!"

The girls wondered if Marie's ridiculous *don* assignments actually had a secret purpose.

"Wow, Mom, that's awesome!" Julie replied. She turned her attention to the pot on the stove where a few pieces of freshly popped corn leapt from the hot oil.

"*Palomitas*. That's what they're called here: butterflies," Cecilia said to Marie, picking up popcorn that had flown onto the counter.

"That's fitting, don't you think?"

"How so, Mom?" Julie said, making a second batch of popcorn.

"Well, a kernel of corn is transformed by heat into popcorn, which has the shape of a butterfly like the metamorphosis of a caterpillar into a butterfly . . . don't you think?" Marie added a stack of napkins to the tray.

"Mom, you're so poetic." Julie rolled her eyes.

But Cecilia wondered if her own metamorphosis would turn her into a dead thing like Little Cecilia, or one of the unpopped but burnt kernels that sometimes flew out of the pot and onto the floor.

"Okay, the coffee's ready!" Lebna turned off the burner. "Now, hand me the cloth inside the bag," she instructed Cecilia.

After stretching the cloth over the mouth of the pot and holding it there to serve as a sieve, Lebna began to fill the cups on the tray with the coffee. Heat rose from each cup, drawing lines of steam that floated in the air like streamers at a party.

Cecilia watched the streamers come together into one.

After Lebna had placed the coffee pot back on the burner, she spread her open hands over the cups and said in a low, solemn tone: "There, it's done."

Cecilia then asked Marie about the two other mothers, to complete the ritual.

"Pray to Mary, the patron saint of *dons*," Marie replied. "And, as for the third mother, let's all commit to finding our *dons*—however difficult that might be." The group nodded, held hands around the coffee cups, shut their eyes and prayed.

"I'll go tell Doña Mercedes that everything's ready," Cecilia said as she opened her eyes. "And I'll move the table where the coffin sat. We can put everything there."

The others nodded as Cecilia disappeared down the hallway. Then they exchanged a baffled look.

"I can't believe she's using the same table they put the coffin on." Julie shook her head.

"Remember that Micaela's in heaven now," Marie responded, giving her daughter a gentle pat on the back.

With that, they picked up the coffee service and popcorn and marched solemnly into the living room where everyone waited in total silence. Lebna carefully set the coffee down on the table in the middle of the room. Four white, tapered candles flickered and tossed looming shadows onto the white walls. Julie placed the popcorn bowls beside the coffee tray and Marie set the smaller tray with spoons, sugar and napkins to one side.

After everyone had taken their seats, Doña Mercedes approached the table, spread her hands over the steaming cups and closed her eyes. She said that they would ask, now that Micaela was in heaven, for the urgently needed *don*. She dropped her hands and opened her eyes, then she asked them all to come up, to take a cup of coffee and to drink it slowly, thoughtfully, with this special request in mind. The popcorn, she added, was to feed and fire up their souls.

Cecilia took her cup in both hands and silently toasted her little sister, who was now apparently a soul in heaven. She took a sip. The hot liquid slid down her throat, and she was invigorated by its strong, rich taste. She took a deeper gulp and glanced around. Everyone stared at her.

Later, as the girls and Marie helped tidy up the kitchen, Julie put down the cup she had just dried and remarked to her team, "Well, the good news is that we're all still alive. Right?"

Cecilia groaned and continued to sweep the floor, while Marie and Lebna didn't even bother to respond. They thought that Julie had reverted to being flip out of fear. They finished the cleanup, and Marie, Julie and Lebna said their goodbyes to Cecilia's grandparents.

When Cecilia accompanied them to their car, Julie was bubbly. "Boy, I can't wait for the Day of the Dead. I bet it'll be really interesting!"

"Either way, I guess you're right," Lebna snickered after she exchanged a quick look with Cecilia and Marie.

"What do you mean?" Julie asked.

"What I mean," said Lebna as she opened the car door, "is that I'm sure it'll be interesting, whether we welcome the visiting souls or whether we're the souls who come visiting."

Julie hung her head.

To lighten the mood, Cecilia changed the subject. "Let's focus on our science project. We really need to get going on it. I'll be over early in the morning to work on it."

As Cecilia hurried back inside, she recalled that her parents had said that she needed to stay in Santa Cecilia for the Day of the Dead to fully understand why they couldn't have simply buried Micaela in San Jose.

Just then, her heart sank as the fear of the curse overcame her.

CHAPTER 39

Early the next morning, Cecilia and her grandparents sat around the kitchen table having *pan dulce* and hot chocolate for breakfast.

"Do you really believe that souls return on the Day of the Dead?" she asked her grandmother.

"Come on now, tell your granddaughter," her grandfather urged. "Tell her how your mother went from being the worst heretic to becoming the biggest believer in the Day of the Dead."

Her grandmother nodded, then began: "My mother was named Josefina and was known throughout Santa Cecilia as a very practical woman. When my father's mother died unexpectedly just days before the Day of the Dead and he had to travel to Mexico City on urgent business, he gave my mother money to honor his mother on this day.

"Being the practical woman that she was, Josefina thought the Day of the Dead rituals were just plain silly. That it was wishful thinking or Mexican superstition to believe that souls actually returned to visit on the Day of the Dead. So, she used the money to fix their leaky roof instead.

"Then one morning, while she sat in her kitchen and darned a sock, she was startled by the continous ringing of the church bells. That's when she realized what day it was and remembered the promise she had made to my father.

But, again, being a practical woman, she soon shrugged and went back to her sewing.

"But as the bells kept ringing, which is the town's traditional way of welcoming its departed souls for their yearly visit, Josefina began to feel the tiniest bit of guilt. She glanced around and noticed the *nopal* cactus right outside the window. She got to her feet, grabbed a knife and plate, stepped outside and lopped off a big cactus pad, thorns and all, and plunked it on the kitchen table. She then snatched a picture of her late mother-in-law, set it next to the cactus pad, and lit a candle. After that, she went back to her sock.

"Three days later, she answered the front door and found her husband glaring at her with spooked, bloodshot eyes. Thinking he was having a stroke, she grabbed him by the arm so he wouldn't fall, but he pushed her off and demanded to know what she had done to honor his mother on the Day of the Dead. Stunned, Josefina feared that if she told him the truth, it would surely kill him. Therefore, she looked him square in the eyes and said that she had prepared not only a pot of *pozole*, his mother's favorite dish, but also turkey *mole*, her second favorite. She said she bought her favorite flowers, the whitest candles and had even made an altar, where she had placed her picture and presented her with all these offerings.

"Somewhat satisfied, my father lumbered over to the kitchen table and dropped into a chair. And after he drained his second cup of strong coffee, he sat up, rubbed his swollen eyes and said in a barely audible voice that, on his ride home, in the middle of nowhere, he spotted what looked like an old woman walking in the distance. As he got closer, he could hear her crying, so he hurried his horse over and asked if he could help her in any way. The woman stopped, then slowly raised her head and looked straight at him. That's when he fell off his horse, shocked to see the face of his own mother, clutching a thorny *nopal* to her chest. And then she disappeared right before his eyes."

☙ ☙ ☙

Later, while Cecilia knocked on the door of her friends' hotel room, she couldn't wait to tell them about what she had just heard at the breakfast table.

"You're not going to believe it!" she exclaimed when Julie and Lebna opened the door. "This morning my grandmother told me something that's going to break your *piñatas*."

"What?" Julie grimaced. "Something spooky, I bet."

"I'm afraid so," Cecilia said. "Look, I don't want to scare you. But this just might help us with the science project . . . *and* explain why my parents, grandparents and Carmen insisted I stay to experience the Day of the Dead."

"Okay, what is it?" Lebna asked impatiently.

With great detail, Cecilia re-told the story about her great-grandparents.

"Oh my god!" Julie slapped her open mouth with her hand. "That would turn me into the biggest believer in the Day of the Dead too."

"Yes, but how is this useful for our science project?" Lebna asked.

"I don't know . . . not exactly," Cecilia answered. "I'm hoping to start getting some clues first thing tomorrow, when we start to prepare for the Day of the Dead. But, for now, let's get cracking on our science project, brainstorming at least, since we need to document all the clues we can find."

❧ ❧ ❧

The next morning, Marie, Julie and Lebna joined Cecilia for breakfast with her grandparents. Afterwards, they accompanied Cecilia and her grandmother to the plaza to shop for the Day of the Dead, while Cecilia's grandfather set off to get the things needed to build the altar.

The square was dazzling. Streamers of elaborately cut-out paper, called *papel picado*, fluttered overhead; shop windows glowed with bright treasures; and heaps of orange marigolds or *cempasúchil* were everywhere. The delicious fragrance of chocolate wafted from one corner of the square and the aroma of spicy *mole* from another. People darted from shop to shop, and the air was pulsing with energy.

Cecilia's grandmother and entourage stopped at one shop for chocolate, at another for flowers, at the next for candles and then, at the last, to buy *pan de muerto*, a loaf of egg bread shaped like a sleeping baby with a baby's face.

When they got home, they found Cecilia's grandfather in the living room, tying two tall cane poles together at the top and shaping them into an arch. Marie immediately accompanied Cecilia's grandmother to the kitchen to help her prepare *tamales* and a big pot of turkey *mole*. The girls dashed back and forth. They helped Cecilia's grandmother prepare the food and they helped her grandfather create an altar by stacking boxes of narrowing widths, one on top of the other, then draping a blanket over them and finally overlaying each step with a different color of *papel picado*.

The boxes were transformed into a glorious pyramid with a total of nine steps to the top.

❧   ❧   ❧

On the Day of the Dead, everyone gathered at the church to follow the other-worldly procession of solemn-looking children dressed as skeletons, witches, vampires and other dark creatures to parade through the streets behind a loud, thunderous brass band.

"They purify the town so that the souls feel safe to return. Today the children will return and tomorrow the adults," Cecilia's grandmother explained.

What a contrast, thought Cecilia as she recalled the thrill and silly costumes she associated with Halloween.

At twelve noon, right after the procession wound its way back to the church, the bells began to ring and ring and ring.

"They're ringing to welcome them back," Cecilia's grandfather said and raised his eyes to the sky.

Cecilia glanced up and gasped. A shaft of light beamed down to form a slide for the baby souls to return. Her friends could not believe it either. They stared wide-eyed into the heavens and felt they were witnessing something from another world.

"Let's hurry home," the grandparents said in unison and started across the plaza with the others close behind. After they stepped inside, Cecilia's grandfather rushed off and returned with a photo of Micaela, which he placed at the very top of the pyramid altar. Then he brought the two framed pictures that hung in Cecilia's room—Carmen's and

Nica's deceased little sisters—which he put next to Micaela's.

"Come," Cecilia's grandmother said as she twined her arm in hers. "It's time for you to make Micaela a cup of chocolate."

Soon after, the girls placed three cups of hot chocolate and bowls of rice pudding on the altar by several flickering candles. Then they sat down quietly at the foot of the pyramid. Cecilia gazed at Micaela's photo and wondered if she was already there. She turned towards Marie and found her looking sad. *Is she thinking about her lost child?*

As dusk approached, Cecilia's grandfather suddenly rose to his feet and left the room. He returned shortly with a sack over his shoulder and a broom in his hand. Marie jumped up to get her bag. Cecilia's grandmother hurried to the kitchen after her.

The girls traded baffled looks. When Cecilia's grandmother and Marie reappeared, her grandmother carried a big straw basket and Marie held a small bundle in her hands. Cecilia insisted she carry the basket for her grandmother and found it much heavier than she expected. Marie waved Julie away, saying she didn't need any help to carry her bundle. She refused to tell anyone what was inside.

The group left the house and walked up the hill to the cemetery where they had buried Micaela days earlier. The graveyard was brilliantly illuminated. The sweet perfume of flowers permeated the air. Festive music played. The somber-looking graves were now laid out like stately dinner tables, with dishes of delicious foods, drinks and sweet treats. Family members of the deceased sat all around them. They ate, they laughed, they talked.

Cecilia's group arrived at Micaela's grave, where a white marble headstone and slab had just been laid. Cecilia's grandfather quickly dusted the slab with his handkerchief, before her grandmother took a white tablecloth from her basket and spread it on top. She then put down a dish of steaming *tamales* and a thermos of hot chocolate, along with plates and cups. Once Cecilia finished pouring a cup of frothy chocolate for her, they all sat around the decorated grave and feasted while they thought about Micaela.

We're inside an amazing, heavenly ballroom, thought Cecilia, as she looked at the countless families celebrating all around, at the luminous moon and dazzling stars above, while the perfumed breeze seemed to weave everyone and everything together. Then she saw her grandfather wave his hand in the air, and, a few moments later, a troupe of *mariachis* appeared in sparkling outfits of white and gold to serenade Micaela with the lovely song *Las Mañanitas*.

As the night grew darker, the cemetery felt even more other-worldly with the flickering of the hundreds upon hundreds of candles around them. Their glow projected the vibrant colors of the flowers into the night sky. Looking up, it felt as if distant stars had come to watch and join the festivities.

Marie turned to Cecilia's grandmother. "Doña Faustina asked me to adopt an orphan grave and said that I should ask you which one to pick."

Startled, Julie stared at her mother. She did not believe what she had just heard. Cecilia's grandmother gestured towards a tiny grave four down from Micaela's that was dark and crumbling.

"Can we come too?" Julie asked.

Marie nodded, and the three girls rose to their feet.

"So how do you adopt an orphan grave?" Julie asked as her mother set her bundle next to the tiny tomb.

"Watch and see," Marie said. She took a brush out of the bundle and scrubbed the moldy, dirty slab and the cracked headstone on which was etched the name of Pablo Reyes.

"It's to honor the soul I lost," Marie uttered while she snipped off the weeds that grew all along the sides of the grave with a pair of clippers.

"And what's that?" Julie said, watching her mother pour liquid onto a sponge and wipe the headstone, turning it whiter and whiter.

"A mixture of vinegar and water," Marie said.

Then Marie dried the headstone and slab with a towel and covered the slab with a white linen cloth. She set down a cup of hot chocolate, which she poured from a thermos in her bundle, along with a lit candle and a dish of candied fruit that sparkled like diamonds. Afterwards, Marie slowly lowered herself beside the festive tomb and closed her eyes, which prompted Julie to tear up.

Cecilia exchanged a quick look with Lebna, then left her sitting quietly with Marie and Julie. She walked back to Micaela's grave.

"Your grandmother is attending to our other two babies," her grandfather said. "Now, come with me. I want to show you something."

They crossed to the far side of the cemetery, where the adults were buried. Cecilia's grandfather said, "Tomorrow this section will be as alive and magical as the children's section is today, since that's when the adult souls return. Here," he continued while he pointed to two tombstones, side by side, "is where your great-grandparents are buried—Josefina and Jorge." He walked to another section where there was what looked like an ancient, abandoned grave, grown over with thorny, tangled vines and littered with trash. "And over here . . ."

"Why is this one such a mess?" Cecilia asked. "Did his family die off? Or does trouble over the border mean no one comes back to celebrate anymore?"

"No, it's because he's buried upside down," her grandfather said with a short laugh.

"Why?"

"That's the grave of the first curse . . . where he's buried, the evil man. And he's buried upside down so that, on each and every Day of the Dead, he can continue digging himself deeper and deeper into hell."

Cecilia stared at the grave and felt a chill when she realized that the devil had actually been present in Santa Cecilia.

At midnight, on their way back home, Cecilia and her friends were surprised to hear her grandfather say that many families spent the entire night at the cemetery, keeping company with their childrens' souls.

The next day, after they helped Cecilia's grandparents place their ancestors' favorite foods on the pyramid altar and honored them at their graves, Cecilia, Lebna and Julie helped Marie clean and decorate the orphan grave of a woman named María Ruiz who had been singled out by

Cecilia's grandparents. Marie told the girls that she had
adopted this grave to make her own soul feel whole again.

The day after that was All Souls Day. To celebrate, the
team placed a picture of Junípero Serra on the pyramid
along with twenty-one candles, one for each of the missions he and his fellow friars had founded all along the California coast. Then they presented him with a steaming cup
of *chipotle*-spiked hot chocolate, sat quietly at the foot of
the pyramid and silently asked him for guidance on how to
stop the new curse. They didn't want the planet to be
destroyed . . . and they didn't want to be destroyed, either.

Afterwards, sitting around the kitchen table, the team
wondered what to do next and felt as clueless as ever. They
were even more dejected than before because they had
really expected to be struck with all kinds of dazzling clues
and insights during the Day of the Dead festivities.

After a long awkward silence, punctuated with heavy
sighs, Julie suddenly jumped up and announced: "I got it!
Let's do a raffle of ideas!"

Lebna rolled her eyes and Cecilia let out the longest,
heaviest sigh before Marie leaned forward and said, "Girls,
since no one has a better idea, why not give Julie's a try?"

"Okay," said Cecilia, after she recalled Marie's uncanny
ability to predict the future. She went to her backpack and
took out paper and pens for the team.

Then, as if their lives depended on it—since they
believed this might truly be the case—they jotted down
their best idea for defeating the new curse, based on all the
impressions, thoughts, dreams and nightmares that they
had had so far. When they finished, they folded up their

slips of paper and tossed them into a bowl. They agreed to follow through on whatever idea was picked, regardless of how impossible or ridiculous it sounded. Finally, the girls insisted that Marie be the one to close her eyes and select the winning bet, since she had not only adopted orphan graves, but also given car rides to all the dishes, cleaning supplies and other things that had eventually been used to honor their dead.

CHAPTER 40

"Santa Claus?" Marie asked after she read the slip of paper.

"How can that possibly help us?" Julie said.

Lebna sighed. "Come on. We agreed to follow through, regardless."

Later, on the flight back to San Jose, Cecilia turned to Julie and said, "At least the curse hasn't killed us . . . yet, though we're still light years away from completing our science project."

"Don't say that—about the curse!"

"Julie, don't worry. As long as Doña Faustina lives, we'll be okay," Lebna reassured her.

"How do you know?"

"Well, Little Cecilia, by ending the first curse, allowed Doña Faustina to continue helping others, and now she's training Cecilia, so . . ." Suddenly, Lebna stopped talking and shot Cecilia a worried look.

"What's wrong?" Julie asked and pitched forward in her seat.

"Eh . . ."

"Out with it. You know the rules," Marie declared.

"I don't know for sure . . . but I think we're safe from the curse so long as Doña Faustina lives. But . . . if she dies, before she has trained Cecilia . . ."

"What?" Julie said.

"Nothing, that's what," Cecilia said with a laugh, "because the moment we land, I'm going straight to Doña Faustina's. That's what Carmen called about: to tell me that Doña Faustina wants to speed up my training."

"Can we come too?" Julie asked.

"Sure," Cecilia said and shut her eyes. She tried to forget what Lebna had said.

After they landed in San Jose, Cecilia's stomach dropped at the sight of her father standing by himself and looking unusually tense. *Where's Mom?*

Cecilia rushed towards him. "What's wrong?"

" . . . Doña Faustina," he said in a subdued tone before he gave her a hug.

"What about her?"

"She's in the hospital . . . in a coma," he said quietly before he greeted the others.

Julie turned pale.

"Is there anything we can do?" Marie said.

"Yes. Pray for her. Carmen found her slumped on her kitchen table. Nica and Carmen are with her now."

"Can I go see her?" Cecilia said.

"Your mom and Carmen will be home soon. Ask them."

An hour later, Cecilia ran to the front door at the sound of her mother's voice.

"How's Doña Faustina doing?"

"Still in a deep coma." Nica gave her daughter a kiss on the cheek.

"But we talked to her," Carmen said as she forced a slight smile.

"What?"

"Hearing is the last sense to go, so she can still hear us, even in a coma. Now let me make us some tea." Carmen darted off to the kitchen.

"Do you think the curse attacked Doña Faustina?" Cecilia asked her mother.

"M'ija, I don't know. Ask Carmen."

After they drank the pot of *manzanilla* tea, Nica said she was going to cook for tomorrow's route. At that, Carmen took Cecilia to her apartment for a *plática*.

"Is the coma a sign of the curse? And am I . . . I . . ."

"Next?!" Carmen switched on her kitchen light.

Cecilia stopped cold. "Are you serious?"

"Sit down," Carmen pulled out a chair at the table for her, then fell into the opposite one.

"What's going to happen next?"

"I should be asking you."

"Why?"

"You're the one who was being trained. But, now . . ."

"What?"

"I don't know. Let's pray that she snaps out of her coma . . . and for you."

"Me?"

"You were her apprentice."

"What about the others? Are they in danger too?"

"I don't know. Father Ramón was at the hospital when we were there, and he alerted Father Gómez. So we'll hear if anyone else gets hurt or dies."

"What should I tell my friends? Julie's already as scared as a spooked cat."

Carmen simply shook her head.

"Does Santa Claus mean anything to you?" Cecilia asked. She realized her team might be in real danger.

"What are you talking about?"

"It's a crazy clue we got."

"Ask Father Ramón. Christmas is around the corner, and that's the time he starts decorating the church with all kinds of mysterious things."

"Like what?"

"Flying angels tossing orbs of light all around the nativity scene he sets up."

"Should I talk to Mom too, since she was named after Saint Nicholas?"

"No. You're dealing with the curse, *El Diablo* and his demons—the opposite of what your mom represents. On the other hand, Father Ramón, I understand, was given a *don* angel to protect him as a priest. So he's the one to talk to."

"What's a *don* angel?"

"Another mystery, but one you'll have to ask him about."

"Can I take my friends?"

"Ask him. Father Ramón knows you were being trained by Doña Faustina, so I'm sure he's anxious to help you in any way he can."

The next day, Marie picked the girls up after school and drove to the rectory, where Father Ramón agreed to meet them.

"Oh my god!" Julie said as she turned around and gazed at Cecilia and Lebna in the back seat. "I wonder if Father Ramón is going to tell us his *don* angel helps him fight demons, like in *The Exorcist?*"

"Sweetie, calm down." Marie tapped her on the knee. "He's been nice enough to have us tag along, so you need to—"

"We're not just tagging along! The curse is after all of us! Right, Cecilia?"

"I don't know what he'll say." Cecilia tried to ease the tension. "Let's take it one step at a time."

"I agree," Lebna added, exchanging a quick look with Cecilia. "And let's let Cecilia lead the discussion."

When they arrived at the rectory, Father Ramón greeted them at the door, then led them down the hallway to his kitchen, where he poured them each a cup of freshly brewed coffee.

"Doña Faustina is still in a coma," he said and joined them at the table. "But I bet her soul is here, visiting us right now."

"Oh my god!" Julie gasped and frantically looked all around.

Marie gave Father Ramón a flustered look.

The priest chuckled. "It's no problem. The Lord knows I've uttered many gasps and groans throughout my life's work." Then he asked Julie, "Do you want to ask me something?"

"Um . . ." Julie cast Cecilia a nervous look.

"Don't worry about Cecilia. I'm asking you."

"Well," Julie said, "I saw *The Exorcist* once. I was wondering . . . whether your *don* angel ever helped you exorcise demons . . . like in the movie."

While the others stiffened, Father Ramón grinned at Julie and said, "Only small ones."

"Oh my god!" Julie said.

"But let's focus on the particulars of your visit." He turned to Cecilia.

"Right," Cecilia replied. She wondered what to say.

After an awkward silence, Father Ramón waved Cecilia on. "Now that you know I've dealt with demons you shouldn't hesitate to tell me what's on your mind. I also know about the first curse, about what happened to Little Cecilia, and that Doña Faustina was training you as her apprentice. So, don't beat around the bush. We're working against the clock, and this is a life or death situation."

Cecilia took a deep breath and explained how Doña Faustina had made them into a team to fight the curse. She also shared that "Santa Claus" was a clue that would supposedly help.

"But we don't understand how, that's why we're here: Carmen thinks you might be able to help us."

"Did she say anything else?"

"She mentioned your Christmas decorations . . . the orbs of light and flying angels."

"I see." Father Ramón tapped his chin in thought. "You were in Santa Cecilia for the Day of the Dead, right?"

Cecilia nodded.

"Did you see the children's procession?"

Cecilia nodded again.

"That was to cleanse the town for the souls to return."

"Yes, I remember hearing that."

"Well, the decorations I put up for Christmas represent what happens on *that* holiday, which might sound like a fairy tale to you. But I know it to be true."

"Because of your *don* angel?" Julie blurted out.

"Hold on. Let me tell you about the orbs of light before I get on the topic of my *don* angel, since it might help you. See, every year, during Advent, many angels descend and hover close to the earth. They toss orbs of light to cleanse it so the Christ child's soul can return. The kids' procession cleanses the community for the returning souls on the Day of the Dead, while the angels' orbs purify the earth for the returning Christ baby on Christmas. Do you follow what I'm saying?"

"I think so, but . . ." Cecilia's voice drifted off.

"You don't believe me?!" asked Father Ramón and he arched his brow.

"Ah . . ."

"Don't worry. Just think about what I'm saying."

They all nodded.

"If there are good angels, are there bad angels too?" Julie interrupted the silence.

"Sweetie . . . ," Marie said.

"No, that's a good question, because the man from the first curse was possessed by a terrible demon. Let me explain. I was a young man when this all happened and was, of course, shaken by the sudden death of twelve people in a single day. But I told myself there weren't demons or a Devil . . . until I encountered one myself."

Julie gasped.

"Like Saint Ramón," he continued, "my mother died giving birth to me, and, several years after Little Cecilia liberated the town from the first curse, my father fell gravely ill. I looked after him, being his only child, but it was really hard because he asked me again and again if I believed in God. That's all he wanted, he said, to die knowing that I believed.

'Yes,' I told him over and over, but he knew I had said it to only make him feel better.

"One morning, he yelled for me and I ran over. He was sitting up, pointing at the wall with the biggest smile on his face.

"I looked where he pointed, but didn't see anything.

"'Don't you see him?' he said, all excited.

"'Who?'

"'The Lord, he's come for me!' The next moment, he fell back, dead.

"I was devastated. And, throughout the entire burial process, the funeral and rosaries, I couldn't sleep, however exhausted I was. My life spun out of control. I started to hallucinate. I saw some good things, but I sensed and sometimes saw a demon loose in the town . . . provoking fights . . . over the stupidest things imaginable. Best friends, for instance, would stop talking to each other over a cheap, borrowed hammer because it was returned with a tiny nick—something sandpaper could've brushed off in a second. Or the closest of *comadres* would suddenly start to slander and accuse one another of witchcraft over a missing button.

"On and on, I saw the handiwork of this demon, who must have been whispering to people's bad angels, causing them to lash out at others with hate. So, yes, there are demons. And, in addition to this, every person not only has a good guardian angel, but a bad one as well.

"But to get back to this terrible demon and the chaos it caused across the town . . . I honestly didn't believe what I had seen. I thought I had simply lost my mind because I still couldn't sleep. That's when Doña Faustina knocked on my door. She'd known my mother and father for many years.

She pushed past me and dragged me to the kitchen, where she made me sit down and tell her what had happened to me.

"I was so tired I told her everything, not caring what she thought.

"'You're lucky—the whole town is lucky—because the demon is a little one; he stirs up fights and troubles, but hasn't killed anyone.'

"*Whatever*, I thought, because the only thing I cared about was getting some sleep.

"'Since you see the demon,' she continued, 'can you chase it away?'

"I had no idea what she meant, but she promised to help me sleep if I just tried.

"'Find the demon and confront it. Say, In the name of the Lord, I order you to leave this town.'"

"I thought it was a total joke. I thought the demon only existed in my sleepless mind.

"Off I went. And as I passed the *cantina*, I saw it!

"'Hey, you!' I called out. It turned and glared at me with its red eyes ablaze. It hissed, and, as it leapt at me, I held out my hands and yelled out what Doña Faustina had told me to say: 'In the name of the Lord, I order you to leave this town.'

"*Poof!* It disappeared, just like that." Father Ramón snapped his fingers. "I was more astonished than the demon must have been. I ran and told Doña Faustina what happened. Three days later, after two full days of sleep from a relaxing tea Doña Faustina had a *curandera* make for me, all the fighting had ended. Doña Faustina told me the happy news that I had delivered the town from the demon.

"That's when my journey to the priesthood began, which brings me back to my *don* angel. Listen closely, since this might be helpful, too. As you can imagine, the town was stunned when the chaos suddenly stopped. But then, late one night, during a torrential storm, I was awakened by loud pounding on my front door.

"A man was shouting, 'Help us! Please help us!'

"It was so dark I couldn't make out his face. He said that his wife was being attacked by the Devil and that Doña Faustina had told him to come get me.

"I had no idea why she thought I could help, but I went anyway. When we got to his house, we went into the bedroom. There, I saw a demon on the bed. He was kicking a woman's stomach, over and over again.

"Suddenly, Doña Faustina rushed up to me and said, 'Do you see a demon?'

"'Of course,' I replied and pointed. 'Don't you see him? Right there!'

"'No. That's why I sent for you. You must drive it away.'

"So I yelled, 'Go away!'

"But the demon narrowed its fiery eyes and laughed—a hideous, evil sound. The very next moment, it attacked me, kicking, clawing and biting me all over.

"Somewhere far off, I heard Doña Faustina's voice telling me to repeat, word for word, 'In the name of the Lord, I command you to leave!'

"I was in shock. I couldn't even open my mouth as the demon hammered my head. Doña Faustina screamed for me to repeat the words.

"To this day, I don't know how I did it, but I said the words and—*poof!*—the demon vanished, just like the first one had.

"The woman and the unborn child she carried survived the attack. But I was shattered by the whole thing. Doña Faustina and others looked after me, and, when I could finally walk again, I still trembled all the time because demons were no longer simply figments of my imagination. And I had many questions, like why did commanding it in the name of the Lord cause it to leave?

"Doña Faustina eventually told me why. 'Only the Lord,' she said, 'has power over demons. The Lord and those who believe in him.'

"This hit me like a punch in the gut because, at the time, I wasn't sure God even existed.

"So what happened next? People knocked on my door. They thanked me for ridding the town of yet another demon. Then, when the elderly parish priest fell ill, he sent for me and asked if I would consider the priesthood.

"'That's crazy,' I said, 'because I don't believe in God!'

"'But you brought such peace to the town,' he replied.

"'I don't want to spend my life fighting demons!' I shouted.

"He smiled and told me the demons I had chased off were just little ones, and not to be afraid, because I had a *don* angel to protect me.

"All he could say was for me to go see Doña Faustina, which I did. She told me that a few fortunate people are assigned a *don* angel. And this *don* angel becomes a gift for everyone in the community.

"I didn't believe my ears. If God really existed, why would he grant me a *don* angel? I wasn't anyone special.

"She smiled and said, 'Only you can discover your true *don*. But, when you are ready, I will try to help you with my coffee ritual.'

"I laughed this off. In order to get the townspeople off my back, I started to hang out at the *cantina*. I thought that, if I acted like a ruffian, they'd soon give up treating me like priest material. I still had scars from my fight with the second demon, but, after I drank too much tequila, my mind got screwed up and I convinced myself I'd been attacked by a mad dog.

"And that's when I met my bad angel."

"Oh my god!" Julie exclaimed. She looked pale.

"What do you want us to know about the bad angel?" Cecilia asked. She had to focus on what needed to be done.

"It's important to live in line with the golden rule, to follow your conscience, to be guided by your soul," Father Ramón explained. "God created many invisible things. Your guardian angel, for instance, inspires you with light and hope. But be aware that you have a bad angel too—everyone does—driven by self-interest and your materialistic mind. If you are guided by your good angel, your bad angel will be kept at bay. On the other hand, if you fall under the control of your bad angel, as I did in my *cantina* days, bad behavior will come to feel normal. Your guardian angel will weep when this happens, because you've essentially cut your soul off from God and become a tool for darkness, for El *Diablo*."

"How will we be strong enough to fight the curse when we don't even know our *dons*?"

Cecilia was embarrassed by Julie's bluntness, but she had exactly the same thought.

"I hear you," Father Ramón said with a nod. "Live by the golden rule, or at least try your best. This will protect you from the slings and arrows of your bad angel and from most minor demons. Also, we're coming upon the Advent season, which is the best time to strengthen your guardian angel, since that's when the heavenly angels start tossing their orbs of light. It's the best time to turn things around for everyone. The food, music and other Christmas traditions make people remember the joy of their childhood selves."

"What about Santa Claus?" Julie said. "What do you think this clue means?"

"I don't know exactly, but Saint Nicholas is the patron saint of children, and Christmas seems to bring out the child in everyone. Think about that."

After they thanked Father Ramón for his time and thoughts, the team got in the car and headed back to the apartment. Two blocks from home, a van cut right in front of them and caused Marie to slam on the breaks.

"Oh my god!" Julie screamed.

"Is everyone okay?" Marie asked. She pulled over and let the car idle while her heart raced.

They all finally mumbled a faint, "Yes."

"Where did the van come from?" Cecilia asked as they turned into their building's parking garage.

"It came out of nowhere. And, if I hadn't slammed on the brakes . . ."

"Was the curse trying to kill us?" Julie asked.

"Let's stop creating more monsters than we can handle," Lebna insisted.

"So what do we do?"

"I'll call you, Julie, once I hear how Doña Faustina's doing and talk to Carmen," Cecilia said as she got out of the car.

"But . . . I'm scared," Julie said. She refused to get out of the car.

"Sweetie, come on," Marie said as she opened Julie's door.

"No!" Julie said and pulled the door shut.

"How is staying in the car going to help?" Lebna asked, tapping on the window.

"At least there aren't any demons in here!"

"So what do you want us to do?" Cecilia asked with a heavy sigh.

"Let's go talk to Doña Faustina."

Cecilia was worried that Doña Faustina might have died while they were with Father Ramón. "Marie, can I borrow your phone? I just want to see where everyone is."

After a brief moment, Cecilia returned from behind a stone pillar and said, "Everyone's there, at the hospital, and Carmen says it's okay to come over."

❦   ❦   ❦

"Julie, what do you want to say to Doña Faustina?" Marie asked as they entered the hospital's parking lot.

"I want to ask her about Santa Claus, how that's a clue."

"How can she tell you if she's in a coma?" Lebna jumped in.

"Didn't Father Ramón just tell us about invisible things, that God created these too? So, if we ask, she might respond in a way that's invisible but that we can figure out."

Suddenly Julie screamed. A dove had fallen out of the sky onto the hood of the car.

Marie quickly pulled into a parking space and jumped out of the car to examine the bird. It was dead, all right. But what killed it?

Cecilia gently took the dove by its wing and put it into a plastic bag she found on the ground. She wished she had time to bury it properly, but instead she placed it into a nearby trash bin.

Lebna and Cecilia exchanged a worried look as they followed the others into the elevator.

"We can't all cram into Doña Faustina's room, especially since others are already there," Marie said. They exited the elevator and headed towards the waiting area. "So, how about we wait here while Cecilia checks things out?"

Cecilia hurried towards the nurses' station. A moment later, she waved them over. "Let's go. My parents are in the cafeteria and Carmen thinks it's okay to talk to Doña Faustina."

When they got to the door of Doña Faustina's room, Julie hung back.

"What now?" Cecilia said in an exasperated tone.

"I've never seen anyone in a coma . . . and . . ."

"And what? It was your idea to come."

"I know, but . . . but it's spooky to talk to . . ."

"Come on." Cecilia pushed the door open. She tensed at the sight of Doña Faustina in the hospital bed. There was a tangle of tubes and Doña Faustina was surrounded by all kinds of beeping machines.

"Doña Faustina," Cecilia said as she walked up to the bed. She leaned close. "It's me, Cecilia, along with Julie, Lebna and Marie. Carmen and Father Ramón said you can hear us."

Julie tapped Cecilia on the shoulder. "Ask her about Santa Claus."

"Julie," Marie said reproachfully.

Cecilia pushed Julie forward. "Go on, you ask her."

"Me?"

"You!" Cecilia stepped aside.

With a spooked look, Julie took a deep breath. Then, hovering over Doña Faustina's ear, she whispered, "Doña Faustina, it's me, Julie, Cecilia's friend. We're all so sorry that . . . that you're in a coma. We love you and are praying for you. And we think the curse did this to you. We were attacked, too, when a van almost killed us, and it just killed an innocent white dove that fell on our car.

"We need your help to stop the curse. We don't know what to do. Can you help us? Please. I'm really scared. Do you know what 'Santa Claus' means? It's a clue we got. Father Ramón said that God created and speaks through invisible things. Can you give us a sign? How about a *don* angel who can help us? And . . ." Julie turned and glanced at the others, not knowing what else to say.

Just then, the door swung open and Carmen walked in. She asked whether the girls had talked to Doña Faustina.

Cecilia nodded.

"But we don't know if we said the right things," Julie said, hanging her head.

"Don't worry, she can hear your souls."

"What do we do now?" Cecilia asked.

"Watch for a sign."

"Like what?" Julie asked.

"Someone saying something or seeing something that strikes you. A dream, perhaps."

Great, thought Cecilia, *more mysteries*.

"Let me take you girls home so others can visit," Marie said.

❧ ❧ ❧

Back at the apartment, Julie hesitated as she exited the car.

"Not again!" Marie cried. She was clearly annoyed. "We did what you wanted, so come out of the car. Don't tell me you're still scared of seeing a demon?"

"Stop it!" Julie said, suddenly jumping out of the car and running to the stairwell.

"How about coming over tomorrow for an early breakfast meeting?" Marie asked Cecilia and Lebna before she hurried after Julie.

❧ ❧ ❧

Weeks passed while Doña Faustina remained motionless in her hospital bed. The girls visited regularly, and sometimes when they prayed for her, they sensed that she could hear them.

They also prayed for themselves, the planet and finding their *dons* to fight the evil still haunting them.

They thought back to their time in Mexico. One evening, Cecilia pulled out the paper bag with the nine stones Don

Diego had given them at the chili shop. "I used to think a stone was just a stone," she said. "But now I see that the stones are a way of remembering that our *dons* are about helping others . . . what Junípero Serra intended his missions to do."

"But what about Mom's *don?* Julie asked. "How does driving dishes around help others?"

"No, no," Marie replied. "Those absurd exercises got me to where I was no longer focused on myself and my woes, but on trying to show the dishes how beautiful the outside world is. From there, I started to think of how I could do something to make the world better for other people. The drives shook me out of my mind and into my heart."

"And how does that explain Ms. Bellow's approving the proposal?"

"Well, it turns out she believes in angels. She told me in one of the calls I had with your school while homeschooling you in Mexico."

The girls added a section to their science project report describing Marie's journey.

And every time they visited Doña Faustina, Julie took her hand, told her she loved her, then asked what the "Santa Claus" clue meant.

❧   ❧   ❧

"Oh my god! You're not going to believe it!" It was Julie on the phone super early one morning.

"What?" Cecilia said.

"Doña Faustina appeared to me!"

"No way!"

"I saw her . . . or dreamt her . . . or something. I feel like she told me something!"

Then Cecilia heard Julie groan and Marie's voice come on. "Cecilia, this is Marie. Come over so we can all talk."

Julie was bursting with excitement when she opened the door. She rushed Cecilia down the hallway to the kitchen. Lebna was already there with Marie, drinking coffee and nibbling toast.

"I'm so glad you're finally here," Lebna announced, shaking her head. "Marie was having a hell of a time trying to keep Julie from blurting out whatever she can't wait to tell us."

"I told Julie we need to hear this as a team," Marie explained.

"Can I start now?" Julie bounced in her chair.

"Go ahead." Marie poured Cecilia a cup of coffee.

"Do you remember that song, "*We are Santa's Elves . . . We are Santa's Elves?*" Julie said, singing the words.

"That corny song?" Cecilia rolled her eyes. "*That's* what you're all excited about? I thought you said Doña Faustina appeared to you."

"Let me finish!" Julie thrust out her arms. "You heard me ask Doña Faustina for help, right? And both Father Ramón and Carmen told us to look for signs, right? Well, this morning, I turned on the radio and this song came on! I couldn't believe it. I used to play this song over and over as a kid."

"Julie, Christmas is just around the corner, so of course they've started playing that music. What's the big deal?"

"It's a very big deal because it's the answer to what I asked Doña Faustina!"

"Are you for real?" Cecilia snorted.

"Let her finish," Lebna responded. She gave Julie a supportive nod.

"Tell us what you mean, honey," Marie said.

"Remember how I loved everything about Christmas and Santa Claus, and how I was crushed when I discovered he was all made-up? And how thrilled I was later to learn that Santa really did exist, that it was Saint Nicholas who did good things for others?

"So, what I think Doña Faustina is trying to tell us through that song is . . . is that we need to be like Santa's elves. By doing good things for others, we can show others how to have Christmas year round—like each of us having our own Santa Claus inside."

Marie, Cecilia and Lebna looked at each other, not knowing what to think.

"Stop it!" Julie said, thumping the table. "You think this is just a fantasy? Let me tell you something that will freak you out!"

"Sweetie, calm down." Marie patted Julie on the back.

"No!" Julie yelled, twisting away from her mother. "I'm serious! Doña Faustina is going to say something to prove that her message to me is real."

The girls wondered whether Julie thought Doña Faustina was going to awaken. But they couldn't wait around to see what might happen. They were in danger, so Cecilia spoke up, "We need to stay focused."

"Advent—the time to prepare for Christmas—starts tomorrow, so how about going over and asking Father Ramón how we can catch some of those orbs of light? We could sure use some of that right now," Lebna suggested.

"Oh my god! I just thought of something!" Julie declared.

"What, now?" Cecilia said.

"If Father Ramón sees demons, can he see angels, too?"

"Good question," Marie beamed at her daughter. "How about I pick you up after school and we go see Father Ramón?"

With that, the girls drained their cups and hurried to the bus stop.

      ▵   ▵   ▵

When Marie's car pulled up, the girls froze at the sight of her somber expression.

"I'm afraid I have some very sad news," she sighed. "Father Ramón just called to say he won't be able to meet with us . . . because he's at the hospital. Doña Faustina's condition is worsening, rapidly."

"That means we have to get there, fast!" Julie insisted.

"Get where?" Marie asked.

"To the hospital!"

"We'll be in the way."

"Mom, it's important we see her. She might say something, like I told you this morning. And, if Doña Benedicta's there, she might tell us what spirits have come."

"Your mom's right. Let's wait in the apartment," Cecilia felt defeated.

"No!" Julie shot Cecilia a fierce look. "If the curse is real, we are in big, big trouble, and so is the planet. We need to act as if our lives depend on it. Because they do. I swear she came last night and told me something to help us."

"Why not give it a try?" Lebna asked. "If they tell us we're in the way, we can always go down to the cafeteria."

Marie glanced at Cecilia through the rearview mirror. "What do you think, Cecilia?"

"Fine," Cecilia said. Doña Faustina's illness was overwhelming.

"This might also provide us with all the data we need for our science project," Julie chimed in.

"Julie, this is really not the time for that," Marie admonished. Julie slumped down in her seat.

The group was not surprised to find the waiting area crowded with members of the Santa Cecilia community. Cecilia spotted Carmen and hurried over.

"How is she?" Cecilia said.

"She's going home."

"I thought she was . . . dying," Cecilia said and whispered the last word.

"That's what I mean."

"Oh."

"She's well enough to go home! Oh my god! That's great!" Julie said and bounced on her toes, beaming.

"Home as in heaven . . . home with God," Carmen said.

Julie stepped back.

"Who's with her now?" Cecilia asked.

"Father Ramón, Doña Benedicta and *comadre* Guadalupe. Your parents and many others are in the chapel, praying."

"Who's Guadalupe?"

"The member of the prayer group who sees spirits."

"To see if a welcoming committee has come for Doña Faustina?"

Carmen nodded.

The team took seats next to Carmen, then stared blankly at the wall, not knowing what to do.

Suddenly the doors into the hallway flew open and Father Ramón burst through. "Ah, good!" he said and hurried towards them. "Come with me! She's calling for you!"

"Who's calling for us?" Cecilia asked as they all jumped to their feet.

"You'll see." He hustled them back through the swinging doors.

They found Doña Faustina sitting up in her bed.

"Julie, is that you?" Doña Faustina asked in a thin, raspy voice.

Julie froze.

"C-come here."

Marie grabbed Julie by the elbow and pulled her towards Doña Faustina.

"I visited you last night," Doña Faustina said in a barely audible voice.

Julie stared at Doña Faustina as though she were a ghost.

"D-don't be afraid."

After taking a deep breath, Julie squared her shoulders, stepped closer and took Doña Faustina's hand. "I'm . . . not afraid, Doña Faustina. I knew it was you . . . last night . . . but I'm not sure what you told me."

Doña Faustina nodded.

After a long silence, Julie squeezed Doña Faustina's hand and began again. "Did you tell me something about Santa Claus? That to defeat the curse . . . everyone has to awaken their own Santa Claus?"

"Y-yes . . . and their *don*." Doña Faustina then called Cecilia over.

Cecilia took the old woman's other hand. "I'm here."

"Junípero Serra is here too . . . and Micaela," Doña Faustina rasped.

"In the room?" Cecilia glanced around and saw Guadalupe give her a slight nod.

Doña Faustina's breath suddenly got shallower and her eyes closed. Cecilia asked, "What should I do now . . . if I can't continue training with you? And how can we stop *El Diablo?*"

Doña Faustina nodded slightly. Then she continued in a halting whisper, "If everyone reconnects with their souls . . . their *dons* . . . and starts living with the help of their good angels . . . the planet is safe. Start with your own soul . . . your own life . . . become an example. Focus on love, not fear. Stay positive and hopeful. Junípero Serra and Micaela will help you. So will San Nicolás. Return to being the child who marvels at Christmas. And, once I reach heaven, I will help you, too.

"Yes, there is evil in the world. A van cut into your path, something killed the dove. Those things are past. Junípero and I have helped to cast out the demons that plagued you and our community. But . . ." Doña Faustina closed her eyes.

After a long silence, she opened her eyes again and looked at Cecilia. "Remember that Junípero sought a happy death. And . . . I'll be back . . . to visit . . . on the Day of the Dead." She then extended her arms, smiled and said, "I'm ready!"

Just like that, she left us.

CHAPTER 41

Afterwards, for an entire month, the team felt attacked and challenged and overwhelmed with even more mysteries. But they forced themselves to stay hopeful and positive as they focused on finding their *dons*. Father Ramón even postponed Cecilia's Confirmation so she could concentrate on this "most important mission."

⚜ ⚜ ⚜

For the Epiphany, Nica baked the most amazing *pan de rosca*. Topped with a rich assortment of candied fruit, it shone like a glorious stained-glass window. And Cecilia prepared the coffee just like Doña Faustina had taught her.

After Cecilia cut a slice, Carmen walked up and handed her an envelope with her name written across it in bold, black letters. Anxious, she hesitated, then opened it and read:

Dear Cecilia,

 You SUCCESSFULLY passed your *don* test.
Congratulations!

Sincerely,
The Don Testers

(Carmen—your Confirmation sponsor—will now present you with your *don* stone.)

"Oh my god! Finally, we all have one!" Julie cheered as she, Lebna and Marie lifted their *don* stones in the air. Days earlier, they too had received letters with their stones. Cecilia beamed, raising hers. "And now we're ready to take on the world—to save her!"

"I knew you'd pass," Marie said, giving Cecilia a big hug. "Without your *don* coffee *pláticas,* none of us would've discovered our gifts." Julie and Lebna nodded as they hugged Cecilia.

"What else do you foresee: with your *don* to foretell the future?" Cecilia asked.

Marie's face dropped. "Well . . ."

Julie slapped Marie on the back. "Out with it, Mom. Remember, no secrets allowed."

Marie cleared her throat. "On the positive side, I foresee that Junípero Serra will be declared a saint. However, on the negative . . ."

"Go on," Lebna said in an encouraging tone.

Marie shook her head and sighed. "The Third Sandy will indeed strike, years from now. And it will be brutal. A worldwide plague, I think. It will kill many, many people."

Julie gasped.

"But, if we crush this dark force—a big if, I also see the dawning of a New Golden Age."

"Then we don't have a minute to lose!" Cecilia blurted out. "I'll start doing what Doña Faustina did: help others awaken their *dons* through her coffee ritual, like I did with you. By the way, Ms. Bellows, after reading and raving about our science project report, asked me to have a *don* coffee *plática* with her. And she expects others in the class will too, once they read it."

Lebna clapped. "That's great! And I'll start hosting more Ethiopian coffee ceremonies. Father Ramón already wants me to hold one at the church, another at Santa Clara Mission and says the other missions will soon follow."

"So that's the meaning of the *pilón* stones," Marie said excitedly. Then, pointing at herself with a grin, she added, "And as for me, I not only foretell futures. But I also know what it takes to go from barely surviving by existing in your head, for yourself, to really thriving by living every moment through your heart and soul, for others. So if I ever catch any of you reverting to head existing, I have a big batch of dishes for you to carry around for a ride—being that you're all still too young to drive."

"What about me?" Julie said, looking troubled. "How can I use my *don*?"

"What do you mean?" Cecilia uttered, clapping her friend on the shoulder. "You've got the funnest *don* of all: all you have to do is to just keep on being you—your joyous Santa Claus childlike, marvelous self!"

Cecilia now threw a fist in the air and declared, "Okay, team, let's get cracking. We've got a magical—life and death—mission to accomplish!"

They cheered, then raised and clinked their *don* stones together.

The next minute they heard Julie squeal, "Oh my god! I found the baby Jesus doll in my piece of cake!"

OTHER BOOKS BY VIOLA CANALES

Orange Candy Slices and Other Secret Tales

The Tequila Worm

The Little Devil and the Rose: Lotería Poems /
El diablito y la rosa: Poemas de la lotería